AMBER LEIGH
WILLIAMS

—

A Place with Briar

<H> HARLEQUIN® SUPER ROMANCE®

Recycling programs
for this product may
not exist in your area.

ISBN-13: 978-0-373-60842-3

A PLACE WITH BRIAR

H HARLEQUIN®
™ www.Harlequin.com

Printed in U.S.A.

ABOUT THE AUTHOR

Amber Leigh Williams lives on the Gulf Coast. A Southern girl at heart, she loves beach days, the smell of real books, relaxing at her family's lakehouse and spending time with her husband, Jacob, and their sweet blue-eyed boy. When she's not running after her young son and three large dogs, she can usually be found reading a good romance or cooking up a new dish in her kitchen. Readers can find her on the web at www.amberleighwilliams.com!

First and foremost, I dedicate this book to my sister, H.P.W. As always, here's to reading 'til midnight, eating too much ice cream, and living like there's no tomorrow. Life wouldn't be the same without you.... (Olivia is for you, Boo!)

I would also like to thank my father and mother, who moved the family to Fairhope in the early '90s and were full of encouragement when I began writing shortly after....

To my husband, J.J.S.—there's a lot of *us* in this book, babe. Thank you for being the inspiration I needed to tell this story....

And finally to the brave volunteers of the 2010 Deepwater Horizon oil spill cleanup. Endless gratitude for making our coastline beautiful once more.

"There's something you need to know...."

Cole's lips curved as he turned back to the bike. "I know."

"You do?" Briar asked, sounding astounded.

"You've never ridden a bike before."

"Is it that obvious?" she asked, rubbing her palms on her jeans.

"A little," he said wryly. "Just lean with me into the turns. And hold on."

Hell, if he didn't coax her on now, she'd probably run for her life. And while that might have been better for the both of them under the circumstances, he found himself jerking his thumb behind him, motioning for her to get on.

After a brief pause, Briar dropped down her visor and stepped to the bike. Gripping his offered hand for balance, she climbed on behind him and placed her feet on the small passenger pegs.

Just this once, he was going to give Briar Browning the ride of her life. God help them both.

Dear Reader,

For fourteen years, Fairhope, Alabama, was the place I called home. While brainstorming *A Place with Briar,* I often found myself in my car driving toward the Eastern Shore of the Mobile Bay, where my hometown rests, snug on a sweeping, green bluff. I drove the scenic route that still makes my heart soar...maybe because I was retracing my first motorcycle ride, which a cute nineteen-year-old boy who would someday be my husband took me on.

I'm proud of the place I once called home. I love the pace of life in Fairhope, the view of the bay from the scenic bluffs along the shore.... It's a dreamer's paradise. As a girl, it was where I discovered my love of reading and writing. From the sailboats gliding across the bay, to the grand homes lining the streets, to the couples strolling hand in hand, growing up on the Eastern Shore jump-started my imagination. My mind has not stopped painting stories since. I had little doubt that one day I would share the stories I conjured there with the world.

I'm thrilled I finally get to share *A Place with Briar* with you, readers! This story is close to my heart in so many ways. Like Briar and Cole, I fell in love on the Eastern Shore. (I might even somewhat re-create my first motorcycle ride within its pages!) It was such a pleasure bringing in a haunted outsider like Cole, who needed a good dose of healing, and giving him the home and love he never knew his heart needed.

I hope you enjoy Briar and Cole's story. I always love to hear from readers! You can find me on the web at www.amberleighwilliams.com or contact me via email at amber@amberleighwilliams.com!

Happy reading!

Amber Leigh Williams

CHAPTER ONE

COLE SAVITT HAD MADE a deal with the devil. He did so willingly because the prize far outweighed the cost.

That is, if the devil stuck to her end of the deal.

The devil, in this case, happened to be his ex-wife. If the past three years had taught him anything, it was that Tiffany could be the most manipulative person he'd ever met. He didn't at all like that his fate was in her hands—or that he'd been the one to lay it there all over again.

But if she did stand by her end of the bargain, not only would his life be his own again, he would also no longer be barred from seeing his son.

Though it had been months since he had seen six-year-old Gavin inside a courtroom as an unsympathetic judge gifted Tiffany with full custody, stripping Cole of any visitation rights, he didn't need a picture to remember his son's face. The young visage so like his own was stamped across his temporal lobe—memory of all that had been, all that there was, and reminder of what could be.

The Fairhope pier was calm and deserted but for

the early fishermen reclining in beach chairs. Their lines drooped over the railing into the shallow bay below. The only sounds that penetrated the peaceful lull of silence and the foggy gloom of the morning were the pelicans doing their far-from-graceful dive for breakfast and the heavy splash of crab nets hitting the water.

The bells of buoys trilled over the quiet, and water lapped against the hulls of boats tethered off the restaurant that some clever individual had christened Yardarm. Part of Fairhope's most enduring residential park, the pier had survived hurricane forces and modern industrialization. Along with the adjacent park and the scenic bluff that crested far atop the shoreline, it was an Eastern Shore trademark. One of Alabama's best-kept secrets.

As Cole sat drinking coffee inside the restaurant, his eyes didn't stray to the seagulls that swooped into view, the pelicans dozing on isolated posts or the sailboats that well-to-do hobbyists had taken out early. His eyes were trained on the strip of land half a mile away, waiting for the clouds to part so he could get his first look at the target, a bayside bed-and-breakfast called Hanna's Inn.

Why Tiffany wanted to buy the place so badly was beyond Cole. He knew her family hailed from Fairhope and the coastal cities surrounding it. He also knew that her hard-hitting, real-estate tycoon father had done his best to get his hands on as much land along the Eastern Shore over the course of his business life—and Hanna's Inn had always eluded him. The old man had bitten the dust three years ago, leaving Tiffany in control of his legacy.

That her transformation from loving wife to manipulative bitch had occurred around the same time she came into family fortune and her own business didn't strike Cole as a coincidence. Though looking back, he had to admit there'd been earlier signs of her ruthless ambition that he'd chosen to ignore at the time.

The phone call from his ex-wife that had led him to Fairhope had come at an odd time. He hadn't spoken to Tiffany since that day in court and had planned on putting as much distance between himself and Huntsville, where they had built their so-called life together, as he could. He expected the usual threats and criticism.

Instead, Tiffany offered him an opportunity to make everything right. She apparently couldn't get into Hanna's Inn to do her own legwork without being recognized and blowing the sale altogether. She needed someone to do her dirty work for her by getting her a copy of the inn's financial records. And who better than the ex-husband who had nothing to lose?

The coffee on the table in front of him had gone cold and would've tasted as bitter as his mood if he'd taken another sip. Cole scooted the mug away from him. He had no love for Tiffany, and if she hadn't offered him the one thing he wanted more than anything else in the world, he would have refused her.

There was no price too high that could make him walk away from this one chance to be with his son. Even if Tiffany wasn't planning on upholding her end, he had to try.

The fog and clouds started to break apart, letting the first golden rays of sunlight shine through and unveiling the sandy, green length of the Eastern Shore, one breathtaking sweep at a time. High on a grassy ridge, Hanna's Inn rose like a waterside Tara, triumphant and glorious, distinctive among other houses around her with white wooden walls and tall columns gracing the bayside facade. It reminded Cole of a regal, antebellum bride from another era.

It looked as charming as it was striking, one of many early twentieth-century dwellings that travelers came to admire along this shore. From a distance, it was all that its promotional brochure promised: a serene getaway. *Forget the world,* the glossy trifold had suggested.

Weeks ago, he might have been tempted to do just that. Now he could only think of Gavin and what he had to do to get back his son.

The waitress approached his table. When he glanced up, she asked, "More coffee?"

"No, thank you," he replied. "Just the check, please." He reached for the billfold in his back pocket as she walked back to the counter. He paid for his meal, left a tip and checked his watch as he left Yardarm and began to walk the length of the pier.

Nearly time for check-in.

The air was soft with a briny tinge. Early summer weather this far south wasn't quite as humid or heavy as he'd imagined, though if he lingered he would soon experience lower Alabama's blistering clime.

For now, the wind felt cool on his shaven face, a subtle hint of evening showers. A round fountain slumbered at the park entrance, its still, clear, blue pool and the coins at its base mirroring the sheen of the sun. The labyrinth of roses around it thrived. Their dewy, open petals trumpeted heady, passionate perfume.

Trapping the sultry scent in his lungs, he strapped on his helmet and mounted his Harley. He gunned the machine to life. It roared into the quiet, turning the heads of the few people who'd come to admire the morning's hushed splendor. He didn't cast them much of a glance as he coaxed the bike up the towering slope onto South Mobile Street.

The road wrapped around the Eastern Shore, stretching as far as Pelican Point, which joined the bay with another then reached for Fort Morgan and the cool waters of the blue-green Gulf beyond.

However, he didn't have nearly that far to go.

A white clapboard sign marked the turn for Hanna's Inn. He pulled into the gravel drive and parked in the shade of a magnolia tree. The wide, fragrant blossoms grinned down at him from limbs of glossy green leaves. The sweet, woodsy, quintessentially Southern scent he associated with childhood bliss… and home.

His chest tightened, and he rolled his shoulder to ease the ready ache. Dwelling on home only made him hurt more.

He tucked his helmet under his arm and left his sunglasses in place as he walked into the inn. The bells over the door jangled, and the homey scent of cinnamon tickled his nostrils.

He scanned the empty lobby, admiring the long, painted aerial of old Fairhope spanning the opposite wall. The glass covering the painting was so clean he saw his reflection clearly. The sharp-cut jawline that framed a tan, narrow face; his hair dark and hanging straight. Black shades hid dark, tired eyes. Still, he could see the wear of travel around the wary crease above the bridge of his nose and the lines bracketing his mouth.

He barely recognized himself and wondered if anyone else would at this point.

"Mr. Savitt?"

THE SOUND OF the bells chiming from the entryway woke Briar Browning. She frowned at the first white strands of sunlight peering through her kitchen window. Raising her head from the tabletop where she'd dozed off hours ago, she winced as rigid neck muscles cried out in protest. Pressing a hand over the nape of her neck, she carefully rolled her head on her shoulders, leaning back against her chair and blinking around the room.

One look at the bills and bank statements spread across the table made her groan. She'd fallen asleep while doing the bookkeeping again. Now there was no time to prep for this week's guest.

Briar straightened and a sharp twinge cruised up her spine. The chair creaked as she pushed to her feet. Her arches were still sore from the day before, but she slipped them into the shoes she'd toed off under the table and ran her hands over her hair, hoping she looked at least half-decent in yesterday's clothes. One look at her reflection in the window over the sink reassured her. She didn't look as fresh as she would have liked, but she wasn't going to scare anyone off.

With her unawares, it had shaped up to be a glorious morning. The bay water was moody gray and choppy under a stiff breeze from the north. The north wind served as a relief to those on the Gulf Coast, buffering dangerous tropical weather.

June marked the first month of hurricane season, and like all other business and home owners, Briar had already checked the inn generator and readied the storm shutters. If El Niño came knocking on Mobile Bay's door, she had little to do except stockpile batteries, gasoline, canned goods and water. Then wait for it to be over.

Hanna's Inn had stood the test of weather and

time for over thirty years. Unless any of the tropical waves roiling far out in the Atlantic turned into a storm of Frederic, Ivan or Katrina proportions, Hanna's and Briar would ride it out like any other.

The four guest suites were quiet on the second floor. Briar's stomach knotted, the silence pressing against her eardrums. The local small-business economy had suffered hard over the past few years. She had hoped summer would lure tourists and revenue to the Eastern Shore as well as Hanna's.

It was June and the guest calendar still looked utterly vacant. The only name on the page was a single man's. *Cole Savitt.* She rarely booked singles, this time of the year, especially. Fairhope, with its easy proximity to Alabama's white-sand beaches, was the perfect place to bring a family or loved one for a cozy, Southern-style getaway. Unfortunately, it didn't seem as if many people were getting away.

The man was probably in town strictly for business, she thought. And with the weather behaving strangely well for June, wouldn't that be a shame?

As she moved through the swinging door, she shifted her unease to the back of her mind. She couldn't leave her guest waiting any longer, not to change or ruminate over her financial difficulties and all the uncertainties ahead. Her mother might have died a year ago, but that didn't change the fact that Briar now singularly owned and operated the inn Hanna Browning had built from the ground up.

"Mr. Savitt," she called as she walked into the

entryway. The room was awash with morning light, and the man who stood with his back to her, back-pack slung over one shoulder and motorcycle helmet in hand, slowly turned. There were sunshades over his eyes, but the frown that greeted her stopped her in her tracks.

Her hand fluttered to her stomach and she sucked in a breath. "I...I hope I didn't keep you waiting too long."

BEHIND THE SHADES, Cole's eyes locked on the inn-keeper like heat-seeking missiles, moving only to rove her fair features. Flushed cheeks, honey-brown eyes, a dainty chin and ripe lips he knew would taste sweet just by looking at them.

His throat went dry and his heart rebounded. Her shoulder-length hair fell in natural streaks of gold, blond and fairest brown. Her slender form was covered in a trim khaki skirt and a pink silk blouse.

There was nothing suggestive or mysterious about her beauty. It was vulnerable and soft, a whisper of wind in a rainless summer. Her eyes beamed sincerity and a touch of timidity.

This was *the mark,* as Tiffany had described her. The woman whose financial ruin would be his ex-wife's gain.

Cole wanted to touch her. It wasn't a sensual need—instead, a knee-jerk urge, an instinct from another life to protect, shelter and shield.

When she only stared at him, lips slightly parted,

he realized he was supposed to respond. "Oh. No problem, ma'am. I was just looking around."

All too quickly, she dropped her gaze and walked around the podium. "Welcome to Hanna's."

He hesitated before crossing the room, his own greeting lodged in his throat.

"If you'll just sign here, please." She shifted the leather-bound sign-in book so he could initial. When he removed his glasses, he watched her lips part again in surprise as she searched his eyes.

He dropped them to the page in front of him, knowing all his secrets lurked there in his eyes—a window to his all-too-haunted soul. Without a word, he scrawled his signature on the line she'd indicated.

"Thank you." She opened the drawer of the cabinet behind her and palmed a set of keys. "These are yours, Mr. Savitt."

He pocketed them. "I paid ahead, didn't I?"

"Yes," she said, a hospitable grin twitching the corners of her mouth. "Your receipt is included in this packet."

"I'm sorry the reservation was made on such short notice. I was going to stay at The Grand, but a family member more familiar with the area recommended your place, instead."

"I think you'll find Hanna's more convenient," she told him. "It's closer to town—a quick walk if the heat isn't oppressive. Your stay is for two weeks, but feel free to extend it if you need to. Just let me know a day or two ahead of your check-out date."

"That's great, thanks." His eyes found hers again. They searched for a moment, clinging to the warmth he saw.

She took a short gulp of air and circled the podium. "I'll show you to your room. May I help with your luggage?"

He shook his head, shouldering the pack he'd dropped at the door. "Thanks, but this is it."

"Follow me, then." She led him into a small sitting room infused with more cinnamon and the soothing aroma of fresh coffee. A small half-moon sofa faced windows that beamed soft, natural light.

"This is where most of my guests like to come in the mornings to socialize, read the paper and check the weather," she explained as she took them past this room and up the staircase to the private suites. "I hope you don't mind being the only one here for the time being."

"I like the quiet." That at least was the truth. He pocketed his hands when they itched to finger the silken hair that fell straight to her shoulders. "I'm not much company."

"Me, either," she admitted with a nervous lilt of a laugh. She glanced back at him. "I try to find as many quiet moments as possible. A guilty pleasure, I reckon."

"I imagine that's difficult, finding time for yourself," he said as they stepped onto the second-floor landing. "Operating a place like this." The antique breakfront standing against the wall opposite the stairs added its own cedar scent to the corridor. The spicy aroma made him feel more at ease than the magnolia at the entrance and the evident polish of the interior. "Do you run it alone?"

"Yes." Her smile slipped out of place for a moment before she recovered from the slight hitch and her eyes shone again. "It's been in the family for some time, but it's just me for now."

He frowned. Seemed a great deal for one person to handle. Tiffany would be relieved, however, that there weren't other owners to contend with. *For now,* at least. "It's nice," he offered.

"Thank you," she said, leading him to his suite door. "This is yours. I reserved the best bay view for you."

When he stepped into the room, surprise filtered through him.

The wooden floor gleamed under the morning glow just like the bay water visible through the wide window. The sleigh bed looked plush and oh-so inviting under a thick blue quilt, matching pillows plumped at the head.

There was an antique armoire with one door open to reveal a full-length mirror on the inside panel. Complimentary padded hangers dangled on the rack inside. Stems of flowers flowed out of crystal vases on the dresser, the cut glass shooting sunshine into his eyes. Irises and hydrangeas blessed the room with their sweet, earthy scents.

He couldn't remember what he'd expected. Something more feminine. Chintz or pastels, something out of a Pottery Barn catalog…but certainly not this. A sense of comfort came over him—swift, almost foreign. "It's…perfect."

Small dimples dug into her cheeks as she smiled. "I'll let you settle in. When you're ready, I'll give you a tour and explain mealtimes and other activities."

"Thanks."

"It's my pleasure, Mr. Savitt," she said as she walked around him to leave.

Instinctively, his hand reached up to brush her arm. At his touch, she froze, her face tipped close underneath his. Inches hovered between his lips and hers.

"Please," he murmured, hardly able to grind the words out. "Call me Cole."

An uncertain grin peaked the corners of her lips. His eyes drifted to them. A long, seductive chain heated and coiled, winding from the center of his torso around his navel.

She closed her eyes, breaking the connection and shaking her head as if to clear it. "Downstairs," she said again. "I'll see you downstairs." And retreated.

When she shut the door behind her, Cole dropped his bag to the floor and blew out the breath he'd unknowingly been holding under her gaze. It wasn't strategy or anything other than the blood he felt humming too closely to the surface that had made him want to lean over and taste that sweet, smiling mouth.

Damned if that was the way he was going to go about this errand. His job was to find out if the owner of Hanna's had any investors and what her financial situation was. He wasn't going to sink to Tiffany's level and use the attraction he felt simmering between himself and Briar to get the information he needed. He'd bring out the detective he'd been before his life had gone to smithereens to get what he needed out of her.

And, no. The detective slumbering inside him didn't think that kissing the innkeeper was a wise way to initiate his under-the-table investigation of Hanna's Inn. As pretty as Briar Browning was... after Tiffany's complete and utter betrayal, there was no way he'd risk entering even a harmless flirtation.

CHAPTER TWO

BRIAR CAUGHT HERSELF thinking far too deeply about the stranger in the bay suite. Especially after he chose to forgo lunch in the dining room and took off with a roar on his Harley.

As far as she could tell, Cole Savitt was a middle-aged man with no wedding ring, and apparently he carried all he needed for two weeks in a single backpack.

And when he'd taken off his sunglasses and she got a gander at the pain riddling his dark eyes, her heart reached out to him unequivocally. And...his broad shoulders and trim torso fit his leather riding jacket really well, too.

She cleared her throat and gave herself a mental shake. Damn her heart. It'd always readily reached out to the wounded.

There was no doubt in her mind Cole Savitt was a wounded man. But that kind of information was above and beyond what she needed to know about her guest. All she had to do was make his two weeks at Hanna's as pleasant as possible. In the year she'd worked here, she had never failed to please anyone under the inn's roof.

She hadn't offered more than breakfast in bed to any guests, either, and she wasn't about to start now.

Too much else to worry about.

In addition to Hanna's Inn, Briar owned the adjoining property. At two stories, the building was painted white to match the inn. It held three shop spaces in addition to a roomy apartment on the back half of the second-floor interior. She rented the living space to her cousin, Olivia Lewis, who managed the adjacent first-floor bayside bar, Tavern of the Graces.

Briar leased the street-side shop space to Adrian Carlton, single mother and proprietor of Flora, Fairhope's finest floral shop. Above it, the third commercial space sat on the second level, overlooking South Mobile Street and had been empty for years. Thankfully, someone had finally taken notice.

As Briar stood aside, listening to the clack of heels over tile, a potential investor, Roxie Honeycutt, strolled slowly around the room, doing her final walk-through. The woman had been eager to sign the lease and institute Belle Brides—a bridal boutique that would house the woman's own line of bridal couture. But Briar had insisted on the final formality.

Roxie sighed, whirling to face her. She looked utterly chic in a strapless summer dress the color of money and matching peep-toe pumps. "I said it once, I'll say it again. It's absolutely perfect."

Briar held back a sigh of her own, one of immense relief. "I had an exterminator give it a once-over. No termites or other pest problems. Though I wish I'd had the time to give it a fresh coat of paint."

"Oh, the color will change, anyway," Roxie explained, waving a hand. "I'm thinking pink. With vintage white mirrored accessories. Typical, maybe. But I advertise my gowns on a red-based pink backdrop and it really makes the designs pop."

"I'm sure you'll make the space look fabulous." She shook Roxie's hand. "Welcome to the building."

Roxie beamed, her commercial-straight teeth as perfect as her Victoria Beckham coif and cornflower-blue eyes. "You've just made me the happiest woman this side of the Mississippi. Opening my own shop has been a dream for so long, I can hardly believe I'm finally doing it."

Dreams, Briar thought. It had been so long since she'd contemplated her own, she could hardly remember them. They had slipped through her fingers so quickly, she was no longer sure what she wanted. "When will you get started?"

"I'm hoping to open before July, just in time for the big holiday rush. So as soon as possible."

"Well, if you need any assistance at all the other girls and I will be more than happy to help you settle in," Briar said. "Shall we sign and make it official?"

As they stepped out, Briar locked the dead bolt while Roxie stood back, eyeing the shop face. "I had a bit of a brainstorm last night. I never sleep when I'm excited. Drives my fiancé, Richard, to insanity, me pacing up and down the halls at all hours. If you're up for it, I think we could come up with a package deal."

Briar leaned against the rail overlooking the small parking lot. "How so?"

"On top of designing, I'm a licensed wedding coordinator. I plan ceremonies, receptions, book caterers, photographers, venues, florists, etc. What I was thinking is we each shave a percentage off our prices for my couples—offer them my services and attire along with your honeymoon suite at a discounted rate."

"Have you thought about adding Flora to the package? Adrian's done weddings, and her bridal arrangements are divine."

Roxie held up a discerning finger. "And don't forget the Tavern. I love that wide veranda on the back. It's just big enough for a reception space. With the right lighting, trimmings and that amazing natural backdrop of the bay, it'd be breathtaking."

"I like it," Briar admitted. Something buzzed beneath her skin. Something that felt an awful lot like *possibilities*. Could this be what the inn needed to stay afloat? "You should discuss it with the others."

"We'll all have to sit down for drinks sometime this week," Roxie said as she descended the steps to her waiting Lexus. "Who knows? This could be a lucrative venture for all of us."

The wild roar of an engine snagged their attention. Briar's stomach fluttered as Cole Savitt zoomed in on his motorcycle, coming to an abrupt halt under the magnolia.

As he cut the engine and pulled off his helmet, Roxie raised a brow. "One of your guests?"

"Ah, yes."

"Mmm." She slid Briar a teasing grin. "I might have to pop by sometime while he's here."

Briar laughed as Roxie got into her car. She waved her off then smoothed nervous hands over her skirt. *A lucrative venture.* The words echoed in her head as she stood alone on the gravel drive. The inn and her mother's lifetime of work were slipping away slowly but surely. She had to find more investors before it was yanked from her hands and the state put it up for sale or foreclosure.

She owed her mother at least that much.

Loosening a sigh, she began the walk back to the inn. Her eyes fell on the lone vehicle in the drive, Cole Savitt's Harley-Davidson. Where had it taken him? What all had he seen straddling its black leather seat?

Dreams. She pondered them as she passed through the garden her mother—and now she—so lovingly tended. Once upon a time, her dreams had led her to Paris where she had escaped the obligation her father had been trying to press upon her. Back then she hadn't wanted to leave Hanna's—a long time ago, her dream had been to run the inn alongside her mother.

Her father's wishes, however, had carried her off to law school. Her path had been laid before her. All she'd had to do was walk within it.

Instead, she'd taken a detour from law school in the States to Europe with friends and, to her father's consternation, had wound up settling in Paris for a semester. There she had rediscovered her love of cooking and had enrolled in culinary school. And that had become her dream.

But soon after beginning her studies in culinary arts, she fell into some bad luck. Or, more accurately, she had run headlong into it, eyes wide-open. Since then, her dreams had gone down a rocky path and hadn't returned.

She gazed up at the face of the bed-and-breakfast she had once wanted so much to be a part of. Was it still what she wanted?

Guilt swamped her, as it always did when she let her thoughts wander back to Paris, her culinary dreams and the niggling sense of uncertainty she kept locked up inside her. What did it matter what she wanted? What she *needed* was to keep her mother's dream alive—to make sure Hanna's Inn survived the test of time.

Though judging by the dismal financial outlook

in the inn's books and its empty guest calendar, it seemed as if her bad luck was back to haunt her and tear down the solid legacy it had taken decades for her mother to build.

COLE'S FIRST NIGHT at Hanna's turned out to be surprisingly restful. He sank into the plush bedding with the drugging fragrance of candles and the dim flicker of firelight lulling him into complacency and easy sleep.

He woke the next morning to the pale light of dawn and stepped into a hot shower, unable to remember the last time he'd woken so rested.

It'd certainly been a while since he'd dreamed of a woman's face.

The vivid memory of the pretty innkeeper had lingered all through the night. He rubbed water over his face, trying to get the blood flowing as much as to scrub the vision of Briar Browning from the backs of his eyes.

As he stepped out and looped a towel around his waist, he recalled the way she'd watched him in his dreams. Never saying anything—just watching him with those soft honey-brown eyes. He'd felt their touch like a skin-on-skin caress.

Damn, the woman was making it difficult to focus.

He rubbed another towel over his dripping hair before he wiped a spot on the mirror clear in order to shave. Before he lifted the razor to his cheek, he heard the knock on the door. He paused, and called, "It's open!" Making sure the towel on his waist was secure, he stepped into the room as Briar opened it.

She took one look at his bare chest, shrieked and whirled away. "I'm so sorry!" she exclaimed, gripping the knob. "I'll come back."

"Don't worry about it," he said automatically. "Nothing to see here."

She cast him an *easy for you to say* glance before her eyes veered politely downward. "You have a phone call. It seems rather urgent. And breakfast is ready."

Amused by the way her eyes averted him, he asked, "What's on the menu?"

"Cinnamon rolls," she explained. "And fruit salad. I'll serve you in the kitchen when you're ready."

He nodded. "Sounds great."

Her lips quirked into a brief smile. "Sorry I barged in on you."

"It's nothing," he said with a shrug. When she shut the door, a wide grin broke over his face, though he couldn't have said why as he reached for the phone on the bedside table. "Savitt," he said, raising it to his ear.

"You didn't call yesterday. I was beginning to think you'd changed your mind."

The grin vanished quickly along with all the good feelings left over from his early morning encounter with Briar. "Tiff."

"Enjoying your vacation?"

His back teeth ground together in frustration. "I haven't found enjoyment in anything since you began your dirty deeds. But that's exactly what you wanted, isn't it?"

Tiffany's laugh filtered over the line. "Don't whine, Cole. It doesn't suit you. I called to make sure you haven't backed out of our deal. And to remind you what's at stake here."

How could he possibly forget about Gavin? "For you or for me—because I'm not quite clear on the former."

"The less you know, the better," she said. "Isn't that what you used to tell me when you'd come off a crime scene? As if my delicate, feminine sensibilities would swoon just for thinking about what my flatfoot husband had encountered."

"I'm no longer your husband," he reminded her. And he'd learned well that there was nothing *delicate* about Tiffany. Hard and unyielding, like a hammer, was more like it.

"You've got that right. Though Gavin does seem to miss you, on occasion."

"Don't," he said, the word coming out on a fierce growl as every muscle in his body tightened in defense. "Don't dangle him in front of me any more than you already are." He couldn't stand it.

"All right. Just remember what I said. Get inside her head, her files, whatever you have to do to find out everything there is to know about the inn, the

adjacent property and if she has investors. If she
does, I want to know who and how much."

"Are you going to buy them off, too?"

"If necessary. I'll need a progress report every
night, Cole."

"So you can keep tabs on me, as usual."

"So I know you're doing your job. I'm not paying
for you to stay there so you can lounge under the
sun, drink mai tais and work on your tan."

"Yeah, don't worry. Nobody knows that more
than me. I'm out." He hung up and took a moment
to steady himself. The woman could wind him up
quicker than a Matchbox car. It was sickening. Fighting the urge to put his fist through one of Briar's
lovely walls, he dug through his backpack until he
found something clean to wear.

BRIAR HAD MADE the mistake of looking at him again
as she closed the door to the bay-view suite. And this
time, her gaze had taken its time perusing freely.
Beads of water had rolled down his chest from the
wet, tousled tips of his black hair. The lure felt more
than magnetic—it melted her. Turning away from
the tempting sight, she had shut the door smartly at
her back, hoping her hormones would get the message *No!*

Her legs wobbled on the stairs. When she made
it safely to the kitchen, she managed to sink into
one of the breakfast table's chairs before she could
shrink to the floor.

She fought to cool her heated cheeks, banishing the image of her guest's sculpted chest from her memory.

It had been a long time since she'd been so drawn to a man—and where had that gotten her? Into a whole heap of trouble. The last thing she needed now was a repeat of what had happened in Paris....

Knuckles rapped against the frame of the screen door. Briar glanced up. Relief swelled at the sight of sure distraction.

"Hey, let me in!" her cousin, Olivia Lewis, called through the door.

"I'm sorry," Briar apologized, springing up. She unbolted the screen and pushed it open with a creak so Olivia could breeze through. "I was distracted."

"Yeah?" Olivia said in her characteristically lurid voice. "You looked it." She held up a large crate. "The wine you ordered."

"Oh," Briar said, remembering. "Right." She took a knife from a drawer to pry the lid open, glad for the activity as Olivia made herself cozy at the table. "Staying for breakfast?"

"Yeah. I thought I'd check up on this new guest of yours."

Briar's hands fumbled at the mere mention of Cole. The bottles in her arms clinked together as she elbowed the door to the liquor cabinet open. "Why?"

"He seems like an interesting character," Olivia mused, picking a ripe purple plum out of the bowl at the center of the table.

"What could you possibly know about him?" Briar asked. "You haven't even met him."

"I'm not deaf. You've got a biker living under your roof. I just want to make sure he's not eyeing the family silver."

"You're terrible! He's not like that," Briar blurted. Instantly, she wanted to clap her hand over her mouth. Instead, she broke down the crate and tossed it into the disposal behind the pantry door.

"What do you mean?" Olivia raised a knowing brow. "He's hot, isn't he?"

"Would you lower your voice?" Briar said. "He's right upstairs!"

"I knew it," Olivia said. "One look at those crimson cheeks of yours could only mean one thing. Come clean."

"Let's not do this now," Briar begged as she tucked cinnamon rolls into a bread basket and set them on the table beside a small stack of plates. "Please."

Olivia smirked. "Well, I guess if you're not interested, I might as well take a whack at him."

Briar's cheeks were on fire. She turned to the sink. "Do what you want," she muttered and began to scrub furiously at a cooking pan. "You always do. And I'm *not* interested."

"Yeah, sure." Olivia knew Briar better than anyone. They weren't just cousins. They'd grown up together, Briar's mother managing Hanna's and

Olivia's parents turning Tavern of the Graces into a runaway success.

Olivia had long, blond hair that hung halfway down her back in flyaway curls and her sharp green eyes didn't miss a trick. She stood nearly a head shorter than Briar but made up for it with her boisterous personality, an uproarious, booming laugh and an unchecked streak of righteousness.

Despite their differences, they'd grown as close as sisters over the years. Guilt riddled Briar over the tinge of envy. Olivia could bait the opposite sex with a mere sidelong glance and, by extension, make Briar feel completely inadequate in the men department.

The swinging kitchen door opened behind her and her fingers stiffened around her scrub brush when she got a strong whiff of soap and shampoo. Not quite steady enough to look, she continued to buffer the oven pan.

"Good morning, ladies."

"Hi," Olivia greeted, rising from her chair with a flirty smile.

"Are you staying here, too?" Cole asked.

"Hell, no," Olivia said with a loud cackle. "I couldn't afford a room here if I sold my tavern."

"Tavern?"

"Briar didn't tell you about me? She's certainly forgotten her manners. Olivia Lewis. I own Tavern of the Graces right next door."

"Cole Savitt. You don't look like a bartender."

"Let me tell you something, mister," she said with a roll of her eyes. "I make a margarita Jimmy Buffet would weep over."

He laughed. Briar's insides trembled over the deep sound. She certainly hadn't made him laugh, had she? "I might have to find out for myself," he replied.

"Then come on by later, if you're not busy. Not much to do around this place."

Briar's back stiffened as Cole hesitated. "I might," he repeated. "Are you joining us for breakfast, Olivia?"

"I wouldn't miss the cinnamon rolls for anything," Olivia drawled. "Tell me about yourself, Mr. Savitt. What brings you to Hanna's?"

He settled on one of the seats at the table. "It's personal."

"Hmm. Well, you can't leave us dangling like that. Can he, Briar?"

Briar lifted a shoulder, drying a coffee mug and setting it in the open cupboard over the counter. "It's his business."

Olivia let out an exasperated huff. "Enough with the Sandra Lee. Would you sit down?"

Briar sighed, drying her hands. She turned to the oven. "I'm waiting for the quiche."

"Quiche, too?" Cole asked, brow quirked in interest. "I think I've died and gone to heaven."

"You better believe it," Olivia advised.

Briar took a pot holder off a hook on the wall and opened the door. "Close enough." She pulled the quiche out and set it on the waiting trivet on the table, moving the bowl of fruit to the counter and replacing it with a server of fruit salad. "What would you like to drink, Cole?"

"Coffee's fine," he said, lifting his mug.

"Liv?"

"OJ for me. So did you bring a wife along, Cole?"

"No," he replied with an edge to his voice. "I don't have a wife."

Olivia pursed her lips, curious. "I've never been married, either."

As Briar brought Olivia's juice to the table and settled into a chair, her eyes met his. "What about you?" he asked.

She paused. "Erm…me?"

"Process of elimination, cuz," Olivia quipped, watching her with a sly grin.

"No. I've never been married," she stammered before dropping her face to hide another flush and piled fruit salad onto her plate.

"Briar hasn't been on a date in years," Olivia blurted. "Needless to say, we all think she seriously needs to get laid."

"Olivia! Honestly, that's enough," Briar squealed as Cole choked on a cinnamon roll.

"What?" Olivia asked. "We're all family. No need to hide the truth. Especially when he might be able to help you out with that. Would you mind loosening her up for us, Cole?"

Briar groaned, pressing a hand over her eyes to ward off Olivia's scheming expression.

"I'd love to."

Briar's hand and jaw dropped simultaneously. Her eyes widened, her heart leaping with surprise and… something else. Delight? She saw his playful grin then Olivia's. "Oh!" she shrieked, embarrassment trawling through her.

"I'm sorry, Briar," Cole said sincerely. "Couldn't resist."

"You'll fit right in around here," Olivia decided, slapping him companionably on the back.

"I hope so." He smiled as he scooped a forkful of quiche into his mouth. His eyes flared, softened. "Whoa. Holy smokes."

Olivia's conspiratorial twinkle was back, suggestive as ever. "Look, Briar, he even likes your cooking."

"That's an understatement," he amended, swallowing another bite. He gazed at her. "This is incredible."

Briar's lips curved warmly now. "Thank you."

"She's the best cook in L.A." At his dubious look, Olivia laughed. "That's Lower Alabama, newcomer." Olivia's digital watch beeped and she cursed. Dropping her fork to her plate with a sharp clang, she pushed her chair back to rise. "Duty calls."

"You're going to work already?" Briar asked. "You didn't finish your breakfast."

"I'll survive, Mama." She took her plate to the sink to rinse. "The bar doesn't open until noon. I'm helping that new girl move her stuff into the shop upstairs."

Briar gasped. "I forgot all about that!"

"Don't get up. Two pairs of hands will get the job done fine," Olivia assured her as she dried hers. "And Adrian's going to sneak up when she can."

"I'll head over later to see if you need anything," Briar said. She'd fit it in between fixing a leaky sink and weeding flower beds. "Call me if y'all need me before then."

"You just do what you do best first." Olivia leaned over and kissed the top of Briar's head. "Be good." She sent Cole a sidelong grin as she headed out the screen door. "Don't give her any trouble now, ya hear?"

"I wouldn't dare," he assured her. "I'll come by later for that margarita."

"You do that. First one's on me. See you two lovebirds later."

When the door rapped shut, Briar turned to him with a grimace. "I'm sorry about that."

"She's a feisty one."

"Always has been," Briar said with a weary sigh. "Trust me. There's never a dull moment around here."

"You grew up here?"

"Yes. My mother established the inn after she

married my father. A short time later, Olivia's parents bought the bar from a couple of retirees and rebuilt from the ground up. They lived in the apartment upstairs. When they retired, they handed it all over to Olivia. Ever since I took over, it seems I'm either over at the tavern yelling at her to turn the music down or she's over here making a fool of me in front of my guests."

"You're right. Never a dull moment. Can I have another one of these?"

Her face lit with a quick smile. "Finish them off, by all means." She passed the basket of cinnamon rolls across the table and felt the glow spread from her heart to her cheeks when he took two. "I'm glad you like them."

"Mmm. This is all wonderful, Briar. I don't remember the last time I had a fine meal like this."

In an instant, his eyes clouded over again. She wanted to reach across the table and touch his hand, squeeze it reassuringly. Anything to erase that haunted look from his face.

Before she could react or resist, the phone rang. She lifted her napkin to dab the corners of her mouth. "Excuse me."

He raised a hand to show that her departure didn't bother him.

She sprinted into the entryway. Hopefully, it was another customer calling to reserve a suite. Or an investor. *Please, let it be one or the other.* "Hanna's Inn," she greeted, pulse pumping in her ears.

"Ms. Browning?"

"Yes."

"My name is Jack Fields. I'm with the Baldwin County tax office. I'd like a few minutes of your time."

CHAPTER THREE

ALL THE BLOOD drained from her face down to her toes. She wanted to shrink to the floor. Without a chair, she leaned against the wall as her heart plummeted to the pit of her stomach. "Is there a problem, Mr. Fields?" Her voice trembled. She prayed for control and watched her free hand quiver as it reached for a pen on the podium.

"I'm afraid there is. Is this a convenient time to talk or should we schedule a meeting sometime this week?"

She swallowed. "Now's fine."

"You are the proprietor of Hanna's Inn on South Mobile Street in Fairhope, Alabama?"

"Yes, that's me."

"And you own the adjacent property, as well?"

"I do."

"I'm sorry to say this, Ms. Browning, but you're late on your property tax payment. Are you aware of this?"

Of course she was aware of it. The tax plagued her every thought—along with the inn's other debts. She took a shaky breath. "Mr. Fields, business was very slow this past autumn and winter season. I had to pay an unexpected remodeling charge for one of the shops next door. Plus, there was another hotel established in the downtown area and it took a chunk out of my profits."

"I sympathize, Ms. Browning, but I'm afraid that failure to pay taxes is a serious offense."

She took a minute to gather herself. She had to stand up against this. Had to be strong. "I realize that, Mr. Fields, but surely, there can be an extension on the deadline...."

"We've already offered the extension. Twice. You did receive the notices we sent?"

She'd received them. And she'd scrimped and saved. But then there was the matter of her car breaking down for the final time. Without a vehicle, she couldn't haul groceries or landscaping materials. The down payment on the used Honda had burned a devastating hole in what was left of her savings. "I received them, yes."

"And you failed to comply."

"It's not a matter of failed compliance, Mr. Fields. It's just a matter of simple finance. I have every intention of paying the tax and I will when I have the resources. At the moment, though, I do not have the payment."

"Ms. Browning, you do know what the penalty for failure to pay your taxes is, don't you?"

Her head started to spin. The wallpaper whirled sickeningly. "I—"

"The county can seize any assets you hold in your name to account for the debt. In this case, we would be forced to take the property."

Now she did shrink to the floor. Curling up, she dropped her brow to her raised knees. She struggled to breathe through the panic that assailed her.

"Ms. Browning?"

She couldn't lose the inn. She just couldn't. In an instant, she was transported back to last winter, watching her mother wither away before her eyes. Staring out at the bay as if the sight of sun dappling on its blue-gray waters would bring healing where nothing else could.

Tears burned her eyes. "Mr. Fields..." She took a deep breath, doing her best to steady her voice. "My mother, Hanna Browning, a pillar of this community, lost her life last year."

"Yes, I knew of her illness." The voice softened. "I'm very sorry, Ms. Browning. I'm also aware of the fact that she was under your care."

"As you can imagine, the expense of her treatments and everything it took to make her comfortable during her last few months..." Again she had to take a breath. The quaver in her voice had worked its way into her joints and threatened to tear her to pieces. "It was devastating to both my family and the finances we had accumulated over the years."

"I understand that, ma'am, but—"

"Mr. Fields, please, I need you to understand that

I will pay the tax. I always pay my debts. I…I just need more time."

A long pause followed the waning words. Her heart hammered somewhere between her stomach and spinal cord. The hole it left in her chest throbbed miserably.

"We can give you until mid-July."

She released the breath she'd held on to as a last resort. "Oh, thank you, Mr. Fields. Thank you so much."

"Just make sure you get the payment in. Preferably ahead of time."

"I will. You can be sure of it." Anything to prevent losing Hanna's. "Goodbye, Mr. Fields."

"Have a good day, Ms. Browning."

She stood to hang the phone back in the cradle. For a long moment, she leaned her head against the wall and concentrated on steadying herself. Her knees quaked, and she ordered them to stop. She wiped her eyes before turning to walk back into the kitchen.

A gasp launched from her throat when she found Cole standing in the hallway just beyond. She clapped a hand over her heart. "Oh, for heaven's sake. Mr. Savitt. I didn't see you there."

He said nothing, just scanned her face with a frown.

Oh, dear God, her troubles were no doubt written all over her. How much had he heard?

He stepped forward, into the light. The haunted

look had vanished from his face, replaced with concern. "Are you all right?"

She swallowed, her insides squirming in embarrassment and cheeks heating all over again. "Is there…anything I can get you?"

He closed the distance between them in three quick strides. Startled, she pressed her back against the podium. Her breath caught as he hovered close, gaze intense now as he searched her eyes, seeing too much. "Are you all right?" he asked again.

She sucked in a long, steadying breath. "I'm fine." When he didn't look convinced, she sighed. "Mr. Savitt, you're my guest. It's my job to see to it that *you're* all right. Not the other way around."

"And who sees to it that you are?" he blurted.

Her lips parted. No guest had ever asked her such a question. Certainly not one she had ever met before.

Lips firming, he lowered his penetrating stare. "I…apologize, Ms. Browning."

With a short shake of her head, she fought for words. "It's forgotten."

Hesitant, his gaze latched on to her face once more, spanning her features. "You look exhausted, is all."

Lifting a hand to her hair, she realized she must look a fright. "I—"

"If you need a break, I'll be happy to—"

"No," she refused, finding strength buried beneath the shame. "No, that's out of the question. I thank you, Mr. Savitt, but the last thing I need right now is a break."

Silence loomed over them both. Then he slid his hands slowly into his pockets in a gesture of acquiescence. "All right."

Her eyes avoided his as disbelief again crossed his face. "Really, if there's anything I can do to make your stay more enjoyable…"

His face hardened and for an instant, she thought she saw the muscles in his jaw quake formidably. Finally, he pulled in a long inhale and said, "I told you. Just call me Cole." Turning away, he walked out, the bells jangling over the door in his wake.

She watched him through the windows until he disappeared from view. Then she shook her head.

The man was unbelievable.

And he'd smelled so good up close—like soap, her cinnamon rolls and that very base note she suspected belonged to him alone.

Setting the pen she still held tightly in her hand on the podium, she dragged her fingers through her hair and made her way back to the kitchen.

She stopped short just inside the door.

The table had been cleared. Three clean plates and forks dried in the sink-side drainer.

Did he…?

Something inside her awakened, unfurling, tingling to life. Something that'd been dead for too long to measure.

If she wasn't careful, she could start feeling things

for this man she barely knew. Things she couldn't afford to feel for anyone again—least of all a complete and total stranger.

COLE NEEDED TIME alone to think. Room enough to pace, to burn off the edge from the confrontation with Briar.

He'd seen women in pain. He'd been a member of the Huntsville police department for ten years. That was more than enough regular calls of domestic violence and trauma vics. Yes, he'd seen too many wounded women to count.

But Briar... She was different. Kind to a fault and yet undeniably capable with what he strongly sensed was an unexpected streak of perseverance. She downright intrigued him.

After the past three hellish years... Well, she was like a breath of fresh air. A fine, cool kiss of morning mist.

A ride around town wouldn't cool the burn in his blood. Wrestling with it, he walked away from the inn. Away from her. He couldn't keep encountering her on the verge of tears. Finding her that way, close to shattering, had made him forget completely why he was here. Tiffany's wicked errand and all that came with it.

Damn it, for a moment, Gavin's face had been completely wiped away by Briar's frightened features, and he'd wanted nothing more than to enfold her in his arms and...

Nope, don't go there. Don't you dare go there, Savitt. Dangerous. Under the circumstances, it was just too damned dangerous. For the both of them.

How he could even think about being with another woman again after all the grief Tiffany had put him through was beyond him.

As he roamed around the side of the building, the tidiness of the well-loved garden left him little doubt Briar landscaped it herself. The scent of the confederate jasmine clinging to lattices tickled his nostrils. Bright salmon petunia faces popped out of the soil in cheery abundance. At his approach, a hummingbird flitted away from a butterfly bush. Off the gravel path, a vegetable garden flourished. Squash and tomatoes looked seasoned, a bright slash of color against the lush green landscape.

More of her work there. He saw it, too, in the clumps of daffodils trumpeting up from the mulch between sweet olive bushes. Climbing roses laced their way around porch columns. He smelled the gardenia before he spotted it. The soothing fragrance of the open, palm-sized blooms cleared the way for cool thoughts.

Briar didn't need a man with a past as black as his underlying intentions cozying up to her.

"You son of a bitch!"

Frowning toward the voice that had read his thoughts exactly, he pivoted on his heel to face the long, glass-walled greenhouse between the inn and its neighboring twin structure. Something crashed against the floor and he took several steps toward the paned doors that had been thrown wide-open. More expletives reached his ears as he peered around the jamb.

First he spotted the glass splintered on the damp concrete slab and the long-stemmed crimson roses scattered like blood spatter.

Great. He was likening flowers to something he'd seen at a crime scene. The world-weary detective he'd wanted to bury deeply, forever, was taking over again, little by little.

"Hello?" he called.

Instantly, a brilliant streak of red hair peered over a worktable. "Shop's next door, mister!"

"I heard a commotion," he called back, taking a step farther over the entrance. "Are you okay?"

She emitted a snort before disappearing from view. Something scraped across the floor, followed by the tinkling protest of glass. *Dustpan.* "What are you, my knight in shining armor?"

He grimaced. "More like a concerned neighbor. Temporarily, at least."

The auburn crop appeared again. On second look, her face was round and pixielike with a button of a nose and unpainted lips, which softened the impact of her pronounced bone structure. The eyes that stared back at him were dark and sharp as a whip.

This was no damsel. From the eyes alone, he could tell nothing got past this lady.

The woman stood slowly, revealing a red apron

with the name FLORA embroidered across the front. "I apologize for the outburst. The vase was delivered broken and tried to pick a fight with me."

He tilted his head, eyeing what had once been the vase in question. "Seems you won."

She beamed and propped a gloved fist on her hip. "As a matter of fact, I did." Those sharp eyes narrowed. "Do I know you?"

He scanned her face more closely. After some hesitation, he stepped forward, cautious of the scattered shards. "I'm Cole. Cole Savitt," he said, extending a hand toward her.

Her eyes narrowed as she pried a glove from her hand to grip his firmly. "I don't think I know any Savitts. Are you related to anyone around here?"

He paused. Then decided there wasn't much harm in mentioning Tiffany. "My ex-wife. Tiffany Howard."

"It rings a bell." She nodded, pursing her lips. "I'm Adrian. Adrian Carlton."

"Adrian," he greeted. "Nice to meet you."

"You married?"

He chuckled, unable to help it. "You ladies cut right to the quick around here."

"So you've met Liv, I take it."

"Yeah." He smiled. He sensed from experience that she was a wary soul, but an inherently good one. His instincts had served him well in the past...unless he counted Tiffany and the viper that had lived unbeknownst to him under her polished veneer. "And

I take it you're the Adrian who owns the flower shop next door."

"That's me. Flora, finest flowers in Fairhope. You must be Briar's new guest."

"You heard about me, huh?"

"We don't get many single men around Hanna's," Adrian told him, easing into a smile. "And with somebody like Liv on the loose, nothing stays secret for long. Though since the fact that you have an ex-wife didn't come up in this morning's gossip exchange, I'm guessing I'm the first to know that you're divorced."

He lifted a shoulder, slipping his hands into his pockets in a relaxed stance. "It's not something people like to advertise."

"Don't I know it." At his curious look, she nodded. "We're of the same breed as far as failed marriages are concerned."

"Ah. Sorry."

She shook her head. "Nothing to be sorry about. Especially when your ex is a wife beater hiding behind a badge."

"Please tell me justice was served," he said.

"After long last. Suspension for him and restraining order for me and my son," she said matter-of-factly before tending to some long-stemmed roses. "So what brings you to Fairhope?"

"Much-needed vacation," he lied.

"Workaholic?"

"Actually, I'm kind of between jobs."

"What do you do?"

He hesitated then realized there was no reason to lie, at least about his job. "I was a Huntsville police detective."

Her brows lifted again. "Seriously?"

"I put ten years on the force."

"You know, now that I think about it, you look like a cop," she said with a smug smile.

"Since the wife-beating ex is a cop, too, I'm guessing that isn't a compliment."

She smiled. "I'll trust you and he have little in common other than your chosen careers."

"And I'll thank you for that, Ms. Carlton," he replied.

"Adrian," she corrected. "Ms. Carlton is my mother, which is why I tend to shudder whenever anyone calls me by that particular name."

He chuckled again. Yes, he was growing to like Adrian.

"You thinking of transferring south?" she asked. "I'm acquainted with a few of the officers at the local PD. I could introduce you...."

"No, for now I'm just..." He stopped because he saw understanding begin to creep into her eyes. "This seems like a nice enough place to live, I'll admit. Everyone's friendly. The weather's good—not too hot."

She snorted out a laugh. "Wait until mid-July before you start making weather assumptions. I should give you the grand city tour, introduce you to the right people. You might like it enough to stick."

No. It'd be a while before he could stick anywhere. The thought of two weeks in Fairhope already seemed like an eternity. At Hanna's, anyway—close to Briar and other things too far out of his reach. However, if he couldn't be around Briar without thinking straight then her friends might be able to tell him more than he could wean out of her. "What are you doing tonight?"

She considered. "I could ask Briar to babysit."

"You don't have to do that. I don't want to put Briar out." God knew she had enough on her plate already.

"Oh, Kyle loves Briar," she explained. "He helps her out around the place, gives her a much-needed hand, even if it is with the little things."

He hesitated, weighing the situation. "Well, okay, then. I'll meet you at the tavern around seven?"

"Seven it is." She started to walk off. "I have a customer waiting on these roses. It was nice meeting you, Cole."

CHAPTER FOUR

"YOU GOT A date with the new guy?"

Adrian heaved an aggrieved sigh. "It's not a date, Liv. I'm just showing him around."

"I think he might be able to show you a thing or two," Olivia deduced.

Adrian took a bite out of her tuna sandwich, knowing as well as Briar did that a reply would only egg on Olivia. It was no use trying to budge Olivia once she set her mind to something. Especially if that something was in any way, shape or form promiscuous.

Olivia and Adrian were eating lunch at the inn kitchen table while Briar attempted to fix the leaky pipes under the sink. It didn't take long for Olivia to notice that she was having difficulty using the socket wrench. "You need a plumber."

"Plumbers cost money," Briar said. "Unfortunately, I can't afford such a luxury."

"Come on, cuz," Olivia said. "It's not that bad."

Briar frowned as she gave up on the pipes and the wrench, tucking it away with her other tools and cleaning supplies by closing the cabinet doors.

She washed her hands then walked to the fridge to pull out the makings for lunch. "I got a call from a county man today. Property taxes are overdue."

Olivia and Adrian exchanged worrisome glances. "Did you ask for an extension?" Adrian asked.

"I've already had two," Briar explained, pulling open a packet of bacon. Strips sizzled as she laid them one by one on a hot skillet. The smooth, practiced motions of her hands were at odds with the slight quaver of her tone. "He said that if I don't pay by the middle of July, they'll seize the property to compensate."

Olivia choked on her sandwich as Adrian gaped in horror. "They can't do that."

The last time Briar had felt this tired, drained, was during her mother's last days. "With the way business is going, I don't know if I can raise it. If I don't nail down one of these potential investors soon, I could lose everything."

"We'll fight for it."

"That's right," Adrian assured her, echoing Olivia's sentiment. "We'll fight for what's ours, Briar. We'll help you."

She shook her head. "I'm already bleeding the both of you for rent. Adrian, you had to replace your greenhouse after the last hurricane and I know it ate a hole in your house budget—you barely had enough left over to send Kyle to soccer camp. And, Liv, you're saving up for an addition to the tavern. I have to do this alone."

"You can't do *everything* alone," Olivia protested.

"And that's why I have potential investors." She waved her hands in frustration. "Can we not talk about this right now? So, tell me what you think of the new girl."

Defeated, Adrian lowered to her seat, appetite forgotten. "Roxie Honeycutt. She seems nice, really excited about opening shop."

"Though Lord knows we don't need another bridal boutique around here," Olivia said before taking a big bite out of a banana.

"She also has a license for wedding consultation," Briar added.

Olivia made a face. "They give out licenses for just about anything nowadays."

"Anyway," Briar went on, "she has some interesting ideas—I think she'll do well. And I bet her gowns are gorgeous."

Adrian brightened up. "*And* she plans on using me for all the floral arrangements she'll need."

"I like her," Briar concluded, placing the bacon onto a plate. She took a knife from the butcher block to slice a tomato. "Why didn't you bring her over for lunch, guys?"

"Said she was eating with her hotshot fiancé," Olivia explained with a dismissing wave of her hand. "Some law professor named Richard Levy."

"He teaches in Mobile," Briar blurted. "At South Alabama."

"You know him?" Adrian asked curiously.

"No," Briar said, frown returning. "Daddy was talking about him the last time I visited."

That left another gray cloud hanging over the room—usually any mention of Briar's father did. Any thought of him, really, had the same effect.

It's unimaginable—you running the business by yourself....

She closed her eyes because the terrible words he'd spoken to her that day not but a year before still echoed clearly through her head—on a constant loop.

Adrian recovered the conversation. "She's coming by the tavern tonight to try one of Olivia's margaritas."

"I guess that'll be around the time you skip off on your hot date."

"It's not a date, Liv."

Briar looked up. "What's this about a date, Adrian?" she asked as she began to shred a head of lettuce.

"Oh, she's got one hell of a date lined up," Olivia groused. "With Cole Savitt."

The lettuce dropped to the floor with a crunch. Briar felt the color drain from her face as she bent to scoop up the mess. "Oh."

Olivia watched her cousin closely as she ran the lettuce under the sink tap. "Yep. She beat us both to the plate."

"That's not true," Adrian protested, clearly alarmed by Briar's reaction.

"Did you get the scoop?" Olivia asked.

"About why he has that wounded air about him? Maybe. And it seems to be a recent development."

"And?"

Taking a sip of her mineral water, Adrian watched Olivia's expectant face with a shred of glee. "It's personal."

Olivia groaned. "Can't you just give me a hint?"

"Nope."

"Spoilsport." Olivia took a hearty bite out of her sandwich, eyeing Adrian with mock loathing before turning her attention to Briar. "Would you just sit down and eat? The man has two hands. He can fix his own lunch."

"You know that I provide meals when they're requested," she reminded Olivia. "He wanted to eat here. I'm going to accommodate him."

"Like a good hostess," Olivia said with some disdain. "Personally, I don't think women should cook for men at all anymore. We've progressed too far for that. Let them fend for themselves."

"It's not as if we're married," Briar said, irritation nipping on her heels. "I've never done anything less for any guest."

"If I were in your shoes, I'd serve him right up in a negligee," Olivia said with a knowing smile.

Briar's color was definitely coming back. "You just stepped on your point."

Olivia met Adrian's curious gaze and said, "She's got the hots for him."

"Olivia—"

The screen door creaked open and Cole walked through. "Good afternoon, ladies."

"Cole," Olivia greeted, offering him a Cheshire-cat grin. She patted the cushion of the seat next to hers. "We were just talking about you." She winked conspiratorially at Adrian.

"Ah, so that's why my ears are burning." He settled in the chair. "Something smells good," he commented, craning his neck toward the stove.

"Briar's slaving away again," Olivia informed him. "I hope you like blood, sweat and tears."

Cole glanced up at Briar who was neatly arranging two BLTs on a plate. "Do you need any help?" he asked.

She turned and met his gaze. She swore she was growing pinker by the second. Lowering her eyes, she set a plate in front of him. "Of course not. What would you like to drink?"

"I'll get it," he said, already on his feet. "You don't have a fixed plate here. Go ahead and make yourself something."

"But I'm—"

He smiled and effectively melted the rest of her words away. "I can fix myself a drink, Briar."

"Cole—" Briar began before Olivia cut her off.

"Let the man do what he wants and fix yourself some food. You work to the bone then starve yourself. Soon you'll be nothing but a scarecrow."

"Fine," Briar resigned. "Cups are in the cupboard." When his back was turned, she sent Olivia a seething look. Her cousin merely lifted a shoulder and finished off her sandwich.

As if Briar didn't have enough problems already with her guest getting under her skin and the inn potentially going under. Apparently, Olivia had decided to play the Emma Woodhouse game again.

Since she had returned to Fairhope, Briar had managed to fly under Olivia's matchmaking radar. Adrian, however, hadn't faired so lucky and had a short list of dating calamities to prove it.

By the helpless look on Adrian's face, Briar knew there was little the people involved in Olivia's matchmaking schemes could do but humor her and hope it didn't all end in complete disaster.

TAVERN OF THE Graces was in full swing by seven o'clock. Regulars lined up at the bar, talking to each other overloud. The room was nearly filled to capacity, and the pool table was in use by after-work players. And above the table in the corner where an arm-wrestling match was taking place was a flat-screen television tuned to ESPN and a Braves game.

When Cole walked through the thick wood-paneled doors he was overwhelmed by a blast of Sheryl Crow's "Winding Road."

Jubilant shouts echoed from the men surrounding the pool table. Cole followed their attention to the television and saw that Chipper had hit a homer.

One of the pool players stalked to the bar and

leaned over it, yelling into an open doorway, "Hey, Liv! Your man just hit one out of the park!"

Olivia walked through, carrying a heavy case of beer bottles and beaming. "That means you owe me twenty bucks, Freddie."

"Aw, hell, Liv. I got a family to feed."

"I'll let this one slide—next time be more careful with your bets. Drinks all around, people!"

Hoots and whistles sounded off around the room as she took bottles out of the case and put them into eager hands. Cole stepped up to the bar to take one. When Olivia's face lit on his, she smiled wide and said, "Hey there, cutie!"

Cole raised his voice over the intro to Aerosmith's "Walk This Way." "Hey, Olivia. I'm meeting Adrian. Do you know if she's here yet?"

"Don't think so," Olivia shouted. She stretched the thin material of her black tank top over the exposed line of pale skin at her belly. He caught a glimpse of a small, heart-shaped tattoo buried halfway underneath the beltline of her low-rise jeans. "She's probably closing shop and carting Kyle over to Briar's. While you're waiting, though, I'll give you something more potent than this."

She snatched the bottle out of his hand and gave it to one of the regulars, instead. Then she went to work pouring, stirring and blending. In two minutes, she handed him a tall hurricane glass. "This is the best margarita south of the Mason-Dixon. Brace yourself."

As he lifted the glass to his lips, he was aware that several of her patrons watched him closely. He did brace himself and took a sip. The surprising tang of salt and alcohol made a visible shiver worm its way effectively down his spine. "Wow," he choked.

The nearest regular let out a whooping laugh and clapped a hand over Cole's back. "Knocks your socks right off, don't it, man?"

"Yeah," he muttered, braving another sip. "Sure does."

Olivia let out a bellowing laugh that made heads around the room swivel. She patted his cheek, leaning over the bar and exposing ample cleavage over the low scoop of her tank. "I knew you'd fit right in." Shouting over the music, she announced, "Now who wants to buy me my first drink of the night?"

Excited shouts of "Over here, Liv" and "Right here, baby" echoed around him. Men muscled Cole out of the way in their rush to get to the bar. As he walked backward, he almost toppled over the woman standing close behind him.

"Bit overwhelming, isn't it?" Adrian shouted with a knowing smile.

"Olivia or her customers?"

Adrian laughed and raised herself on tiptoe to brush her lips over his cheek in greeting. "Let's get you another drink."

BRIAR STEPPED INTO the tavern from the door behind the bar just in time to see Adrian give Cole a smooch. Her stomach plummeted to her toes. Determined not to feel crushed, she went to Olivia's shoulder and waited until her cousin downed the two shots the rugged gentleman in front of her had bought. She wasn't at all surprised when Olivia didn't so much as flinch.

"That's the way to start the night!" she shouted, leaning forward to give the man a hard kiss on the lips. "Whew!" She stumbled around and spotted Briar. "Oh, hey there, cuz! What'd you do with the little one?"

"He's napping on the couch in your office," Briar said, nodding back toward the door she'd closed to block out some of the noise. "Didn't take him long to pass out."

"Being a kid's tough," Olivia said. "What are you doing here?"

"Figured you could use some help since it's Monica's night off."

"Could, yeah," Olivia agreed. "Busier than an ant at a picnic." She looked over Briar's shoulder. "You could start by taking their orders."

Briar turned toward the end of the bar and met Cole's gaze. She hadn't noticed him and Adrian grabbing two stools. Whirling back to Olivia, she caught sight of the smirk on her face as her own heated. "Liv, I know what you're doing."

"What am I doing?" Olivia asked innocently.

"They're on a date."

"But notice, his eyes are on you," Olivia pointed

out. "And I'm the boss 'round these here parts." She gave her cousin a good push in their direction. "Scat."

Briar walked toward them on uncertain legs. She answered Adrian's smile of greeting before leaning over the bar and raising her voice. "Kyle's in the back room sawing logs."

"I know you wouldn't leave him anywhere alone."

"What can I get you two tonight?" Briar asked, putting on her brave face.

"We're not going to be here long," Adrian considered. She turned to Cole. "Crown and Coke suit you?"

"Suits me just fine," he said, his eyes never straying from Briar's face. He took out his wallet. "Let me get it."

"No, this is on me," Adrian protested.

He laid a hand on the one she'd used to open her purse. "You're nice enough to show me around town. Let me pay for the drinks."

When she shrugged acquiescence, he turned back to watch Briar mix the drinks behind the bar, pretending she hadn't heard their exchange. A moment later, she set the glasses on the bar. "That's three dollars." She smiled at Adrian. "Olivia says you get the official family discount."

"How sweet," Adrian said with a smile and a wave at her friend across the room, tipping her glass to her lips.

Cole took a ten-dollar bill out of his wallet and handed it over the bar. "No change."

She took the bill uncertainly, eyeing him in surprise. "Are you sure? That's seven dollars."

"A tip for a good bartender," he said as he raised his glass and drank, watching her over the rim.

"Thank you," she said, heart hammering as she walked away. More blood rushed to her face. She bit her lip to choke it back.

Olivia caught up and muttered in her ear, "Wow, what was that all about?"

Briar sent her an imploring, sidelong look. "It didn't mean anything. He was just being nice."

"A dollar is nice," Olivia pointed out. "Three dollars is generous. Five dollars is damned chivalrous. Anything more than that is just plain love."

Briar glanced back to where Adrian and Cole had been sitting. Something inside her shrank when she saw that they were already gone. She tucked the whopping tip in Olivia's jar before turning back to the bar.

Olivia gestured to the couple sitting on the far side. "There's Roxie and her squeeze. Go introduce yourself while I mix a couple more margaritas."

Briar pushed Cole out of her mind and pasted on another smile.

Roxie lifted a delicate hand when she recognized Briar. "I was hoping we'd see you tonight. This is Richard."

"Nice to meet you, Richard. I believe you're acquainted with my father," Briar said as she shook his hand. "Hudson Browning."

"Ah, yes," Richard said. His tall, gangly build towered over his companion's. Briar gauged him to be in his mid-thirties. With his subtle green eyes and dull brown hair, he looked the part of professor in a pin-striped shirt tucked neatly into pressed khakis. "The defense attorney. I didn't realize he had a daughter."

Surprised, Briar's eyes widened. A barb she was all too familiar with dug in against her heart...where it'd been lodged for some time. "I'm sorry I couldn't help you move into the shop today, Roxie. I wanted to, but—"

"I know you're busy," Roxie assured her, sympathy crawling into her eyes. She took Briar's hand and squeezed it reassuringly. "It's a tough time. But I'm as willing as Olivia and Adrian to help."

"Um, thank you," Briar said, uncomfortable. "Olivia should be done with those drinks in just a second." Before Roxie could protest, she turned away to escape into the back room. She bypassed the office and surged into the bathroom, locking the door behind her. She splashed cold water on her face as the fear and humiliation built at the back of her throat.

This was not the time to give in to panic again. She took a minute to breathe. *In and out. Just breathe.*

She looked in the mirror and saw her mother in the eyes staring back at her. The tears came quick, choking her. She covered her face with her hands, shame and regret dragging her under.

The door behind her opened swiftly. "Hey, I thought you were here to help," Olivia said.

Briar clenched her teeth together. "You really need to get that lock fixed."

"What the hell's the matter, Briar?"

Her voice shook. "How dare you?"

Olivia put a hand on her shoulder. "Briar…"

"Don't touch me!" Briar swatted the hand away and whirled. "How dare you tell her about *my* problems?"

"She has a right to know," Olivia said. "She has as much right as I do now that she's a part of this place. And she's willing to help."

"I don't need her damn help!" Briar shouted in a blinding burst of anger. "Why do you all think I'm some weakling who desperately needs saving?"

"No one thinks that, hon."

"You and I know everyone thinks that. You, Adrian, Roxie, her fiancé…even Cole Savitt."

"Cole's just a nice guy who likes you."

Briar shook her head as more tears fled down her cheeks. "Cut that out, Olivia."

"What?"

"I'm not interested in your matchmaking," Briar said bitterly. "All it's ever done is bring Adrian more disappointment. How do you expect it to work out any better for me?"

"You've had your guard up ever since Paris. I would never set you up for a fall like that again."

"Please. I need you to just stop playing games with me and Cole. He's not interested."

"Yes, he is. It's so obvious!"

"I said *stop!* I don't need anyone in my life. Especially not some stranger who's here for a couple of weeks and then gone. If I get one more stone thrown at me, I don't think I'll be able to stand alone again."

"That's what I'm here for," Olivia assured her. "I just want to help, Briar."

Another wave of anger geysered up, fast and blistering hot. "Well, help yourself. You haven't had a decent relationship any more than I have. Spend your time finding someone you don't have to drive away after a month or less."

Olivia's eyes darkened, her jaw firming. For a moment, she only glared. Then she jerked her chin in a resolute nod and sucked in a breath. "You've made your point. I'll leave you alone."

Briar closed her eyes. "I'm sorry. I'm a mess and I'm taking it out on you. I didn't mean that, Liv."

"Yes, you did," Olivia said. "I know you, Briar. You mean everything you say."

Briar sank to the closed lid of the toilet seat and rocked herself. "Maybe. But your love life isn't the issue. I shouldn't have dragged it into this."

Olivia shrugged as a tense silence carried over them. "Yeah, it was a cheap shot." She leaned against the sink, watching Briar's pained face. "Listen, if you really don't want me around the inn anymore, I'll give you some space."

She shook her head. "You're all I've got left."

Olivia slung an arm around Briar's shoulders. "That's ridiculous. You've got Adrian and Kyle, too. We're family, the four of us. And I mean it when I say I'm here for you, cuz."

Briar sighed. "I know."

Olivia patted her cheek. "Are we better now?"

Briar sniffled, nodded. "I think so."

"Then fix your makeup because we've got a bunch of thirsty people to charm before the night's done."

"Right." Briar squared her shoulders and locked composure into place, a practice she'd mastered long ago. "Back to work." Work would save her, even if nothing else could.

"So we've established that you were a detective," Adrian said as she dipped her fries in ketchup.

"Yeah, in Narcotics, mostly," Cole admitted and instantly felt a tightening in his belly. Adrian's tour so far had revolved around Fairhope and the everyday lives of the people who lived here. She had shown him the downtown area, the parks and the most notable restaurants, insisting they stop at one—Fly Creek Café. Since the sun had set and a nice, cool breeze was blowing off the bay into the harbor where the restaurant was cozily nestled, they'd chosen a picnic table on the sand outside.

There was a live band playing and the atmosphere was almost serene.

If he'd been able to relax, he would have really enjoyed it. All night long, though, he felt that he'd had to step carefully around Adrian. She was sharp. He had a good sense the cunning wisdom he saw in her eyes had been gained from experience. Their conversation hadn't ventured that far into the past, and he was thankful for it. It had been a long time since he'd had dinner with anyone new, but he did know that if she opened up about her past, he would be forced to open up about his.

And that was a whole can of worms he wasn't ready to open.

"I can see you in Narcotics," she said with a nod. "You've got this determined look about you."

He took a bite from his shrimp po'boy to cover the fact that his mouth had fallen open at the observation. He'd been so careful. Had she been reading him the whole time? Swallowing, he raised a brow and said, "Which means?"

"I don't know," she said, tilting her head as she studied his face. It was akin to being under the lens of a high-powered microscope. "It's just this vibe I've been getting. Like a 'wary hunter' sort of thing."

"*Weary* hunter is more like it," he muttered, picking up the last of the po'boy and washing it down with the beer in front of him. "How'd you get into the flower business?"

She pursed her lips, knowing he was evading.

She took a moment to wipe her hands on her napkin before deciding to answer the inquiry. "My parents own a plant nursery. Since I was little, they made me work there. Taught me how to grow, nurture, care for plants of all varieties. When I got older, I was in charge of the greenhouses with the annual flowers. I grudgingly started to like it. Eventually, I realized I wanted to branch out and make arranging flowers my business. About five years back, I finally saved enough for a start-up. Briar's mother gave me a good deal on the shop space, and the floral business has been keeping me busy ever since. Mom and Dad deliver peace lilies and ferns for me to display and sell."

"So it's a family enterprise?" he ventured to guess.

Her eyes narrowed. "I like to think of the shop as a solitary effort, but they knew all the best suppliers. I probably would've never gotten Flora off the ground if it hadn't been for them. I admit, it helps having parents who know people *who know people* in the industry."

She didn't like the implication that Flora's success was due to anyone but her, though, Cole noted. "Well, congratulations. You seem to be doing very well."

"Thanks," she said, dipping her head. "Now you again."

"Oh, boy," he said and took another sip of beer.

"Why'd you get out of Narcotics?"

The frown came instantly. He couldn't fight it or the dread that sank into him. He hated to remember how everything had gone downhill. From the divorce to his profession... It was all one big messy blur. But he knew the exact moment things in Narcotics had gone sour. Rarely did he let himself dwell on it.

He took a deep breath, spinning the beer bottle on the tabletop. "You're better off not knowing."

"Did something go wrong?" she asked.

He scanned her face and saw what she was waiting for. "They didn't take my badge, if that's what you're asking."

She nodded and a small relieved light flashed in her eyes. "That's a relief."

"I left for personal reasons," he said. "When you're around cops long enough, you hear a lot about something called 'burnout.'"

"You burned out," she surmised.

"Not completely," he told her. "I could've kept going. But things were unraveling around me. There's a numbness that you have when you're exposed to enough bloodshed. It doesn't completely protect you, but it's usually enough to get you through."

"You stopped feeling numb?"

He paused for a long moment. Was he really going to relive this again? "Something broke through." Clearing his throat, he shifted on the hard picnic table seat. "My partner and I had been tracking a meth lab into the woods outside the city. We secured a warrant, but we were a day too late. There was an explosion, and everyone in the house was killed."

He stopped but couldn't quite bring himself to look at her. His mind was back in the woods outside Huntsville, a place he rarely allowed himself to go. "It wasn't the first time I'd investigated a meth lab after an explosion and seen the dead bodies. But this time there was a family living in the house, too, with small children."

She nodded. "I can see how that would affect someone."

The part he didn't reveal to her was that one of the children had been the same age as his own son and that the meth lab investigation had happened around the same time that he realized Gavin could be taken away from him. For weeks, he couldn't sleep. When he'd finally gone back to work, he hadn't been able to focus on anything but the crime scene photos… and the face of that little boy.

With a court battle approaching, it had been the worst time to lose his job. But without focus, he could see himself slipping up in the field just long enough for his partner to be unprotected. One mistake was all it took. And the long hours he'd spent on the job over the past decade hadn't boded well for him in the fight for custody, either. Tiffany had used that very fact as one of her main striking points.

It was a lose-lose situation, whatever he did. He'd

given up the job he'd dedicated his life to, and he'd lost his son. All in one horrible year.

"How long ago was that?" Adrian asked, breaking the heavy silence that had fallen over the table.

"A little over a year."

"And you're still drifting."

He lifted a shoulder. "I lost my family and my job. It's hard to start over when there's no center."

"Do you think you'll ever be able to move on?" she asked.

Wasn't that why he was doing this wicked errand for Tiffany, for the promise of a new life? "Maybe. But it won't come without…work."

"Speaking as someone who has hit rock bottom—" she lifted her bottle in toast "—it's not easy, but it can happen."

There was the source of that shrewd judgment he'd seen under the surface. She was a single mother who had obviously been through hell with her ex and had come out on top—and all the better for it. Lifting his own beer bottle, he tapped it against the neck of hers. "Thanks."

"Be careful, though," she added. "Make sure the ends justify the means and you don't end up hurting someone you love in the process."

Someone you love. She was speaking of his son. But he couldn't help thinking of Briar back at the tavern. When had he gone from thinking of her as the pretty innkeeper to *someone you love?*

Gavin was that someone. Gavin was his only

chance at a content life, happiness. He couldn't lose sight of that for one second, especially where Briar Browning was concerned.

CHAPTER FIVE

NEAR TEN O'CLOCK, Adrian and Cole made it back to the tavern. Standing outside the doors, the jukebox could be heard blaring an old Hank Williams song. Adrian smiled at him. "Pretty rowdy in there."

"Is it always like this?" Cole wondered aloud.

"Liv lives for it," Adrian said. "She's as rowdy as three drunks on a bad night. She's got help, Monica Slayer, most evenings. On others, we try to lend a hand, whoever has less to do. But if she had to, Olivia could hold this place up with one hand and have strength to spare."

Cole hesitated before asking his next question. As far as Briar was concerned, his curiosity wouldn't stop prodding. Though he and Adrian had talked of little else but the inn and the three shops adjacent to it all night long, he'd managed to keep the subject off the innkeeper. Until now. "And Briar?"

Adrian lifted her shoulder. "She's been doing what she does ever since…well, she had to, really. But it's wearing her down. She refuses help, but we can all see the responsibility of the inn weighs on her, heavily. The past year's been especially difficult."

"Her mother," Cole surmised. Yes, he'd heard more of the conversation between Briar and whoever she'd been on the phone with than he'd have liked. The more he learned about Briar and why the inn was in such bad financial straits, the more he was riddled by guilt over what he was doing there.

"Yes," Adrian said and not much more. Solidarity, he knew. Her dark eyes slit, scrutinizing. "Why are you so curious about Briar?"

Shifting, he glanced out over the bay. "She just… It really seems like she… I don't know. Needs someone."

Her lips pursed. "You're interested in her."

Alarm filtered through him swiftly. "I'm not the kind of man she needs." It was the truth—as much for himself as to assure her.

Adrian lifted her chin in a short nod. "Not everyone's brave enough to share the load she has. Or care for her the way she deserves to be cared for."

Words formed on his tongue, but he stopped them before they could spill out. "You're right about that."

Her hand lifted to his arm. "Cole, I like you. And it's because I like you that I'm going to be completely honest with you. Briar's one of my oldest friends, and I don't want to see her hurt again. If you're just passing through, it's best just to leave things be."

He frowned over her shoulder at the bay again. "Adrian, I never had any intention—"

"I know," she said with a small smile. "But I saw the way you were looking at her today."

Avoiding her gaze again, he stuffed his hands in his pockets. "You're looking out for her. I get it. But trust me. The last thing I want is to cause Briar any trouble." Veering around her to the tavern door, he reached for the handle. "And you're right. That's all I'd ever be to her."

"Cole—"

"Don't worry about it," he said, pushing the door open. "I'll see you around, Adrian." Before she could reply, he shouldered his way in, losing himself in the crowd.

He could use another stiff drink.

The place was twice as crowded as before. Over the heads of the people on the barstools, he caught a glimpse of the two women working there.

Cole edged toward the wall to avoid getting shouldered by any of the people milling about. For a moment, he simply observed.

Briar maneuvered her way through the crowd with two large pints of draft beer in each hand. She took them to a table, set them down and pocketed the patrons' money. The gracious smile she aimed at them sucked Cole in. Made his pulse dance irregularly in that dark place it'd dwelled during the past few years.

Cole watched as a large man with a ruddy face

coated with a prickly red goatee cornered Briar, laying beefy hands on her shoulders. She jerked in surprise, spinning around only to find herself locked
between his solid, two-hundred-and-fifty-pound
bulk and the wall behind her. His booming voice res-
onated across the tavern. "Careful there, little lady.
Don't want you to trip and hurt that sweet face."

"Then you shouldn't stand in my blind spot,
Clint." She tried to outmaneuver him by ducking
under his arm. "Now if you'll excuse me, I have orders to fill."

"Why the rush?" he asked, wrapping an arm
around her waist and steering her toward a table
near the back of the room where lights were dimmer
and Olivia didn't have quite so well a view of what
transpired between her patrons. Cole saw Briar's
eyes flash around the room, looking for an escape.
He took several steps forward.

Clint's meaty paws squeezed her shoulders and
he leered close as his buddies at the table looked
on and sniggered. "Give me some sugar. You know
you want to."

She turned her nose up, digging an elbow into
the man's ribs in another effort to dislodge his at-
tentions. "You're embarrassing yourself, Clint. Now
knock it off so I can get back to work."

He chuckled louder, reaching around to her back-
side and grabbing a handful.

Cole lunged forward, pushing through the other
bystanders, a haze of rage cloaking his vision as

he heard Briar shriek in alarm. Before he could reach them and dispense justice in his own way, she hauled back a flat-palmed hand and struck Clint across the face.

Clint staggered back, not from the force of the blow, but in surprise, gripping his chin and eyeing Briar in a new light. "Well, who knew there was something fiery underneath Minnie Mouse's blouse? I like that."

Before Clint could reach out and touch her again, Cole clapped his hands over the giant's shoulders and jerked him forcibly around to face him.

"Hey, man," Clint protested. Blinking sluggishly, his eyes found Cole's face. Judging by the slow perception and the heavy stench of beer emanating from him, it didn't take a scholar to determine that Clint was well wasted. "What's it to you?" he asked, thumping Cole in the chest with the heel of his hand.

"Leave the lady alone," Cole demanded, his voice low. Someone shut off the music and all eyes tuned in to the action. "Or you'll be answering to me."

"Cole…" Briar began but Clint's mocking "ooooo" broke through her speech.

"What're you gonna do?" Clint asked. "Hit me?"

"If you touch her again, yeah," Cole pledged, his hard gaze never flickering from Clint's face. "I will." His hands were already balled, ready, at his sides.

The man let out an obnoxious laugh, grabbing

Briar by the wrist and trying to haul her against him again. "Is this bothering you, pretty boy?"

Briar clawed at the brawny cuff on her arm in a failed attempt to dislodge it. Her fingers were turning white—the nimrod was cutting off her circulation. "Let go of me, Clint! You're hurting me!"

Panic crossed Briar's face. Cole had seen that same expression on too many victims' faces to count. *Not Briar.* He flexed his fists until the knuckles cracked.

Olivia finally managed to work her way to the center of the crowd. He turned to her in question. "Permission to make a scene?"

"You had to ask?" she said, eyes bright with indignation. "If you don't, I will."

"Come on, mousey." Clint laughed, now using both hands to plaster Briar against him. "You'll like it. Trust me."

"Enough," Cole said, lunging forward. He put a firm hold on Clint's arm, twisting until the man was forced to let go. He blustered, swinging wildly with one arm. Briar ducked, but despite Cole's attempts to shield her, Clint's arm plowed into her, knocking her back into the vacated table and chairs.

Cole saw her go down hard. It was the last straw. Whirling, he raised a balled fist and nailed Clint in the jaw.

The man reeled back against the wall. Spitting blood, he knuckled his mouth. "Son of a bitch clocked me." He eyed Cole with the light of challenge strong in his eyes. "You wanna brawl?" He stood up, squaring his shoulders and planting his feet as he raised his fists. "Let's go."

Cole snapped his ready fist up again and sent Clint reeling once more, this time into the crowd of regulars to his left. They parted and let him fall like a tree with a deafening clatter to the floor.

Cole leaned over him, grabbing hold of the collar of the man's shirt. Again, he spoke low in a menacing tone. "If I catch you even looking at her again, much less bothering her, I'll knock your eyes out. Got me?"

Clint coughed. Blood spittled as he spoke. "She's not worth the trouble."

Cole hauled him into a sitting position and jerked his head in Briar's direction. She sat in a chair with a hand on the back of her head, her expression pained as she eyed the pair of them warily.

Cole twisted Clint's arm behind his back until he shrieked in pain. "Apologize."

"No flippin' way."

Cole twisted the arm harder, making Clint yelp.

"Okay, okay! You're gonna snap my damn arm off!"

"So apologize and save me the effort," Cole warned.

"Fine! Sorry, Ms. Browning. I didn't mean any harm."

Cole held on to the arm a moment longer then

reluctantly let it go. He looked to Olivia. "What do you do with the trash?"

She smirked, helping Briar to her feet as she looked around for two strong regulars. "Freddie, Ty, get rid of this hunk of junk for me, will ya?"

"Gladly, Liv." They scooped Clint up by each arm and hustled him out the door.

Cole crossed to Olivia and Briar as the crowd started milling again, everyone murmuring in the hushed wake of commotion. "You'll let me know if he makes trouble again?"

Olivia nodded. "You did good." She seemed to realize Briar was still leaning heavily against her side. "Come on, cuz. Let's get you cleaned up."

"She okay?" Cole asked, trailing them into the back room.

Olivia steered her into the office and lowered her to the only chair. "She'll be all right, as long as she's not bleeding anywhere."

Cole could see the bruises on the white skin of her wrist and a large purple welt on her shoulder where she'd smacked the table or chair. "Briar," he said, fighting the urge to reach out and touch her. "You all right?"

"My head," she said, reaching back again for it. "I rapped it on something." She pulled her fingers away. They were wet with blood. Cole's heart shrank at the sight.

Olivia parted Briar's hair to get a closer look at

the cut. "Cole, put some cold water on one of those hand towels there and hand it here."

Without hesitation he went to the sink in the corner, listening to Olivia's ministrations.

"We'll find you some aspirin, okay?" she said. "It should help the bump." She turned to Cole with a sneer when he handed her the wet cloth. "That slimeball."

"Does this happen often?" he asked.

"Not in my bar."

Briar groaned when Olivia poked gingerly at the bruise on her shoulder. "That hurts," she muttered. "And I'm a little dizzy."

Cole couldn't help himself. He knelt in front of her, took her free hand and squeezed it. "You might have a concussion."

"I'm not going to the hospital," she insisted.

One of the men who'd hauled Clint off walked into the office. "Hey, Liv. Sorry to interrupt, but some of your customers are getting antsy out here."

"Thanks, Ty. I'll be right out." Olivia went to the sink to wash the trickle of blood off. "Here's a clean towel. Can I trust you to get her to bed, Cole?"

"Go do what you need to. I'll make sure she's all right."

"Thanks. I'll be over to check on her after closing." Olivia patted his shoulder and walked back into the bar.

"Can you stand?" he asked, lifting Briar's head to look at her face.

"Yeah."

He pulled her to her feet slowly. Her knees wobbled, and he tucked an arm around her waist. "Okay?"

"Fine."

He walked her through the narrow hallway to the side door, which opened onto the lawn behind the greenhouse. It was a pretty night. He could smell the jasmine and gardenia of Briar's garden. Moonlight poured down around them, a spectral spotlight.

Briar slumped against his side. He paused, tucked one hand under her knees and scooped her into his arms. "Put your head on my shoulder."

She turned her face into his neck. The touch of her skin against his stirred something warm and hungry in his blood.

Not hungry by Clint's definition. Cole wanted to guard her, protect her from the seedy reality of the world. Her scent filtered through him just as the fragrance of her flowers penetrated the tepid night air. When she wrapped her arms close around his neck, he realized he had her full trust.

The knowledge was potent.

He mounted the stairs to the third level where he knew her private rooms were. Stepping into the living room lit by a single lamp, the smell of lavender struck him. He toted her past the small kitchen on the right and into the first bedroom. Its pale green drapes were closed tight over the windows. The mauve spread was turned down in invitation.

He set her on the edge and went to his knees to tug off her shoes. "Lay back," he advised.

She lowered to the pillows, curling onto her side to face him. He pressed the cloth to the back of her head. "How do you feel?"

"Mmm," she moaned distantly, her eyes closing. "Sleepy."

"Don't fall asleep yet. I need you to tell me if you blacked out at all."

"I don't think so."

He stroked a hand over her hair. "Do you have any Advil? Ibuprofen?"

"In the bathroom cupboard."

He returned with two pills and a glass of water. "Take these." Relieved to see color filtering back into her cheeks, he said, "You already look better."

She gazed at him as he ran the cold rag over her cheeks and brow. "Liv's right. You're a nice guy."

He didn't feel particularly nice. Protective. A bit shaken. But with hunger gnawing at his vital hold on control, *nice* wasn't the word for what he felt.

"What you did to Clint..." She trailed off and swallowed hard. "No one's ever done anything like that for me."

"Assault is something I don't tolerate," he groaned. "No one should."

"It was only a kiss he wanted. He was drunk and things just...escalated."

Cole had seen the greed in Clint's eyes, the way they'd skimmed her torso, the way they lit up when he touched her skin. Fury slunk into Cole and he worked carefully for a moment to contain it. Cole had seen his like too many times to count. The man had wanted more.

"He won't touch me again. Not after you scared him like that." Grinning, she added, "It was sort of funny hearing him scream like a girl."

Relieved to see her smile, he stroked her cheek and watched her eyes flutter closed. Pulling his hand away as if burned, he cleared his throat. "No, he won't touch you again. Not as long as I'm around."

The smile melted from her face and the light in her eyes faded. He knew she was thinking about his check-out date. She cleared her throat and changed the subject, careful not to look at him. "Adrian said you used to be a detective."

"Yeah," he said, his voice surprisingly rusty.

"You'd make a good cop."

Cole dropped the rag from her head, set it aside. "I don't think you have a concussion."

She sighed in obvious relief. "Good. I don't think I could've handled the hospital tonight."

"Still, expect to wake up with a rough headache in the morning. Think you can sleep?"

"Maybe."

He pulled the spread up and over her, tucking it around her shoulders, and switched off the light. "Good night."

"Cole."

As he glanced back, Briar looked too pale in the shadows. Too vulnerable.

"I'd feel better if you stayed a bit."

Swallowing hard, he hesitated halfway between the bed and the door, both calling to him for reasons that dwelled on opposite poles. "You need your sleep," he decided, looking away.

She let out a breath. "You're right. I'm…sorry to have to ask something else of you, but could you lock up downstairs? Liv has a key if she wants to look in on me later."

"Sure," he answered, taking several steps toward the door before he could change his mind. "Don't worry about it. Just get some sleep."

"Good night, Cole."

BRIAR'S ATTACK PROVIDED the perfect opportunity to check out the inn's records and gain some insight into the establishment's shaky finances. And Cole seriously doubted that someone as attached to the family business as Briar was would let it go belly-up without tapping all possible resources, such as buyers or investors.

However, as Cole lay in bed fully clothed in the dark with his gaze fixed on the ceiling, the knot in his throat grew larger.

Yes, it was the perfect opportunity—perhaps his only chance to get in and out of Briar's files unseen. But there was something else at work now.…

Maybe he'd gone soft since turning in his badge because he couldn't motivate himself to invade her privacy—not after the scare she'd had tonight in the tavern.

But she was okay—probably sleeping. Turning on his side to force his attention away from the ceiling—and Briar somewhere on the other side of that white, orange-peel expanse—he tried not to dwell on the fact that concussion victims *could* slip into comas if they fell asleep. No, she was fine. It was time to do what he was here to do.

Driving a fist into his pillow, he sat up and swung his legs over the side of the bed. He stepped lightly to the floor of his suite, careful not to wake the creaky, old footboards beneath him. As he turned the knob of the door, he ignored the knot in the back of his throat and how bad he felt about what he was going to do next.

Gavin, he remembered. All he had to do was think about his son. He pulled the door open and stepped out into the dark hall.

No sooner had he moved onto the landing than he heard the creak of the stairs in front of him.

He bit back a curse. No time to step back into his room and erase his tracks. The top of Olivia's head came into view and he gripped the banister in as casual a stance as he could manage.

Damn, why hadn't he heard her come in? He *was* going soft.

"Cole," she said, surprised as she made it to the landing. "You're up late."

"I heard you come in," he lied. Clearing his throat, he jerked his thumb toward the stairs that led to Briar's rooms. "I just wanted you to know I saw her to bed. She seemed fine, but I'm glad you're checking on her."

She smiled at him. "You're worried. That's so sweet."

He was worried about her. No acting involved there. "I guess," he said for lack of anything better. "Anyhow…" He pushed off the banister and backed toward the door of the bay-view suite. "I'll let you go on up."

Olivia patted his arm as she passed him. "Thanks again, Cole—for everything. You're a real hero."

Disguising the knee-jerk, disagreeable sound in his throat with a chuckle, he opened the door and walked back into his room. Frowning at the bed, he balled his hands into fists again.

Sleep wouldn't come as easily tonight as it had previously in the suite's bed. He consoled himself with the thought that tomorrow… Yes, *tomorrow* he would find a way into Briar's filing system. Then this foul errand, which he already felt tangled in from the neck down, would be over and he could get as far away from Briar Browning as possible.

TWO DAYS LATER, Briar beamed as she hung up the phone in the inn entryway. It was just past 10:00 a.m.

and already she had two families booked for the week. Her sigh wavered with relief, and she felt elated.

Guests meant she was another foothold closer to rising above the treacherous cliff she and the inn were dangling over. It hadn't occurred to her that at some point she'd begun to look forward to bookings because some part of her still enjoyed preparing for them. As she made her notes on how to prep for each family's specific needs, the urge to get back to work and arrange for a full house was strong enough to make her tap her foot against the side of the check-in podium.

The dull headache that had followed the run-in with one of Olivia's tavern chairs was down to a subtle throb, easily masked by a small dose of pain-killers.

With two cups of coffee in her system already, plus the last-minute reservations filling the days of the guest calendar in front of her, Briar's disposition went from cheerful to downright sunny for the first time in weeks.

Lunch. It would be lunchtime soon and Cole would likely be roaring back on that Harley of his. Touching a hand to the center of her chest, her smile faded a bit. Since the night he had gallantly carried her up to bed, even casual thoughts of him were accompanied by the flutter of her heart.

Scrubbing the heel of her hand against her sternum, she closed the guest book and walked to the kitchen. There was no room in her life for feelings

like this. Especially since Cole was a temporary fixture in her life. Less than a fixture actually, because
for the past couple days she'd seen very little of him.

"Roxie," she said, turning around as the door to
the kitchen swung open. "I wasn't expecting you."

Roxie lifted a shoulder. "I had some spare time
and thought I'd drop by. I hope you don't mind."

"Not at all. Have a seat—help yourself to some
coffee." Briar went to the sink to busy her hands. She
pushed her sleeves up and began to rinse the tomatoes that waited in a basket on the counter. "Roxie, I
should apologize for the way I acted the other night
in the tavern. There's no excuse for being rude to
you and your fiancé."

"You weren't rude at all," Roxie assured her as
she joined Briar at the sink. Her eyes widened as she
reached over to pick up one of the tomatoes. "These
are bigger than my mother's. You should sell them."

"I would if I didn't use them all for cooking,"
Briar explained. "They get bigger each year. Soon
I won't be able to get them through the door."

"That's when you enter them in the county fair
and win prizes," Roxie advised. Her warm grin
faded after a moment and she put a hand on Briar's
arm. "Olivia told me that you're uncomfortable with
me knowing about the inn's troubles."

"It's nothing."

"No, I think it is something." Roxie read her well.
"And it's worrying you a great deal. I wasn't paint-

ing pictures when I said I want to help. I can pay more on the lease if you need me to."

"No," Briar said, shutting off the water and drying her hands. "I already charge you girls enough. It's just...this was my mother's place. She's gone and Hanna's has to continue running, no matter what." She gestured to the table. "If you're not in a hurry, I have some leftover biscuits from breakfast if you want some."

"Sure," Roxie said. "Olivia and Adrian rave about your cooking."

"A year and a half of cooking school," she explained. "Anyway, I want to hear more about the boutique. How's it coming along?"

"Wonderfully—quicker than I anticipated. I'm just thrilled with how things are progressing."

"Have you mentioned the package deal to the others?" Briar asked.

"Oh, yes. Adrian jumped on it and had a proposal and spreadsheets lined up for me the next morning. Olivia seemed happy about the veranda being put to good use. We just need to iron out the details and we can start marketing it as soon as I open Belle Brides for business."

Through the screen door, the sound of an uninhibited engine poured loudly through the quiet of the inn. Roxie's eyes widened in glee. "Ooo, I was hoping I'd get to meet your tavern hero."

Briar frowned. "He's been gone most of the morning. Most of yesterday, as well. I guess he's come back for lunch." Her heart did that inconvenient jump when the kitchen door opened and Cole walked in, his brow wet and the front of his plain white T-shirt damp from perspiration. As he glanced around the kitchen, his dark eyes caught the light and flickered. Briar's stomach muscles softened, trembled.

"Sorry, ladies. Am I interrupting something?"

"Not at all," Briar said quickly. *Composure,* she urged as she opened the refrigerator. "I made some fresh lemonade if you're thirsty."

He watched her take down a glass. "Parched, actually." After a moment, he glanced at Roxie. "Cole Savitt."

"Pleased to meet you, Cole," she acknowledged. "Roxie Honeycutt."

Cole stuck out a hand for her to shake then pulled it back when he saw the grease on his fingers. "Sorry. I've been working on my bike for the better part of the morning."

"Nothing like a little early morning mechanics," Roxie commented. "I'm opening a bridal shop above Adrian's florist."

"Oh, right," Cole said. "She mentioned you." Briar handed him the cool glass. "Thanks, this looks great," he said appreciatively and sipped. "Tastes great, too."

"Want some lunch?" she asked.

"Actually, I was going to grab a shower before I stink up your kitchen."

"Do you need fresh towels?" she asked as he turned to go upstairs.

"Just the one will do."

"I'll wash the others," she offered. "Give me a minute to get you a clean stack."

He nodded, lifting the glass. "Thanks again for the drink. It was nice to meet you, Roxie."

"Likewise." As she watched him walk out, Roxie tilted her head to admire the view. "Mmm. Honey, with men like that roaming the earth, global warming is here to stay."

CHAPTER SIX

UPSTAIRS, COLE stripped off his grimy T-shirt and answered the soft knock on the door with, "Come in."

Briar pushed the door open but stopped short when her eyes skimmed over his bare chest. She averted her gaze as she walked in, arms laden with fresh white towels. "I brought three, just in case."

"Thanks."

She set the stack on the edge of the bed then backed away, her eyes still shifting elsewhere. "I'll let you shower."

"Wait," he said quickly, taking a step in her direction. He heard the swift catch of her breath as he closed in. Her eyes caught his and locked. A hand pressed to her stomach and he wondered what was going on under there.

He'd hardly seen her these past couple days. Avoidance. He was avoiding her like the plague. As soon as he'd seen her walk downstairs for breakfast the morning after her near-concussion, he'd run like the paperboy chased by a pack of neighborhood dogs.

As for his plans for breaking into her filing system? He hadn't yet found a safe moment. She was always there, the subtle but no less devastating scent she carried on her skin leaving him no room for clear thought or instinct.

On impulse, he moved closer. Briar's lips parted and he bit the inside of his, hoping they would stop tingling in anticipation. Focusing on her eyes, he swallowed to quench his throat. His palms had gone damp, and he rubbed them against his jeans. Nerves held the silence.

What was his move here?

He hadn't been able to get into her files so he had to come up with some other way of getting the information he needed, or something close to it at least. Tiffany was hounding him and his dreams were haunted by visions of both Gavin and Briar, each on the verge of being engulfed by the blackness that lurked in his shadow. The closer he got to either of them, the more they disappeared into darkness. He woke in cold sweats throughout the night with the weight of the black pressing on his chest.

"I was wondering…"

"Yes?" she asked after he trailed off, uncertain.

"I was thinking about taking a ride later."

Her mouth fumbled. "Oh. Right. Well, I can delay dinner, unless you'd like to dine out. There's a restaurant guide in the packet I gave you."

He thought quickly. How could he get her to agree to an invitation he knew she would automatically refuse? "Do you ever go out?"

"Out?" she asked as if the term were foreign to her.

"Yeah. Like with friends, for drinks or dinner. Or just for yourself, even?"

She frowned, perplexed. "What does that have to do with anything?"

"I've already told you I don't need to be waited on hand and foot," he explained. "If you wanted to take the night off and have some time to yourself—"

She let out a short laugh. "Mr. Savitt—"

"Cole," he corrected.

After a moment, she conceded. "Cole. I'd much rather tend to your needs."

He raised a brow, reading way too much into that statement.

So did she, judging by her quick flush. "I meant..."

He cleared his throat and shifted from one foot to the other. "Yeah, I know what you meant."

Firming her lips together carefully, she clutched her hands tight in front of her. Her anxiety was all too apparent.

Riding another rare wave of impulse, he took one more step toward her. "What if I told you that nothing would make me happier than if you went with me?"

"Went...where, exactly?" she asked with a frown.

"Out. For a ride." He watched her eyes go blank and jumped on her uncertainty. "A short one."

She said nothing, just stared at him.

With a nod, he backtracked. "Don't worry about it. I knew it was a long shot."

"Okay," she interjected.

His smile was quick, unexpected. Anticipation built inside him. He wanted her on his motorcycle, behind him. Wrapped around him. Doing his best to shut that line of thinking down, he asked, "You're sure?"

"When?"

"Um, six o'clock?"

"Fine," she snapped.

He jerked his head in a terse nod. "I guess I'll take that shower now."

"And I'll just...go." Her eyes veered down to the dirty towels on the floor by the bed.

He scooped them up before she could. "Here you go," he offered, shifting them into her arms.

She shifted toward the door. "Thanks."

"No problem."

As he watched her walk to the landing and disappear from view, he pulled in a long, steadying breath. That tempting, delicate scent of hers he'd grown to need as much as the woman herself lingered, clouding him all over again. Shutting the door smartly in his own face, he pressed a hand to the wooden panels, bracing and cursing himself.

JUST BEFORE SIX, Briar went up to her rooms. She'd worked in overdrive to finish all the laundry and tidying so she wouldn't be behind.

There were any number of excuses she could've given to get out of her evening plans with Cole. But then he probably expected her to cancel. She imagined him sitting in his suite, waiting for her to knock on his door and pass on her regrets.

She walked into her bedroom, opened the closet and felt a huge lump of dread clog her throat.

What was she supposed to wear for a ride on the back of a Harley? And why had she agreed to it?

It'd almost seemed like a dare. *Do you ever go out?* The question had needled her. And the fact that he himself had called it a long shot....

Still...*motorcycle.* Nerves eating away what little bravery she had, Briar rummaged through her clothes. Stepping back, she saw nothing but muted slacks and unsuitable blouses in linen and silk.... She scrubbed her hands over her face, feeling completely inadequate.

What in God's name could she do with her hair?

There was a brisk knock on the bedroom jamb. Before she could answer, Olivia strolled in. "Hey, cuz. I heard you were feeling better today...."

Briar threw her hands up, exasperated. "I can't find a thing to wear."

Olivia crossed her arms over her chest and propped a hip against the bureau to study her. "You look fine."

"I mean for Cole."

Olivia raised an intrigued brow as she watched Briar pace to the open drawer of her dresser. More blouses of varying hues and fabrics flew dismissively over her shoulder. "You two are...going out?"

"Oh, my God. This is a disaster." Briar sank to her knees and dropped her head to the drawer's edge in defeat.

"Come on. It can't be that bad." Olivia walked over, lifting her up with a firm hand beneath her shoulder. "Where're you going? Wintzell's? The Steamer? Ruby's? That great new Mexican place?"

"We're not going to dinner. I'm going on a motorcycle ride."

A long pause trailed the words, and Olivia's face fell in shock. Then she flung her head back and let out a loud bolt of laughter.

Briar scowled. "You're laughing? Really?"

Olivia answered with more raucous laughter, dropping on the bed and hooting mercilessly.

Briar sighed. "You can leave. Now."

Olivia sat up quickly, her face flushed with mirth. "I'm sorry. Oh, God, I'm sorry."

"You don't look sorry."

Olivia cleared her throat and scrubbed her watery eyes before holding up her hands. "I'm good now. I've had my moment. Let's find you something to wear."

Half an hour later, Briar stared at her reflection in the bathroom mirror, dismayed. "I should just call the whole thing off."

"You've never looked better." Olivia stepped back to admire her creation.

"I look like a teenage girl," Briar muttered, picking at the tight, razorback tank Olivia had rushed over to grab from her own closet. "These jeans are way too tight."

"They look hot," Olivia encouraged. "You've got awesome hips. You should flaunt them more often. No offense, cuz, but you dress like a librarian. What happened to that girl who jetted off to Paris, who wore clothes with color and just the right amount of *chic?*"

"They weren't exactly appropriate for an inn-keeper."

"Whatever! That doesn't mean you have to dress like your mother."

Briar sighed. "Are you done yet?"

"Hold your horses. I'm banding your hair here so it won't get in the way of the helmet."

"Helmet." Briar's eyes clouded with renewed doubts. *"Queasy."*

"Here. Have a stick of gum." Olivia grabbed one from her purse and folded it into Briar's mouth. "It'll help with the nerves *and* make your breath minty. Guys appreciate nice breath *almost* as much as a female who puts out."

"You would know."

"I would," Olivia admitted with a quick, mischievous grin. "Just one more thing. You need some color on your lips." She dug around her makeup bag until she found the gloss. She gripped Briar firmly by the chin and smoothed it on. "It'll make your lips look wet and Cole will spend the whole night thinking about them."

"What if I don't want him to think about them?"

"Don't lie to yourself, Briar. Cole Savitt? I'd be wanting much more than a kiss by sundown."

"You should go in my place," Briar suggested, grabbing on to her last thread of hope.

"He invited you, not me. He's crazy about you."

Briar's eyes widened. "I can't think that. I can't let myself get ideas, Olivia. Anyway, this is far from a date. He's just taking me out for a spin."

"You keep telling yourself that, cuz." Olivia nodded approvingly at the end result before picking up the eyeliner, grabbing Briar by the chin again and smoothing it under her eyes before she could protest. "Look on the bright side. With this makeover, you'll no longer have to worry about your virginity growing back."

"Enough!" Briar snapped, brushing away Olivia's hand. "I'm going. And I'll be back in an hour."

"I want all the deets," Olivia insisted, trailing her to the stairs. "Down to the smallest, most insignificant moan."

"I'm not going to have sex with him," Briar threw over her shoulder, careful of her voice as they neared the front door. She opened it and heard the Harley engine roar to life. Feet failing her, she stopped short, heart pounding. "I'm going to die."

Olivia laughed and gave her a good shove out the door. "Go get him, tiger."

COLE LOST HIS breath. What in God's name was she wearing? He was used to seeing Briar all clean and polished—covered up. The faded jeans hugged her hips and thighs in such a way that tangled his tongue around itself. He nearly swallowed it.

And he'd never seen so much of her skin. The green of her tank suited the tone of her skin.

Her lips were wet. He fought hard to keep from dampening his own.

For some reason he couldn't name, her honey-brown eyes seemed denser, darker. They sucked him in and refused to let go.

He was in serious trouble.

Shifting his numbed feet, he cleared his throat and summoned speech. "You, ah...you look nice."

Lips pressed together, she lowered her head and tucked a loose strand of hair behind her ear. He had an insane urge to press an openmouthed kiss just below the soft lobe. "Thank you," she said.

As her gaze returned to his, he struggled to think clearly. "Are you ready?" he finally asked.

She lifted her hands, awkwardly. "As I'll ever be."

He retrieved the spare helmet from the passenger seat. "I have to take precautions."

With a short nod, she stepped forward so he could fit it over her head.

An enticing note of her perfume hit his nostrils and nearly made his eyes roll back in his head. He fought to focus on his fingers as she lifted her chin and they went to work securing the safety strap. "I, ah...don't want anything to happen to your face— as much as it's a shame to cover it up."

Her eyes lowered to his as they widened...softened...warmed. She held the stare, and the joints of his knees felt loose. His voice was almost guttural when he asked, "Does it feel okay? Not too tight?"

She shook her head and lifted the visor to talk. "Um, Cole? There's something you need to know...."

His lips curved as he turned back to the bike. "I know."

"You do?" she asked, astounded.

After lowering the helmet over his head, he lifted its visor and tightened the strap. "You've never been on a bike before."

"Is it that obvious?" she asked, rubbing her palms on her jeans.

"A little," he said wryly. "Just lean with me into the turns. And hold on."

"Sounds easy," she said slowly, looking completely unconvinced.

He threw a leg over the seat, straddling it. As exhaust smoke tickled his nose, he glanced at her, revving the engine. Fear coated her expression. Her skin turned the color of paste.

Hell, if he didn't coax her on now, she'd run for her life. And while that might have been better for the both of them, he found himself jerking his thumb behind him, motioning for her to get on.

After a brief pause, she dropped her visor down and stepped to the bike. Gripping his offered hand for balance, she crawled on behind him and placed her feet on the small passenger pegs.

It took a moment for her hands to slip over his waist. They clutched his shirt as he toed up the kickstand and revved the engine again, just so she could feel the vibration of the machine beneath her. He thought he heard her whimper and, for some reason, couldn't fight a grin.

Just this once, he was going to give Briar Browning the ride of her life. God help them both.

BRIAR SAW THE quick, dangerous grin curl the corner of Cole's mouth before he hit the gas and sped south down South Mobile Street.

The force of the bike's quick acceleration drove her back on the passenger seat. Her heart pounded in terror as she grabbed him around the waist tight, visions of flying off the back playing out vividly in her head.

Who knew she'd meet her end on the back of a motorcycle?

Once he settled the speed to a calm, leisurely pace, she opened her eyes and braved a look around.

They cruised underneath overhanging branches strewn with Spanish moss. The azaleas, dogwoods and red bud trees were all in full bloom. The setting rays of the sun filtered through the leaves and dappled the pavement in random patches. The houses along either side of the road were old yet lovely and kempt, with shaded porches and tidy garden beds behind their picket fences.

The bay was calm, the early evening clear. Idyllic.

The flashing glare off the bay water obstructed the view of Mobile's high risers, but the sailors were certainly taking advantage of the good wind and the last light, their masts toy-sized silhouettes against the horizon. Brilliant shades of scarlet and magenta streaked the clouds and painted the bay's mimicking surface.

The unexpected feel of her shoulders and thighs relaxing slowly subdued her. People on the sidewalks waved, Southern hospitality ringing true in their easy smiles. She loosened her viselike grip on Cole's waist, loving the way fingers of wind lifted her hair and caressed her bare arms in warm, soothing strokes. Over Cole's shoulder, she eyed the long, curvy road she knew better than the lines of her palm.

Maybe she wouldn't die tonight after all. The key was to relax, which wasn't hard when the breeze smelled of summer blooms and tepid bay—such familiar, lulling scents. She leaned into the corners as he'd instructed, pleased that he slowed when they rolled over bumps.

She began to realize her life might just be in good hands. Her lips curved as she watched those hands squeeze the brake, release then throttle the accelerator. They were strong, capable...just like the sturdy line of his back through his black T-shirt.

She could easily dwell on how close they were. Even better, she could lay her head on his shoulder, close her eyes and let his warmth lull her into wistful complacency.

Too easily she could imagine the heat of his body, skin to skin. The weight of him. His hands making themselves capable in another way entirely. She had little doubt he'd manage her long-abandoned needs as well as he handled the purring machine between his legs.

A sweet, twining sensation sank into her midsection then spread outward, deepening and heating as it wrapped around her, a velvet blanket that simultaneously cosseted and drowned her in heat.

Gasping for breath, she stiffened, realizing her hands had fisted around handfuls of his shirt. She shoved the visor of her helmet up and drank the rushing air until her face and thoughts both cooled.

The mysterious stranger in her arms was turning out to be a dangerous man, indeed.

COLE DROVE AS the lukewarm sundown sank into cool dusk. He stayed on the scenic road, veering right when it forked. They wound their way around the Eastern Shore until it reached the pavement's end and the water's edge at Pelican Point.

The lights on the Fort Morgan peninsula across the way were already twinkling as he parked at the shoreline and cut the engine. He pushed up his visor as Briar's hands retreated hastily from around him and she slid off the bike. "I thought you might need a break."

"A little bit," she admitted. She bent at the knees and rubbed her thighs—they likely tingled from the engine's vibration.

"It's normal," he explained. "You get used to it." As her hands skimmed along the inner seams of those maddening, shapely jeans, he snatched his gaze away and trained his eyes on the water. "Looks like it'll be a nice night."

"Perfect," she agreed, straightening and walking to the edge of the pavement. "I've always liked this spot."

"What's this body of water?"

Gesturing behind him, she said, "That's Weeks Bay. It's linked to Fish River and Magnolia River just northeast of here. This point is where they all filter into Mobile Bay. Then they join the Gulf of Mexico at Fort Morgan peninsula." She pointed to the shadow of the fortress of war on the dimming horizon.

He jerked his chin in the same direction. "I imagine you've been there."

"Fort Morgan?" She shrugged. "Not much to see, really. The beach there is my favorite, though. It's so far removed from Gulf Shores, Orange Beach and all the public beaches, it's usually light on foot traffic." Her lips curved into a smile. "After hurricanes, Olivia and I used to beg one of our parents to take us out there. The storm waves dredge up the floor of the Gulf and wash everything ashore.

We'd find huge unbroken shells, jellyfish, starfish, driftwood—sometimes even boats. Once we found the hull of what looked like an old shipwreck."

As she remained submerged in the past, her smile faded. A frown took hold and she stepped back, distancing herself from the memories. "That was a long time ago."

"You were happier then," he assumed, trying to figure out how best to turn the conversation back to the inn.

Her brow creased. "I don't know about happier, but I felt more in control of my destiny. And I had my mom."

He fought for a moment to find something neutral to say. "I can't imagine waiting out a storm like that. In Huntsville, we'd only get fragments. Rain bands, maybe a tornado would tear through. But nothing like you've experienced, I'm sure."

"It's a fact of life down here," she explained, voice flattening. "We stayed through Ivan and Katrina. We had quite a bit of wind damage, though. A gale ripped one of the storm shutters off and blew it out to sea."

He raised a brow. "You stayed through *that?*"

Lifting a shoulder again, she said, "We got lucky. Katrina practically split Dauphin Island in two and left nothing but pilings on the west end. A row of whole houses and several families' worth of worldly possessions just vanished. Not a scrap of wreckage left behind."

"Christ," he muttered with an unbelieving shake of his head. "You're all nuts for living here, in the eye of the storm."

"Maybe," she said with a soft smile, "but it's beautiful, isn't it?"

Again, he had to tear his eyes away from her profile. "It certainly looks worth it," he replied, then turned the ignition switch. "Wind's picking up. It'll be getting chilly soon."

She frowned. "It's ninety degrees."

"Yeah, but it's cooler riding, especially at night. We better head back." He held out a hand to her.

Hers slipped warm over his, the long, graceful fingers rough around the edges. Though delicate in shape, they were hardworking hands. As his fingers closed around them and she mounted the passenger seat, her slender torso slid into place behind his, snugger, more comfortable than before.

He inhaled sharply and cranked the engine quickly. Rolling the throttle back, he tried to drown out the lingering lust with the machine's reckless roar.

Those hands, gentle in their grip, sweet in their careful altitude between his hips and rib cage, not only reawakened the unsettled hunger, they lit a fire in his head, heart and groin.

He cursed under his breath and snapped his visor into place. Using his feet, he backed away from the pavement's edge, lifted them onto the pegs and gunned it.

Her careful hold on him turned into a death grip, both arms latching tight around his chest as he sped off.

Dark gathered, turning the sky to eggplant. The road was unlit by streetlights and deserted. He gave the eager engine more gas and soared faster underneath the canopy of trees along the narrow road. He didn't take it easy around the bends, and her grip didn't loosen. The tunnel effect of overlapping limbs and dense foliage on either side of the blacktop added a sense of weightlessness.

He only slowed when they reached the road's fork. Then he cut the speed back down to the limit. It took her a while to relax again—he must've scared the daylights out of her. But the adrenaline had thankfully burned off the simmer in his blood.

He felt the chill of her hands through the thin cotton of his shirt as one covered the other to gather some warmth between them.

They had several miles to go yet. He frowned at the cold spot over his sternum. Lifting his hand from the brake, he draped it over hers, his arm cloaking the skin of her bare forearm. It felt frigid under his.

She stilled. Then she ducked farther behind him, hunching out of the wind and laying her head against the back of his shoulder.

Neither of them moved until they neared the inn.

He lifted his hand to squeeze the brake and swerve into the parking lot, coming to a stop under the magnolia tree. She eased back slowly and neither of them said a word as he turned off the bike and dropped the kickstand into the gravel.

He took off his helmet as she rubbed warmth back into her thighs. For form's sake, he checked the gauges before switching the lights off and pulling the key out of the ignition. Shifting to pocket it, he glanced back at her. "You all right?"

"A little warmer," she said in a voice coated in sleep.

He felt the tug again down low and cleared his throat. "Need some help down?"

"I've got it." Still, her hand gripped his shoulder as she dismounted.

Sliding off, he shifted from foot to foot, trying to get the blood moving. Preferably away from his pelvis.

Cole followed her up the steps to the inn as she unlocked the door, holding it open for him to enter then shutting it at his back. She flipped the latch behind them and switched on the entryway light. "I guess I should thank you, Cole."

With a short smile, he led her down the hall to the kitchen. "Only if you enjoyed yourself."

"I did," she said, a little surprised. "I'm sorry to say I didn't expect to."

As the stove light fell over them and he turned to face her, he let out a laugh.

"What?" she asked, alarmed.

He gestured up. "You're, ah…still wearing the helmet."

Lifting a hand to it, she gasped. "Oh, shoot. I forgot all about it."

When she struggled with the strap, he stepped forward to rescue her. "Let me get it."

She closed her eyes. "I can't believe I forgot. It felt so awkward when I first put it on."

"You were relaxed," he told her, making quick work of the strap.

"I admit, when I warmed up, I got kind of numb." She pried off the helmet, running a hand over her loosening ponytail.

He began to step back then couldn't. His blood sang at the sight of her flushed cheeks and heavy lids. As she pulled the band from her hair, raking it with her fingers and teasing the strands into place over her shoulders, the scent enveloped him.

Everything he'd felt that night swamped him again, leaving little room for rational inhibition. He moved in, no warning. Her breath had barely caught before his lips captured hers.

A small sound of surprise escaped her throat as his hands closed over her hips, maneuvering her back against the counter. She gripped his shoulders but didn't push him away. After a shocked second, her fingers curled into his shirt.

Her lips were soft, plusher than he'd imagined. Sinking in, he didn't progress further. He could've gulped, taken, plundered, demanded. But he held back because her breath cascaded over his face. He opened his eyes and saw the pinched bar between hers. As if, like him, she fought a costly, silent inner battle.

He lifted his lips but didn't step back, waiting for her to look at him.

It took her a minute. With a great deal of effort, her lids pried back from her stirring, honey irises... and heat kindled in them, throwing a lit match on the dry brush inside him.

She pressed her lips together and searched his eyes. They parted once then twice before she whispered, "What was that?"

His heart thumped heavily between them, and he didn't think he could stop it. "I...I'm not sure."

Her teeth latched on to her lower lip in a move that tormented the hell out of him, and her gaze lowered to his mouth. "Maybe you could...do it again?"

No mistaking the request. The plea. Glutton for punishment, he gazed at her lips. Wanting. Needing.

Facing once again something he could not have.

"I'm sorry," he groaned. He let it register, watched her eyes ping back to his in surprise then distress before he backed away and cast his face downward.

Careful not to look again, he lifted his helmet from the table and retreated into the sitting room. All the way up the stairs, he ignored the hand inside him that reached for her, threatening to wrench him in two.

CHAPTER SEVEN

BRIAR WAS STILL in somewhat of a confused daze the following morning. So much so that as soon as she finished preparing the garden suite for the first family on the guest calendar—the Josefstines—she found herself tiptoeing around the door to the bay-view suite to take a walk.

She wound up at Flora. Adrian had propped the front door of the shop open to invite in the early morning breeze. Flowers all but poured out of the door in perfusion. There was a chalkboard easel on the sidewalk announcing the latest sale. Silver buckets of colorful gerbera daisies sunned in the dappled light along with sprigs of iris and lavender. Briar stopped to trail her hand over the soft, white lilies of the valley nearest the door before entering the cool air of Adrian's shop.

Her summer assistant, Penny, a high school junior whose family had connections to Adrian's, looked up from behind the glass checkout counter. "Hello, Briar!" she greeted, her face lighting up instantly.

"Penny," she said. "How are you?"

"Great." Penny beamed. "Just great. Are you here to see Adrian?"

"Yes," she said. "I thought I'd order some new centerpieces for the entryway and dining room. Is she around?"

"In the back," Penny said, gesturing beyond the front room with its potted plants and glass-fronted display coolers filled with Adrian's many impressive floral arrangements, corsages and bouquets.

"Thank you," Briar said, going through the archway that led into the work area. Adrian was not at her usual post, the preparation counter where she worked her unique brand of magic every weekday and Saturday. "Adrian?"

"In here!"

Briar walked into the office all the way in the back of the shop where Adrian was sitting at her desk. "Catching up on some bookkeeping?"

Adrian huffed as she pulled off a multitasking headset. "Well, I *was* until bridezilla called, sobbing." She took a breath, held up her hands. "Crisis and cold feet averted."

Briar grinned. There was no one more equipped at calming distressed brides than Adrian Carlton. "You could've been a therapist."

"Trust me. It's me who needs the therapy," Adrian said, reaching for the last dregs of coffee in the coffeemaker at her right. She shook her head, filling her mug. "Replenishing centerpieces?"

"I can come back later," Briar offered. "With mimosas. And pâté."

"You know my weakness. But have a seat. I could use a calming presence."

Briar felt far from calm, but she scooped a handful of floral design books off the only other chair in the room and sat down. "I do need centerpieces... but I don't think that's why I came over...."

Adrian lowered her mug before she could take a sip. "Something's wrong."

"No. Well, not exactly." She pushed her hair from her face, frustrated with her own restlessness. Lifting her hands, she realized there was no better way of getting it out in the open so she blurted, "Cole kissed me."

Adrian's mouth fumbled. Very carefully, she set the mug down and swiveled her chair around to face Briar fully. "He kissed you," she said after a moment's contemplation.

"Yes," Briar said, brushing her hair back again, this time from her brow. "I...I don't think he meant to. It just happened." She exhaled on a shaky rush. "It wasn't an overt kiss...it was just... It was... perfect." She frowned over the word as it slipped out. "Yes," she said on second thought. "It was perfect. But then he got distant and backed away...practically ran away. And now I don't know how to act or what to do about it or him or anything...."

Finally, she raised her eyes to Adrian's and felt her cheeks color when she saw her friend's pursed lips and studious expression. "I'm sorry to drop this on you, Adrian, especially after the morning you've had already. I just need an objective opinion."

Adrian nodded, pressing her lips as she picked up her mug again, this time holding it between both hands. "So…he kissed you, without really meaning to."

"Yes."

"Then he backed off, without explaining himself."

Briar thought about it. "Pretty much. But in a way that was almost…respectful." She scoffed over the word. "You'd think I would appreciate that kind of behavior…but it made me a little mad."

Adrian lifted a brow. "A little?"

"More than a little," Briar admitted. "I didn't sleep at all last night, I was so angry and conflicted."

"Briar…" Adrian's gaze dropped to the coffee in her hands. "I need to tell you something."

"About Cole." She took a deep breath, straightening in her chair. "Uh-oh."

"It's nothing bad, really. It's just that after I gave him that tour around town, we were standing outside the tavern, talking. Your name came up. He didn't come right out and say it, but…I think he has feelings for you."

"No," Briar said with an unbelieving shake of her head, even as her heart fluttered at the thought. "The man just got here. I'm his innkeeper. There hasn't been time to develop anything more serious than a professional relationship. There's hardly been time for that, really."

"Okay, if you really think that, ask yourself this. Do you have feelings for *him* outside of your professional relationship?"

Briar's lips parted then she snapped them closed. "I don't know."

Adrian studied her in what looked like something close to pity. "Yes, you do."

She lifted her hands helplessly. "I have these little flutterings…and moments where I can't particularly breathe around him. And, yes, when he looks at me it feels like my knees are melting into hot liquid. I'm dealing with it, though."

Adrian's face softened into something of a smile. "You realize if Olivia were here, she'd be jumping up and down."

Briar rolled her eyes. "Last night she told me to sleep with him."

Adrian let out a short laugh and she shook her head. "So I'm assuming since you didn't go to her, you need someone to talk you out of it."

"Not sleeping with him," Briar clarified. "I know not to sleep with him. At this point. At any point… it won't even come to that, I'm sure. I just need someone to tell me that this is all foolish, that he'll go away and whatever flutterings and moments I'm having are just temporary."

Adrian narrowed her eyes. "Let me talk to him."

"No! What? I didn't ask you to do that."

"Somebody's got to," Adrian insisted. "The man's a good one, but there's trouble there. I saw that a mile off."

"I don't want anybody cornering him in the garden, interrogating him about his intentions toward me, Adrian," Briar said sternly. "Frankly, I'm starting to think all this was better off in my head. And he is a good man. He's a survivor because whatever trouble he came through to get here, he went through the brunt of it alone. I can see it in his eyes."

"Are you sure you need this right now?"

"No, I'm not," Briar admitted. "It's the very last thing I need right now. But…you're right. It's there and I have to live with it."

Adrian's frown deepened. "Just be careful. Please. In my experience, when a man's hiding something, it's not because he's being respectful. It's because he doesn't want you to see what's underneath."

YES, SHE'D asked to be talked down. And she'd gotten a talking down to. Adrian had given her exactly what she wanted. But still she felt conflicted. Still she felt those angry dregs left over from her sleepless night humming under the surface.

Briar decided to put it all aside and let it ruminate while she greeted the Josefstines at noon.

To commemorate the Josefstines' first evening at Hanna's she planned a formal dinner, placing a roast into the Crock-Pot soon after their arrival. What little space she had in her head for thoughts of Cole got crowded quickly when Mrs. Josefstine presented her with a laundry bag and asked if she would mind doing the wash for them.

For the first time in weeks, the inn felt like itself—full of bodies and chatter. The Josefstines' daughter quickly changed into a bathing suit and went to lie out in one of the padded lounge chairs on the boat dock while Mrs. Josefstine left to explore downtown.

There was no room for Cole in her head, and yet as she transferred the fresh clothes from the dryer into her basket to whisk them upstairs for ironing, she thought about him. She heard canned voices from the television in the sitting room. Mr. Josefstine had made himself right at home, taking a seat on the sofa with a glass of red wine in hand after driving eight hours from Savannah. He didn't seem like the kind to stay underfoot. With that in mind, Briar forced Cole out of her head and began timing her duties until dinner.

Ironing, half an hour. Just in time to start the potatoes. Then the gravy and green beans. Serve at six in the formal dining room. Allow time for conversation and clearing. Then dessert by six forty-five.

As she carted the basket toward the stairs, she slowed. Cole stood midway down, eyes on the television. Mr. Josefstine had flipped to the weather radar. It showed a turbulent tropical system forming just off the tip of Florida. Brett, they were calling it. The meteorologist projected a northeasterly path that placed the cone of impact between Panama City and New Orleans by Friday morning.

Mr. Josefstine grunted, glancing sideways at Briar. "Might have to cut our stay short."

Cole jerked out of his trance, seeming to realize she was there. She'd seen neither hide nor hair of him since his blatant retreat from the kitchen the night before. He'd left her shaken, wanting and bemused. Meeting his gaze, she couldn't look away even as leftover need and anger formed a twisted knot inside her.

When he said nothing, Briar forced herself to look away and offered Mr. Josefstine a reassuring smile. "No worries, Mr. Josefstine. Wherever it does go, there will be plenty of advance warning. A day at least. But I assure you, Hanna's has stood through many storms, and even the meteorologists are saying Brett is too disordered to become any kind of serious threat before landfall."

He grinned at her. "They should get people like you to do the weather. It seems you locals have seen enough to know whether we should head for the cellar or hunker down and ride it out." He switched to the Braves game and propped his socked feet on the ottoman. "I won't worry until you do, doll."

"I'll be back down in a moment," she promised. Sucking in a bracing breath, she took the first few steps and met Cole's cautious stare. "Dinner will be served at six tonight in the dining room if you'd like to join us, Mr. Savitt."

His frown deepened and he jerked his chin in wordless agreement. Before he could make a sound, she breezed past him, toting the Josefstines' laundry up two flights of stairs.

IT WAS AMAZING how she could cut him down with little more than a few courteous words.

He deserved it after his performance the night before. Sleeping on it had proved impossible. He'd spent the night tossing, turning and cursing himself profoundly before jerking off the covers and searching his pack for the penlight he'd brought with him.

Down the stairs he went, padding on light feet. He'd already memorized creaking boards on the landing and stairs and steered around them. When he made it downstairs, he crept through the dark, senses tuned to movements upstairs and ignoring the guilt prickling in his gut. It had to be done then—she'd told him that another family was coming.

He picked the lock to her office door and spent an hour behind her desk, going through the files.

He found nothing of value. Nothing but bills showing how far she was backed up. As he'd looked at them, he hadn't thought of Tiffany and how pleased she would be at the news that Briar was indeed drowning in debt. He thought of Briar and what the struggle must be doing to her.

The most interesting thing he came across were medical bills in staggering amounts. They were addressed not to Briar but to Hanna Browning—her mother. Before he could clearly discern what the bills were for or what had happened to Hanna, he put everything back where he found it. It wasn't his job to find out where the bills had come from. It was his job to find out what Briar planned to do about it.

And Tiffany hadn't been pleased to hear in the next morning's progress report phone call that he'd turned up no information whatsoever on the latter.

Are you taking this seriously, Cole? Have you forgotten what's at stake or do I need to remind you?

There was more at stake now than ever. He had to find out Briar's intentions because the sooner he got away from Hanna's Inn, the sooner he could stop dwelling on what her mouth tasted like. The sooner he could get back to building a new life—with Gavin.

He could skip dinner tonight. After all, Briar had left the invitation open-ended, clearly stating she wouldn't mind, or likely care, either way.

Yet, not going down at six seemed downright cowardly. He changed from his uniform of the past few weeks of T-shirt and jeans to brown cargo pants and a black button-up. Staring at his reflection, the shirt struck him as overdone. He quickly unbuttoned the cuffs and rolled them up his forearms, leaving the waist tails untucked.

On the way downstairs, he heard the Josefstines already packed around the table. The room was lit by the single chandelier over the long antique oak top with its eight patterned chairs and gnarled claw feet. She'd covered it with a burgundy tablecloth that set off the white, scalloped linens folded prim and proper under gleaming silverware. Silver trivets and lit tapers already lined up along the table's center showed how much she'd put into the occasion.

Cole unbuttoned his collar and made a beeline for one of the empty chairs on the far side of the table.

"Oh, you must be Mr. Savitt," Mrs. Josefstine said, holding out a hand. "We were starting to wonder if our chatter chased you away."

He smiled and shook her hand then Mr. Josefstine's in turn. "Not at all, ma'am. Pleased to meet you both."

"This is our daughter, Jane," Mrs. Josefstine introduced. "You'll have to excuse her. Can't seem to go anywhere without her iPhone."

Cole nodded to Jane, who lifted her fingers and waved before going back to texting. "How long are you in town for?" he asked.

"If the weather stays as fine as it was today, we hope a week and a half," Mr. Josefstine replied.

Cole felt a lick of relief. He wouldn't be alone with Briar before he left, from the sounds of it.

The swinging door to the kitchen opened and Briar appeared, carrying a large serving platter piled with roast and potatoes. She'd dressed up for dinner, too, her hair piled on her head in a neat chignon and her figure adorned in a belted, sleeveless purple dress. She wore two-inch heels and still moved with her usual proficiency despite the small hitch he caught when she spotted him at the table.

"Ah, doll," Mr. Josefstine said as Briar laid the platter carefully over the trivets. "Smells divine."

"You've outdone yourself," Mrs. Josefstine added as Briar pulled the lid off a serving dish of green beans she'd no doubt picked fresh from her own garden and produced a ladle for the wafting gravy boat. "A fine Southern home-cooked meal without the labor. This is certainly a treat."

Briar offered her a grin as she placed a floral-patterned plate in front of each of them then proceeded to fill their wine goblets. For Jane, she poured sweet tea over a glassful of ice. "I hope everyone enjoys it. Make sure to leave room for dessert. The coffee cake's cooling. And if there's anything you need, just let me know."

"There's no place setting for you, dear," Mrs. Josefstine noted, brows winging together.

"I'm not hungry just yet," she explained. "But please, dig in. I'll be in the kitchen."

The hell she wasn't hungry. He'd heard her working in the kitchen for hours. And had seen her dealing with the family's laundry before that. There was no telling what else she'd managed to talk herself into doing around the inn since her last meal. "Why don't you sit down, Briar?"

As her eyes shifted to him, they narrowed slightly. Before she could turn him down, Mrs. Josefstine chimed in. "We insist! If not to eat then let us at least pick your brain."

Pursing her lips, Briar folded her hands over her belt, considering what little choice she had. Then she nodded silently and took the empty chair at the head of the table. Two seats away from him.

"Here," Mr. Josefstine said around a mouthful, lifting the wine bottle. "Have a glass."

"Oh, thank you, Mr. Josefstine," she said then leaned back, crossing one knee over the other, and sipped. Cole tried to ignore both the movement of her long, smooth legs and how perfect she looked in candlelight with her hair drawn back from her exquisite face. "How do you like the roast?"

"So succulent," Mrs. Josefstine murmured, closing her eyes to savor it. "I haven't had anything so fine since my mother passed away."

Briar's eyes softened. "I'm so sorry, ma'am."

Mrs. Josefstine waved a hand. "It's been seven years this September. Her heart wasn't ever strong enough to support her ambitions. My sisters and I were surprised she held out as long as she did without slowing down."

Briar's lips curved. "Sounds like she was a force of nature."

Mr. Josefstine chuckled knowingly. "To say the least."

"Did you do the decorating yourself?" Mrs. Josefstine asked, looking around the dining room.

"Some," she explained, picking up the gravy boat

and holding it out to Jane so the girl could easily ladle it over her serving of roast. "Most of it hasn't changed since my mother ran the inn. She had much more of an eye for such things than I do."

"Family business," Mr. Josefstine grunted between forkfuls of potatoes.

"Very much so," she agreed. "I try to stay true to her vision."

"From what I see, you've done a fantastic job," Mrs. Josefstine said. "Is your mother retired?"

Briar looked down at the tablecloth, absently brushing away a speck of lint. "I'm afraid she passed away, too. A year ago this past winter."

Mrs. Josefstine patted her arm. "A shame. She must've been so young. Was it an accident?"

"Cancer," Briar replied. "By the time they found it…despite treatment, it was too late."

Cole stopped eating. His stomach twisted at the grief still prevalent in her eyes. And the guilt he'd begun to feel the night before overwhelmed him now when he thought again of the medical bills. *Cancer. A year ago.*

Despite his efforts not to find out why Briar was losing the inn, it now became so clear. He could say nothing as the Josefstines offered their condolences.

"And you've run the business on your own since she passed?" Mrs. Josefstine asked.

"Well, of course there was family who pitched in at first."

"Your father?"

This time Briar's eyes darkened before they lowered again. Her voice dropped, tightening. "No, my father had other priorities. My aunt helped mostly. Her daughter, my cousin, owns what was once her and my uncle's business, Tavern of the Graces, next door."

Mrs. Josefstine shook her head. "Still, I imagine that was a tremendous burden placed on you."

Shifting in her chair, Briar cleared her throat. "I wouldn't call it a burden." A faraway glint entered her eyes. "When I was younger, I wanted nothing more than to live here and work here. And a part of me has always known that if ever my mother were to retire, I would be the one to take her place as innkeeper. I suppose I just didn't expect to be taking her place so soon."

Mr. Josefstine nodded. "Kids nowadays don't know the first thing about hard work." Nudging Briar with an elbow, he murmured discreetly, "You could teach our Janie a thing or two."

She laughed at his conspiratorial wink. "More wine, anybody?"

Plates cleared ten minutes later. Briar stacked them and took them into the kitchen. It took Cole less than a minute to rise and follow her.

Small dessert plates were already laid out on the round table. She was slicing the coffee cake and transferring a piece onto each. When she looked up, her hands froze at the sight of him. "Need something?"

"I'll take those," he said, lifting the first two plates. She frowned after him as he carted them into the dining room. She followed him with the last two and he took one, setting it under Jane's nose.

"Don't you want some?" she inquired as she headed back to the kitchen.

"You aren't having a slice," he pointed out, brushing pointedly by her.

The kitchen door swung shut at her back and her polite tone sharpened to cleave. "What are you doing?"

The dishes piled in the sink caught his eye. He picked up the first plate and scraped the leftovers into the waste disposal. "When you sit down and eat, I'll join you."

She sighed, her heels clicking fast across the floor. Her hand gripped his wrist, stopping him. "This is just silly."

He raised his hard gaze to hers. "Sit down and eat, Briar."

"This is *my* kitchen!" she yelled, exasperated.

He let the plate clatter into the sink, anger rearing its ugly head. "For Christ's sake, what good is that when you're too weak to stand, much less fix a four-course meal and keep ignoring that gaping hole in your stomach?"

Mouth dropping wide, she gawked at him, speechless.

"Sit down and eat," he said again, slowly.

She stared him down for several seconds then dropped to the table with a huff and filled a plate with far less than her usual poise.

Relieved, he continued to clean the dishes until they were stacked on end in the sink drainer. The silence between them hadn't cooled at all by the time he finished drying his hands.

She dropped her fork with a clatter and moved her chair back to rise. "They're probably done with dessert."

His hand closed over her shoulder, keeping her in place. "I'll get it."

"Cole—"

"If you want to avoid another argument, Briar, I suggest you stay and finish eating," he warned.

She looked at him, brow furrowed. "I don't need your pity."

He rubbed his back teeth together then took a deep breath. "I just want to see you eat a full meal for once."

"It's not your job to look after me," she muttered.

"Then who the hell else is going to do it?" he demanded. "You work too hard."

"I do my job, and nobody ever had any complaint about it until now."

"That's because nobody's ever taken the time to look."

"Why do you?"

Damned if he didn't know. "Just finish eating. Please. I'll take care of the Josefstines."

BRIAR FUMED SILENTLY over Cole's behavior. The only reason she'd allowed him to help her serve dessert was to avoid making a scene in front of the Josefstines, who'd been watching the exchange with great interest.

Yet the tirade she'd worked herself up to while shoveling food down her throat under Cole's watchful eye slowly died as she cleared the silver from the dining room and scrubbed the kitchen until even she had to admit it was spotless. She tucked away the leftovers, glad the Josefstines had finally retired upstairs and Cole had disappeared, giving her time to brood.

She'd hated the greasy humiliation that had coated her when Cole demanded she sit and eat everything off her plate—the goading words still itched beneath the surface. But under it all had been genuine concern. Whatever he'd said, however grating his tactic, his intentions had been good. She'd been so hungry…and yet there'd been so much to do.

After setting the coffeemaker's timer, she realized her work downstairs was done. With a sigh, she walked into the sitting room, repositioned the sofa's toss pillows and folded the throw blanket. Reaching down to switch off the lamp, her eyes snagged on the figure standing on the sun porch.

Her heart rate doubled in both alarm and pleasure. She dropped her hand from the switch, hesitated then crossed the threshold and walked to him.

The inn lawn beyond the room's panorama windows was spotlighted by the moon. The white beam of it dipped over the bay, waters undulating under its pallid caress. For a moment, she stood next to him, arms folded across her chest. Then she spoke, voice lowered reverently. "When it gets quiet like this and the light shines on the water like that, I remember her most. I hear her voice. I feel like I'm that little girl again, before everything got too heavy…too real. For a moment…it's like nothing in the world can touch me. It reminds me why I'm really doing all this."

As the words lingered between them and he offered no response, her cheeks heated. Feeling Cole's eyes on her, she shook her head. "Sometimes it's as if she's been gone such a long time…and at other times it's like she was here just yesterday. I hate how alone I feel when I realize it's been eighteen months."

"Cancer," he said, frowning at the view in front of them. "I can't imagine it made things any easier around here, financially."

"It was devastating." She nodded. "In every way."

He blew out a breath, shifting his feet as if he were uncomfortable. There was something like a grimace on his face as he continued. "Are you doing all right now? With the inn, I mean?"

She thought about the bills on her desk, the messages on her answering machine demanding late payments, the interest on all those payments that kept stacking higher and higher the longer she was forced to put off those payments. Yes, he'd overheard quite a bit of her conversation with the county tax official, hadn't he?

Rubbing a finger against the line between her brows where a dull headache had dwelled for much of the afternoon and evening, she said simply, "It's nothing I can't handle."

"Isn't there anyone who can help?"

She looked at him. It was as if his face were etched from stone—so hard and rigid. "It's not your problem to worry about, Cole."

He looked at her, lips parted to say something. Then he stopped. His face slowly softened as he stepped close, so close she could smell the bay on him. Clearly, he'd been out walking the shore. "She must've been beautiful."

She blinked. "Who?"

"Your mother."

Swallowing hard, she nodded. "In her own warm, quiet way, she was very beautiful."

"Like you."

She blinked in surprise. "Excuse me?"

"You're beautiful."

Her gaze dropped from his quickly. "I think the wine's gone to your head."

"No." He shifted closer.

Her pulse leaped into overdrive. Oh, dear Lord, he was going to kiss her again.

"I think you're one of the most beautiful women I've ever met. And I'm not just talking physically.

Inside, Briar, you outshine everyone around you. Do you know that?"

She closed her eyes, began to shake her head in denial.

He blew out a short laugh. "Of course you don't. You see everyone but yourself."

"Cole..." Her breath hitched and she stopped to gather it. "I need you to know...I've been taking care of myself, and others, for a long time. That's my job."

"That's just the thing, though," he intervened, eyes growing pained again. "Knowing now what you said at dinner, how long you've been holding this place together, especially under those circumstances... Adrian's right. You need someone to take care of *you*."

Her lips parted. "Wait. What? Adrian...?"

His expression cleared, obviously realizing what he'd said too late. "We were just talking..."

"About me," she said, locking her arms together again in a stance she damn well knew was defensive. "At the tavern."

"Yes, at the tavern. And she only said you've been running Hanna's capably and single-handedly. But at the end of the day most people need someone. You said it yourself just now.... You *are* alone here."

Her chin rose swiftly. "You two discussed this in detail, did you?"

He held a hand up. "Please, Briar. Don't get upset.

She's concerned. Hell, I'm concerned and I've been here less than two weeks."

"Did Adrian happen to mention that she runs a business and goes home to a bed as empty as mine? Not to mention she has a son who she drops off and picks up from school Monday to Friday, and takes to soccer practice twice a week? Oh, and how about that she spends every waking hour worrying that her abusive ex-husband is going to show up and snatch her boy away from her?" She threw her hands in the air. "And you, Cole? There's no ring on your finger. As far as I know, there's no one waiting for you. How dare you try to tell me I need someone in my life when you're just as alone as I am."

He looked away quickly. "This isn't about me."

"No, you're right," she snapped. "Because we don't talk about you, do we? At least I'm honest with the people around me. You have some nerve jumping on my case when it's obvious that you're hiding something from me."

He shook his head, pivoting toward the stairs. "I'm going to bed."

With a scoff, she gestured him out. "Of course you are. Good night, Mr. Savitt."

He stopped, planted a hand on the archway leading into the sitting room and pushed himself around to face her again, eyes hot with pain. They pierced her straight through the heart. "You want the truth, Briar? I'm a thirty-five-year-old man who floats around on a Harley with no clear destination. And yeah, I'm running from the past miserable three years of my life. Years, I spent in divorce court watching the woman I was married to for nearly a decade lie to a judge and strip me of everything that ever mattered to me. For the past few months, I've had no set address, no home and no idea what I'm supposed to do with myself because the life I lived—the man I made myself into and counted on being for the rest of my life—doesn't exist anymore."

As she stared, dismayed, he lifted his shoulders in a terse shrug. "Not only am I going up to an empty bed that belongs to me for the next few days, *I* am empty. Now tell me...who wants to live with that?" Before her mouth could do more than fumble open, he answered, "Nobody."

A breath shuddered out of her and she shook her head, ashamed now that she knew, that she'd galled him into telling her. "Cole...I'm..."

He held up a silencing hand, lowering his head. "Don't. I don't want your apology. I won't pity you so long as you don't pity me. You know, you've got something here, Briar. Permanency. People willing to stick by you through it all. A purpose. You have everything to live for."

The grim silence hung between them. Her vision blurred with tears and her breath hitched on a quiet sob.

Cole cleared his throat and looked directly at her.

"I've decided not to stay any longer than the two weeks. I'll be checking out Friday."

"Cole," she whispered. Oh, God, what should she say to him? With all her might, she wanted to beg him to stay. With her, now—after the two weeks were up. It hurt to think of herself alone again after he was gone.

To think of *him* alone again.

"Good night," he said and turned away to return to his room.

CHAPTER EIGHT

HE MISSED BREAKFAST, which gave Briar pause. Cole rarely missed breakfast. When she finished serving the Josefstines, she went to the entryway windows. Her heart sank—there was no Harley parked under the shade of the magnolia.

An ache had carved out a home for itself in her chest since they parted the previous evening. She caught herself rubbing it as she opened the door to Cole's suite and the scent of him all but slapped her in the face.

It took her a moment to step into the room and go about her chores. He hadn't requested she freshen the room, but she did so, anyway, stunned by how neat he was.

If not for the clothes in the armoire and the toothbrush and razor in the bathroom, he might have never dwelled there.

She stripped the bed, tossing the lived-in sheets into the waiting basket before carefully—with far more care than usual—covering the mattress in fresh linens. The flowers in vases around the room were drooping. She threw them out and added fresh buds she'd clipped that morning, arranging them carefully and adding a sprig of jasmine to each.

After some hesitation, she gathered his dirty clothes and added them to her laundry basket. She loaded everything into the machine downstairs before rushing back up to dust and polish the suite's furniture.

She dared not think about the fact that she would have to do it all again soon. Only the next time, she'd be washing every trace of him away for the next guest.

Fighting the ache, she scrubbed his bathroom until every corner gleamed. Then she locked herself out of the suite and went down to finish his laundry.

She was sorting it, folding it piece by piece when Mrs. Josefstine peered into the laundry room. "I'm sorry to bother you, dear, but there's a man in your kitchen. Says he has an appointment."

"Oh?" she asked, mouth firming into a frown. She set the last shirt on top of Cole's pile and made her way to the back of the house. As she swung through the kitchen door and caught sight of the reedy man towering over the table, her pulse careened to a halt. "Daddy?"

It shocked her how old he looked. Even though his thick brown hair had thinned and grayed years ago, it still caught her off guard. His once-solid shoulders slumped slightly forward. His eyes were creased. They matched the permanent, somber line his mouth was firmly tucked into.

There was no flicker of affection in his eyes. They regarded her gravely. Nothing warmed inside him—she imagined nothing so much as stirred. "Briar."

She pressed a hand to her stomach, suddenly feeling sick. And words he'd spoken after her mother's passing came floating back to her like an ill wind....

"It's unimaginable—you running the business by yourself.... You won't succeed."

"I know full well there's a possibility that I could fail. But I won't let that happen, Daddy," Briar rebuked. *"She didn't let it happen—neither will I. We owe it to Mom to keep it in the family. That's what she would have wanted."*

"You want to live with ghosts," her father tossed back. *"Well, I won't be here to help you. Are you prepared for that? You've made your bed, Briar, but I can guarantee that you'll never be happy here...."*

Chilled, she caught herself brushing her hands over her arms. Lowering them, she searched for something—anything—to say. "I—I wasn't expecting you."

"I need an excuse to see you?" Hudson asked. His voice was deep and patchy. Familiar, except for the stoic tone he wielded like a blade. She didn't think she would ever grow accustomed to that.

She pulled in a careful breath. "No, of course not."

"You have several guests."

"Yes. The Josefstine family checked into the garden suite yesterday. For the past week and a half, Mr. Savitt has been staying in the bay view."

"But business isn't well."

She opened her mouth and locked her hands together. "I'm fine."

He shook his head, eyes censorious. "Don't lie to me, Briar."

She lifted her hands then clasped them again. "I'm handling it."

Hudson scowled then gestured to the figure in the corner. As her eyes darted to him, she saw it was a man in his thirties dressed in a gray suit and blue tie. She blinked at him, seeing him for the first time. It was as if he'd tried to melt into the wallpaper as the tension between father and daughter mounted into an acerbic air of foreboding. Now she wondered how a man so big could have escaped her attention. "This is an associate of mine," Hudson told her.

"Byron Strong," she said with a nod in his direction. "We've met."

"In law school," Byron explained to Hudson. "It's good to see you, Briar."

"And you," she said, though she didn't feel it. Not that Byron hadn't been perfectly nice in law school. He'd actually been quite the campus catch. Frankly, she was surprised he remembered her at all. But what was he doing here with her father?

"Sorry to barge in like this," he said when her father offered no such apology.

She lifted a shoulder and fought not to grit her teeth. "Any friend of my father's has always been welcome here at Hanna's."

"Byron's my new partner," Hudson told her.

Her brow furrowed. "I see." Yes, she saw perfectly. Her father had finally given up on his dreams of making her a distinguished lawyer and had installed Byron Strong in the office he'd no doubt been reserving for her all these years.

It didn't upset her that he had replaced her with Byron. What galled was that he'd brought the man here to tell her he'd found the son he never had.

"He also has some experience as an accountant," Hudson went on.

"Is that so?" she asked, looking from one to the other. Though there wasn't a trace of emotion in her father's eyes, Byron looked almost embarrassed. He, too, knew *exactly* what was happening here.

"Sit," Hudson said. He motioned them both to the table. It wasn't a welcoming gesture. It was more routine—businessman to potential client.

She was nothing more than that now. Despite the fact that the inn was in her name and that he'd made sure nothing of himself remained here, her father commanded authority like he would in his office, a classroom or courtroom.

"I got a call from a friend of mine the other day. Jack Fields."

Briar's stomach went from tight to slippery as she settled into the chair. "Did you?"

"He says that you're late on your property taxes, that he has extended the deadline for the last time and he'll be forced to seize Hanna's, the tavern, the shops and surrounding land if you don't pay by the end of the month."

She couldn't look at him. Not when he laid it all out like an accusation. "I told you I'm handling it."

"Jack says this isn't the first year you've had trouble paying. He says you've been under close watch by real-estate companies. Briar, they've always had their eyes on this place and they'll be closing in now, breathing down your neck. You're going to lose the inn eventually. The best thing to do is to try and sell before the banks get hold of it and you can no longer avoid foreclosure."

Her eyes came up to his, swift and indignant. "You act like I've already lost Hanna's. I *will* pay by the deadline. I won't abandon it like you did."

Hudson moved past the insult without so much as a flinch. "If you hang on too long, you could bury yourself in a hole. And I won't be there to scrape you out of it."

"I won't need you to," she replied, finding strength within that she hadn't known was there. "I've never needed you to help me, have I? Whatever stake you think you have here is gone—you took it away a year ago. And you made sure I knew your faith in me was lost, that it was my loss. Well, I've cut *my* losses and I've moved on. Maybe you should, too."

"I'm not the one who ever had difficulty moving on," Hudson said, voice tightening. "You've buried your head in the inn, Briar. It'll take you down with it."

"We'll see."

"What exactly do you plan to do? You do have a plan?"

"Of course I have a plan," she said, voice rising with each word. "There are people who would be more than happy to invest in a business like this, especially considering its location."

"You have investors?"

"I'm still ironing out the details—"

"Which means you don't have a single one."

"I think it's time that you leave. I have guests to tend to."

He stood, his chair scraping loudly across the floor. "Don't delude yourself into thinking I'm wrong like you did a year ago. When it's all said and done, think of what you'll have left. Absolutely nothing. Less so than you have now, which I'm sorry to say isn't much."

"Ah…" Byron Strong rose to his feet, too. "Maybe I should give you two a moment alone."

"No, Byron," she protested. "Please stay right where you are. You've come a long way—there must be a reason my father brought you here."

"I brought him for your sake," Hudson told her as Byron hesitantly settled back into the chair behind him. "He's here to act as an accountant for you. I want you to use him for whatever needs to be done to get the inn's affairs in order. We'll get as much out of this sinking ship as we can manage at this point."

"You…hired him as an accountant," she said

slowly. Fury frothed from a live, foaming pit inside her. Her blood boiled with it. Her ears rang with it.

It was the final straw. "I want you to leave," she said in a quiet voice that shook with rage.

"I won't leave until you agree to—"

"You will leave," she demanded. "And you won't come back. You are no longer welcome here."

Face hardening, Hudson slowly picked up his briefcase. "After all I've tried to do for you...this is how you end it?"

"You ended it," she reminded him. "Remember, Daddy? When I needed you most, you walked out on me and *this*." She lifted her hands to encompass the inn. "You walked out on *her*."

"Don't you dare accuse me of abandoning your mother!"

"You were ready to throw all her hard work, every dream she ever had, in the dirt because you were too damn busy to grieve. To feel. You got as far away from her, from me, from everything that reminded you of our lives together as you possibly could because you were too much of a coward to face it. I said it once, I'll say it again—I'm not like you. I can't snap my fingers and pretend like she never existed, like this life never existed. And I loved her too much to give up on her dreams."

His eyes boiled, but he was perfectly calm, as always. She'd never seen him yell or lose his temper—how she wished he would. Maybe then she could believe that his life with her and her mom had meant something to him. Maybe then she could believe that he remembered what it was like to be happy. "I loved your mother very much, Briar."

"But you refuse to honor her by preserving her legacy," Briar reminded him. "This is all that's left of her, and I won't throw it away."

"You already have," he said, turning toward the door. "Trust me, you have."

She gripped the edge of the table as the screen door slapped shut at his retreating back. There were so many live wires loose inside her, she could hardly contain herself. Taking a deep breath in, she turned to Byron Strong, who'd been quietly observing the scene. "I'm sorry you had to see that, Byron."

"Not at all, Briar," he said quietly. "Think nothing of it, please."

"I wish I could," she told him. "I'm also sorry you had to come all this way for nothing. I won't be needing your services—not at this time."

"I'm sorry we couldn't have met again under better circumstances," he replied.

She saw genuine sincerity in his eyes and sighed. "You can leave your card, if you like. My father's right. This is a sinking ship. And if for any reason… in the end…"

He shook his head before she could go on. "Your father was wrong. Family should stand by family, especially in situations like this." Reluctantly, he reached into his breast pocket and pulled out a card. "But if you need anything…"

She nodded, taking the glossy rectangle with his business name and address. "Thank you."

He dipped his head again in apology before he, too, made his exit.

She shrank back into her chair. No sooner had she settled than she was up again, pacing from one end of the kitchen to the other. Before long, she trudged through the swinging door, up the stairs to her rooms.

No time to dwell on her father's words or her own—nor the implications behind them. Work, she thought. There was work to be done and she would damn well do it.

NO SOONER HAD Cole returned from his afternoon drive than he saw Olivia crossing the parking lot from Flora. She waved, shoes crunching across the gravel toward him. "Hey there, good-looking," she greeted when he shut the Harley's engine off. "Where've you been?"

He pulled off his helmet, offering a short smile as he slipped off the bike. "Nowhere in particular. Thought I'd ride before it got too hot to enjoy it."

"Yeah, it's heating up fast," she warned. "Thanks to that system in the Gulf. You're about to get real acquainted with the breath of hell. Wednesday's supposed to be a hundred and one."

He whistled low. "I'm already sweating."

She smirked, raised a brow and eyed the dampness on the bare skin of his neck and the front of his T-shirt. "I can see that. You decide to stay on another week?"

His smile melted fast. "No, I leave Friday. Pretty sure I've overstayed my welcome."

"I seriously doubt that," she said. "This place will miss you."

It was his turn to smirk. "You say that to everyone who passes through?"

"No, just the hot, single, male variety. And they're few and far between."

He chuckled. "Well, I'm flattered. I think." Glancing over his shoulder, he lifted his hand to the Josefstines as they walked out of the inn.

Olivia frowned. "Howdy, folks. You going for a ride, too?"

The family matron, topped off by a bright pink straw hat, ambled forward, all smiles. "We thought we'd drive down to the Gulf and eat out. It's about time we gave our pretty innkeeper a breather."

Olivia snorted. "I'm sure she was distressed to hear it."

"I'm afraid I've not yet told her," Mrs. Josefstine confessed and lowered her voice. "She's been out in her garden, working for hours. She hasn't been as bright-eyed since that gentleman came to see her today."

Cole stopped short, several feet from the front steps. Gentleman?

"What gentleman?" Olivia demanded, echoing his train of thought.

"A man in a suit came to see her. Tall. Mid-fifties, maybe. A bit stiff around the edges. Looked like a lawyer of some kind."

"Oh, hell," Olivia muttered. "Thanks, Mrs. Josefstine. I'll pass on that you folks won't be needing dinner and make sure she's back to rights before y'all return."

As the van drove off and Olivia beat feet toward the side of the house where they could already hear Briar's WeedWacker at work, Cole fell into step with her. She stopped and gripped his hand. "You let me worry about this."

"Who was he?" Cole asked, concern and indignation fusing under the surface of his skin. Someone had upset Briar and he had to know who. What he would do with that information, he was less sure....

"Most likely? My uncle Hud, whose sole purpose over the past year has been to drill his disapproval into Briar until she breaks. Now you go on inside. She's either going to be weepy or spitting mad, and I know she'd kill me if I let you see her either way."

He frowned. "If she's upset, I should—"

"What?" she asked. When he remained silent, she patted his arm. "I love the quick initiative, Cole. And I would be happy to let you ride to my cousin's rescue again. God knows she needs a bit more chivalry in her life. But situations like these are best left to family."

He scanned her face. Even before he examined her set features and measured the grave light in her eyes, he knew she was capable of taking care of Briar. He nodded acquiescence. "I'll be inside if she needs anything."

"I'll let her know," Olivia assured him with a smile before she walked off in the direction of the garden, leaving him alone on the gravel drive.

KUDZU. IT was attacking her vegetables. Briar was all but buried in it, ambushing the vines that had managed to creep their way into her garden without her noticing.

Damned kudzu. She hacked at it, breathing hard through the heat of late afternoon, oblivious to Olivia's approach.

Her cousin planted her hands on her hips as her shadow fell over Briar and her WeedWacker. "What did he say?"

"Who?" she bit off through clenched teeth. Her face was flushed with color and her heart was pounding hard and furious, but she kept wacking.

"Uncle Hud," Olivia prompted.

Briar blew out a frustrated breath. "I'm a little busy, Liv."

"What did he say to you?"

"What he's *always* said," Briar snarled, wrestling vines away from her precious squash. "That I'm not strong enough to hold this place up on my own, that the inn is a sinking ship, that he's right and I'm wrong and I'll come running to him when I lose everything."

Olivia sighed. "Stand up."

"I'd *really* like to be alone."

Olivia didn't back down. Instead, she hauled Briar up with a hand under her shoulder and shoved her back a foothold. "You let him get to you. Don't bother," she snapped when Briar opened her mouth to argue. "I told you not to let him get to you anymore. Every time he comes around he either leaves you in tears or a snit, and I'm tired of it. You're going to call him right now and tell him not to bother you anymore."

"I did."

"What?"

Briar gazed into Olivia's determined face. Somehow, her mouth twisted into what she feared was a grin as mad as she felt. "I told him."

Olivia narrowed her eyes. "You told him to leave you alone? You told him not to come around here anymore?"

"I did." A burbling laugh escaped her. She swiped a hand over her beaded forehead and shrank to the nearest garden bench, hands propped on her knees as she rocked forward and back, once, twice. "I told my own father he isn't welcome in our family home."

Olivia raised a brow. "How did it feel?"

"Good, in a way. And bad. He's my father."

"I know." Olivia sat and slung an arm around Briar's shoulders. "You did good. Real good."

"I don't feel too good," Briar admitted, pressing a gloved hand to her head.

"I think you're a little dehydrated."

"No. I just feel like the part inside me that Mom took when she died, the hole she left, just keeps widening."

"She's not gone, Briar," Olivia assured her. "She's here. She's always been here. She's with you, and she's proud of you. And if Uncle Hud can't see that, he's a damn fool."

"You're right," Briar said with a small grin. "You're always right. But I'm still living in her shadow. No matter what I do, I can't measure up. I can't fill the space she left."

Olivia squeezed her shoulder. "I know what you need—a hot bath, a good glass of Chardonnay and a romance novel."

Briar let out a laugh. "I wish." She shook her head. "No, I've got too much to do. Look at my vegetables."

"That kudzu isn't going to take over completely in the next twenty-four hours."

"But the Josefstines—"

"Went out to dinner. It's just you and the hottie in the bay-view suite."

Briar caught the mischievous gleam in Olivia's eyes. She frowned. "He'll want dinner."

"Yeah," Olivia chipped in. "And you'll both want dessert."

UPSTAIRS, IN THE bay-view suite, Cole's cell phone rang. Reluctantly, he walked to his bedside table.

Though he already knew what name he would find on the caller ID screen. He reached for the phone and answered, "Yeah?"

"I haven't heard from you in over twenty-four hours. This incommunicado bullshit is starting to get on my nerves, Cole."

"I said I would contact you if I had any new information. I don't."

"Again, I'm starting to think you aren't taking this seriously. I think it's time for a reality check."

Cole frowned. "What is that supposed to mean?"

"Gavin and I decided to take a little trip south this weekend."

Cole's grip on the phone tightened as his heart pounded. "Where are you?"

"A cute little beach house on Ono Island," she told him, sounding downright gleeful.

Cole's heart stopped. The world shifted and he reached out to plant a hand on the wall.

When he remained silent, Tiffany said, "He's asking for his daddy."

Cole sucked in a long breath as the teeth of pain gnawed at his frayed nerves. "You are the one who made certain I could never see my son again. And now you're offering him up to me on a silver platter? I don't buy it."

"It's called visitation. I'm his legal guardian. His sole guardian. If I see fit to let you back in his life then that's my call. You're a good daddy, Cole. I'll give you one day to spend with him. To remember what it is that you could possibly lose here. Nothing like a little motivation to make you do what you're told."

The hand around the phone balled into a fist. It was a wonder the cell didn't shatter into a million pieces. He tipped the phone away from his mouth to catch his breath. It was blackmail, again. And again he succumbed, willingly. Practically on bended knee. "Where?"

"Meet us tomorrow, ten o'clock at the public beach in Gulf Shores."

"This better not be a trick, Tiff," he ground out.

"Temper, temper," she tutted. "We'll be there. Trust me."

"I don't." He ended the call and shrank to the edge of the bed. Again, he stared at the screen as it faded to black. Fighting to breathe, he reached to the bedside table for his billfold.

He kept only one picture in it. If Tiffany had known, she'd have taken that small token from him, too. He stared into the eyes that matched his own—those sober, dark eyes. The brown, straight cap of hair that grew like weeds and always fell in the kid's eyes. The wide shoulders that promised more breadth than height.

Anyone could see the boy belonged to him. Anyone but his ex-wife.

The knock on the door startled him. He looked up as Briar opened it and peered in. He closed the billfold and dropped it on the pillow beside him, hiding it from view.

She wore a pink-and-blue-checkered apron and had changed from her gardening clothes to a sleeveless coral blouse and white slacks. "Hi," she said with a small smile. "I just wanted to check on you."

He only stared at her, unable to find words. How could he have ever thought he could have any part of her, even temporarily?

The smile melted when he didn't reply. "I'm about to start dinner. We'll eat in an hour."

He looked down at his hands. "You know, Briar, I'm not all that hungry tonight."

A slight pause followed the grim admission. "Are you sure? You didn't eat breakfast again...."

"I'm sure. I think I'll just turn in early. A full night's rest will do me good."

"Is the bed okay?" she asked, lacing her hands together in that uncertain way of hers. "If you're not sleeping well on it, I could remove the mattress pad. It might be—"

He stood, crossing to her in a handful of strides. She trailed off, lips firming together at his quick movements. Standing close, he leaned over her and murmured, "The bed's fine. It couldn't be more comfortable. I just need some space."

Hurt flashed in her eyes before she lowered them to his shoulder. "If...if this has anything to do with last night... Well, I'm sorry—"

"Damn it, Briar," he said, scrubbing a frustrated hand through his hair. "Last night has nothing to do with this."

She didn't look altogether satisfied. "Well…if you need anything at all, Cole, please let me know how I can help."

Did she know how undeserving he was of the understanding and the entreaty in her eyes? He swallowed hard. "I want you to take the night for yourself. Do whatever it is *you* do when the inn is taken care of."

She began to protest, her lips parting. Then she sucked in a breath and closed them. She nodded. "All right, if you're sure."

"Thank you," he murmured. Suddenly, he wanted to kiss her, so he took several steps back. "I won't be here most of tomorrow. Don't worry about feeding me."

"When will you be back?"

"I don't know."

She hesitated then gripped the doorknob, backing out. "Rest well."

He lowered back to the bed and dropped into the pillows, Gavin and Briar weighing on his mind.

Several minutes later, he glanced out the window at the sunset and saw his innkeeper strolling alone toward the boat dock, a glass of wine in one hand and a small bowl of salad in the other. She sank into one of two waiting Adirondack chairs, the last light of day falling in gilded, blinding pinpricks on the bay's listless waters and casting the perfect woman in a lonely silhouette.

THE WOODS HAUNTED him. The high wind rustled through the treetops of the pines that closed in around him and his partner as they approached the small cabin with its blown-out windows and blackened roof. The pine needles underfoot stirred, restless, a brown carpet that never rested.

Yellow police tape was tied from one tree to another. He ducked underneath it to enter the crime scene. The coroner was there as was the crime scene photographer. Other officers milled about in his periphery as he climbed the rickety steps to the open front door.

He knew the smell well. In the past ten years, he'd been no stranger to meth lab explosions. This one, however, he could see instantly was one of the worst. Holding his breath, he moved around, taking note as the homicide detective beside him rattled off the particulars.

The meth lab had been in the kitchen. The walls of the room had blown clean through. There the coroner had already tagged and bagged the three bodies of the dealers he and his partner had been investigating for some time now. Frowning, he felt the bite of defeat. If the warrant had come through a day earlier, they would be behind bars now. Not on their way to the morgue.

Moving away, he followed the blast radius. Walls were gone, exposing beams that had buckled and now stood crooked, making the shanty roofline unstable. They wouldn't have long to comb through what was left and log their information away with photographs.

He moved from the small living room into what appeared to be a young child's room.

He frowned. It was the closest to the kitchen. The small twin beds were blown askew. The window here was busted, too, its black-out curtain now lying somewhere in the forest. There were few things left that were recognizable. He knelt down and reached for the smudged face of a teddy bear that lay on the floor at his feet.

Before his fingertips could graze over the surface, he saw the body lying on the other side of the bed. It had already been discovered by the officer first on scene—he had known it would be there. But he hadn't been prepared for this. The face was turned to him, eyes flat and dead. So young—just four or five.

He blinked several times when the face of the child blurred into a familiar one. The one of the child he'd kissed on the forehead that morning before leaving for the precinct. His gut churned and he fought for breath. No matter how many times he blinked or looked away, the face didn't change. It was Gavin's face. His boy, he was there with him in the wreckage. And he was gone....

The grief bound him, tied him in place and squeezed until he thought his ribs would shatter. Gripped by pain and terror, he fought the invisible force that bound him in his bones. He was losing it. He had to get out of there. Out of that house...out of those woods...away...far away...

"Cole?"

He tore through the remnants of sleep, sitting up in bed. Drenched in sweat, he hitched in a breath. Phantom pain lingered in his lungs and ribs. He exhaled in an unsteady rush, raising his hands to his face to scrub the memories from the underside of his lids.

The light at his bedside came on and he blinked at the beam of it. A figure hovered over him. "Briar?"

"Shh," she murmured. There was a rag in her hand and when she pressed it to his brow, it was cool.

His heart still pounded. He looked down at the twisted sheets, saw they were as wet with perspiration as his T-shirt. Embarrassment broke through the dregs of panic. "I'm sorry...."

"Hush," she said in a gentle voice. Moving the cloth to his neck, she pressed the cool, soothing rag to his skin. "You're all right now. Everything's all right."

He was calming, leveling off enough to know that she was right. "I'm sorry," he said again. "I'm sorry I woke you."

"You didn't," she assured him. "I was going up to bed and I heard you as I passed by your door."

He dropped his head and braced his hands on his knees. "Just a bad dream."

She said nothing, just continued to press the cold cloth against the heat of his skin until the chill of it finally broke through. Then she asked, "Feeling a little better?"

He raised his gaze briefly to hers. The humiliation still clawed at him. She'd found him twisting and turning in his sheets like a child. But there was nothing in her eyes to suggest that she thought of him that way. There was only concern and the warm light of reassurance. "Yes," he replied. "Much."

She nodded. "Here, hold this." Her hand touched his, guiding it up to the cold compress. "I'll get you a glass of water."

"You really don't have to…" He trailed off when the words didn't stop her from going into the adjacent bathroom. Closing his eyes, he pulled in a careful breath as he heard the tap gush to life. He still felt a bit shaky. It would take some time for that helpless feeling to go away. It *would* go away, though. It had to. As she came back, he lowered the rag and took the glass she handed him. "Thank you."

After a moment's hesitation, she lowered to the edge of the bed and watched him gulp half the water down. "More?" she asked when he set it on the bedside table.

"No," he replied and cleared his throat—his words

were still coming out like his throat was coated in shards of splintered glass. "You've done enough. More than enough."

Her hand latched on to his. The warmth of her fingers bled into his skin, into the bones beneath. The sick, shaky feeling he desperately wanted to dismiss fell to a mere near-forgotten backdrop as he watched their hands join.

Despite the humiliation, he was glad she was here. He didn't know how he would face her in the morning...but he was glad for her presence nonetheless. She'd calmed him much more effectively than he could have calmed himself. She'd pulled him from the dream before it had become something worse and he woke the whole house.

When he finally lifted his face back to hers, she was smiling. "You're fine."

He nodded, drinking her in. The goodness in her compelled him. It pushed away the black of his dreams and everything else that was dark in his life. She was a good person, so unlike the other woman in his life. And his deception would ruin her. The light of goodness in her might never recover. What the hell was he doing?

His gaze lowered to the curved line of her mouth. What he wouldn't give to taste her right now—to graze his lips over that sweet, bowed line and lose himself completely.

Wrenching his thoughts out of that dangerous

track, he trained his eyes on their hands and watched his pull away from hers. "Thanks again."

She lingered for a moment, gauging him as if to make sure he was all right. Then she took the compress and folded it neatly on his bedside table beside the glass. "Please...let me know if you need anything else."

Unable to summon any further speech, he gave a short nod and watched her depart. The door clicked closed behind her and he lowered himself against the pillows piled at the head of the bed, releasing an uneven breath and scrubbing his hands through his hair.

It had been months since the recurring nightmare had crept up on him. At first it had been a nightly torment, then it had begun to fade. Now it came when he least expected it, when he was on the verge of forgetting....

He saw that face, those eyes, and forced his thoughts elsewhere. Briar. Briar's face. Briar's eyes. *Just Briar.* He closed his eyes. He could see her, as she'd been sitting on the edge of his bed. He could all but feel her there.

He would have thought it impossible, but it wasn't long before he drifted off to sleep again, Briar's face leading him back into dreams that wouldn't wake him in cold sweats and panic. Dreams that would heal, nurture.

Dreams that, in sleep, he wasn't afraid to wish were real.

CHAPTER NINE

THE MORNING WAS cloudless, the sun overbright and baking hot. The wind blew out of the south, and Cole wondered if the hair-raising breeze was the breath of Tropical Storm Brett itself, spinning steadily into the middle of the Gulf, hundreds of miles south of Alabama's coastline but traveling at a sure north-easterly pace.

Yellow flags flew on the beaches. Waves crashed ashore, rolling in on blue-green crests not yet violent enough for local officials to change the yellow advisories to red, banning people from the water.

Surfers took advantage of the light action, riding the swells for a short distance before sinking into the water and paddling back out to wait for another. The beach itself was packed with adolescents playing a game of volleyball, couples and small bunches of women lazing on beach towels or lounge chairs, men tossing footballs or Frisbees back and forth, and children dancing in the lapping surf. Some had brought floats and foam noodles to bob between crests. Others zipped by on Jet Skis. In the distance, two people parasailed far above the water, pulled by a long recreational boat.

The sand was white, fine and warm under Cole's bare feet as he walked toward the shore, combing the inhabitants' faces.

He saw Gavin first and the ache inside him seared. He wore a white T-shirt to protect his pale skin from sunburn and a pair of dark blue swim trunks.

God, he'd grown taller. Three inches, at least. For all the time that had passed, it could've been a foot. Someone, probably Tiffany, had cropped his hair short, almost to the scalp. The militant cut didn't look quite right on him.

Gavin wore a smile as he took his boogie board for a spin, washing to shore on its back before rolling off and getting up to wade out and try it again. Boundless energy. Cole had forgotten how active Gavin was—a force of nature all his own.

A barb dug into Cole's chest. *He'd already begun to forget.* It'd been months since he'd sat across from Gavin in a courtroom. Eight long months since he was barred from him altogether. It'd felt like forever…but what kind of a father forgets?

"Well, you showed."

He glanced up, jolting to attention. Tiffany wore a bright blue sundress and aviator shades. Her long, white-blond hair was held back with some kind of Jackie O bandana. The sand hadn't stopped her from wearing a pair of wedge heels so her long legs looked even leggier.

Disgust coated him from the inside out when he saw that she'd been watching him, smiling, from a beach chair close by. "You knew I would," he muttered bitterly.

"Like I said last night, I was beginning to wonder...." She followed his gaze to where Gavin played in the surf. "He does miss you."

"I won't mistake that for an olive branch," he told her, looking back at her with a scowl. "It's sickening the way you have no problem using our child to blackmail me."

"What's sickening, Cole, is how fast you take the bait," she said, taking several steps toward him. "Makes me wonder if the man I fell in love with all those years ago exists at all anymore."

"I doubt you were ever capable of love, Tiffany," he battered back. "All I was to you was another mark, even then. Just like Briar Browning."

"Don't be ridiculous, Cole," she said flippantly. "I rushed into what we had, but I did love you. Blame the fact that it all went to hell on my youth and naïveté. Despite what you may think, I'm not that great an actress. I fell in love with your strength, your refusal to take crap from anyone. Somewhere along the way, that alpha male in you turned into something weak and malleable. The man I loved no longer exists."

She raised a hand to shield her eyes and tilted her head, studying his face. "I've been thinking about it. There has to be more to your reluctance to dig into sweet Briar's records. Though you *have* always been a softie for a victimized female."

He took a threatening step toward her. "You don't know a damn thing about Briar. If you did, and you had a scrap of decency left in you, you would back off for mercy's sake. She doesn't deserve this."

Tiffany's thin brows lifted over the rim of her glasses. "You do have feelings for her. You want my advice, Cole, here it is. Choose wisely. Either the innkeeper—" she nodded toward Gavin "—or your child."

Cole glanced out over the white sand. A lashing wave sent Gavin skidding off the board. His dark hair bobbed over the surface after a moment and he waded his way back to shore, rubbing the stinging salt water from his eyes and dragging the board behind him. He lowered his hands and finally spotted Cole.

Though rushing water still pulled at his calves and ankles, the kid stopped short, arms limp at his sides, expression unreadable.

Cole took off his sunglasses and offered what little smile he could conjure. "Hey there, chief."

Another moment of wary hesitation passed as Gavin dripped and stared. Then he lugged the board into the wet sand, dropped it and broke into a run.

Cole's heart squeezed as he caught Gavin on a running leap. He spun him in a quick circle before he crouched and hugged him tight to his chest, not giving a thought to the dampness that soaked clean through his shirt. Everything inside him swelled and, for what felt like the first time in months, Cole could breathe right again.

It took him a while to let go. He leaned back, kneeling in the sand to take a good, long look at what he'd missed more than anything from his old life. Thick black eyelashes framed hazel eyes, an embodiment of the clash between his parents. They winked with tears, but a huge grin highlighted several new missing teeth. Working furiously at the knot in his throat, Cole ran a hand over his close-shorn head. "It's been way too long."

"I missed you," Gavin said, rubbing the back of his hand over his mouth to hide the quiver of his chin. "Even when they told me I shouldn't, I missed you, Dad."

Cole pulled him close again, placed his chin on top of his son's head as he always had when comforting him. "I know. I've missed you, too, Gav."

"Mom says I can spend the day with you?"

Because it came out a wavering question, Cole let a real smile soften his face. "Of course. The whole day's ours. Wherever you want to go, whatever you want to do."

"Tomorrow, too?" Gavin asked hopefully.

Cole's smile faltered. He felt Tiffany's shadow fall over the both of them. "We'll see," he offered. "Come on, let's get you dried off."

As Gavin ran for a beach towel, Cole stood slowly but couldn't quite face Tiffany again. Sliding his hands into his pockets, he released an unsteady breath. "Thank you," he said, barely able to keep his voice from cracking with emotion.

"You get one day," she said. "It shouldn't take you that long to make your decision. Have him back here by sunset. I'll be waiting."

COLE HAD STOPPED by the local Harley shop to buy Gavin a kid-sized helmet, but he'd been worried he wouldn't want to ride the motorcycle.

To his surprise, Gavin took to it with his characteristic eagerness and peered around Cole's shoulder as they cruised Gulf Shores. When they both decided lunch was in order, they grabbed some takeout and drove to the nearest park. Only a mile from the beaches, it was surprisingly quiet, the playground shaded by thin, towering pines that idly swayed in the southerly breeze, scattering green needles and their woodsy scent around them.

As it turned out, Cole didn't have to worry about communication. Gavin readily launched into conversation as if the year's ordeal had never taken place, laughing, kidding, teasing and answering questions about home.

"How's school?" Cole ventured after wolfing down a cheeseburger.

For the first time, Gavin's smile fled. "Sucks. Mom took me out of public school and put me in that prissy academy. I have to wear dorky uniforms and I don't have any friends there."

Cole frowned at that but knew anger would be

useless. Any say he had in Gavin's life had been mercilessly uprooted. "How're your grades?"

"Okay, all except for math. I made a C the last quarter. Mom was upset. She wants me to get a tutor next year."

Guilt pricked under the surface. "It'll get better, buddy." Gavin had inherited Cole's numerical dyslexia to Tiffany's heavy disapproval. He hesitated for a long moment before adding, "You mentioned that your mom's seeing someone. What's he like?"

Gavin grimaced, eyes falling. "Chad. He's a jerk."

"Is he treating you okay?"

He lifted a shoulder. "He doesn't hurt me or anything. But Mom wants me to call him Dad and gets mad when I don't. He's moved all his clothes in, and he sleeps in her room."

"It's nice that your mom's seeing someone, but there's no reason to call him Dad if you're not comfortable with it."

"You're my dad," Gavin said in answer to that. "Chad doesn't even come close to you."

Despite himself, Cole felt his lips twitch. He picked up a napkin and handed it over the table. "Wipe that ketchup off your lip."

Gavin grinned as he scrubbed his mouth. "Where're we going next? Waterville? I've always wanted to go there."

Cole tossed the paper wrappers into the garbage can. "If that's where you want to go..."

"And then we could go goofy-golfing at that cool

pirate place. And then to The Track—the go-karts look fun."

He scooped the kid over his shoulder and hauled him back to the parking lot. "Whatever floats your boat."

"Hey, Dad, can we go parasailing?"

Cole chuckled heartily. "Okay, I lied. I draw the line at parasailing."

"Ah, man." As Cole set his feet on the asphalt, Gavin grabbed his helmet. "I really like the bike. Maybe after The Track we could go for a really long ride?"

Bending down to latch the strap under Gavin's chin, he considered. "We could do that. Someone told me about this abandoned Civil War fort a couple miles from here."

Gavin's eyes rounded in awe. "With ghosts?"

"What's a creepy old fort without ghosts? We'll ride down that way and check it out."

Gavin whooped, hopping onto the passenger seat. "This is the best day ever!"

The best day ever. Cole wanted to echo the sentiment. Having Gavin with him after so long apart... it was a gift. Before the day was over, he knew what he had to do. And dreaded returning to the inn to face the last person he wanted to hurt.

BRIAR STEPPED OUT the kitchen door with a basket in hand. The garden vegetables were so heavy they were practically falling off the stalks. She savored the sight of the new tomatoes. She and her mother had nurtured them from seedlings. There was nothing so rewarding as watching them grow and remembering those last few months that her mother had been able and active.

By the time she finished plucking and weeding, a nice bunch of fresh produce filled her basket. She began to walk back into the inn. And stopped.

The colors drew her. Hot, electrifying waves of light splashed across the sky like paint on a canvas. She set the basket by the door and slowly walked down to the dock.

It was breathtaking. She never took the time to watch the summer sunsets anymore.

But tonight's was one of those that drew everyone out to ogle. She leaned against the rail on the boat dock and watched the hot ball of red flame descend from the sky. Bands of hot pink, bright orange and untamed yellow jetted in its wake in a series of colorful tufts that faded into the east.

As the sun lowered just over the far west bank of Mobile, its light hit the water at exactly the right angle. With a catch of her breath, she watched the light dance on the still waters around her. It was magic, those sparkling lights.

Fairies. Fairies dancing.

The memory came back to her, blazing her with warmth and her mother's love. Closing her eyes, she felt like a little girl wrapped in a parent's loving embrace, heart bursting with wonder and magic.

"Fairies. Fairies dancing," her mother said. "You only see them when the sun comes out full and bright like that. They hide in the rocks until the rays hit the water. Then they dance."

Briar smiled up at her. Their eyes locked. Glee bounded in her young heart as her mother squeezed her shoulder. In that moment, she knew fairies existed and it was their secret to share.

Tears filled Briar's eyes as she felt her mother's presence envelop her again, a protective shell nothing could penetrate. She let it fill her up, a glowing pool. And she yearned for what had been—simple, carefree days.

The boards of the dock creaked behind her. She turned and saw Cole. Her heartbeat didn't settle, only stumbled and cantered. She let out a laughing breath. "You're always sneaking up on me."

"Sorry," he said, voice tuned low, as if he didn't want to intrude upon nature's exhibition or her enjoyment of it.

When she saw his hesitation, she gauged the grim light in his eyes. No, not a grim light, but sadness. Deep, unequivocal sadness. Reaching out to him, she touched his arm. "What's wrong?"

He let out a breath and shook his head. "Have you ever been so sure of what you wanted…but you lose sight of yourself trying to get there?"

Her eyes softened and she nodded. "It's like you've read my mind."

He reached up to the hand she'd touched him with

and gently took her fingers in his. "Briar, whatever happens...I need you to know that I care about you. I've only known you a short time, but it doesn't matter. Sometimes all I see is you."

Her heart lifted, fluttered at the words. "Cole..."

"If I had my way, I'd never hurt you. I'd never let *anything* hurt you."

His eyes were damp. With her other hand, she touched his face. With her heart, she reached out to him, enfolded him, refused to let go. "Where's this coming from?" When his eyes dodged hers, she lifted her other hand to frame his face. "Cole, it's okay. I know you'd never hurt me."

Before he could say a word, her mouth covered his fully. Her world tipped off its axis and went into free fall. Stunned, she swayed back against the rail. After a moment, Cole cupped her face and spread his fingers over her cheeks. Warm, so warm...

Her lips parted and something shot to life inside her, a rocket of flame that sailed from the tips of her toes to the top of her head. His tongue stroked hers ever so lightly and she quivered, breath quickening in surprise.

He shifted back on his heels. Mindless, she gripped the front of his shirt and pulled him flush against her again. "Don't stop." She kissed him deep, praying the fluttering, unsteady, heating sensation in her joints would never fade. Praying she would always feel just like this.

With a groan, his arms banded around her tight.

He dipped into her, not to taste this time but to take—until he chased all semblance of Briar's thought and reason away. How had she ever gone through one day of her life without knowing the shape of his mouth, the taste of it and the desire that spilled free now that she was with him, uninhibited?

He lifted his mouth from hers, seeming to wrench himself away. "Briar, I want you."

She sucked in a shocked breath, faltering. "You... you want me."

"I want you." He said it more vehemently this time, seeming to damn himself for doing so.

She sighed. "This is so fast. But for once, I don't care."

He stopped her from kissing him again with his hands on her shoulders. Eyeing her mouth, he said, "We should take this slow."

Letting out a laugh, she shook her head to clear it. "I'm sorry. You're right—I don't know where my head's gone."

"I lose mine too often around you, Briar. I lose everything when I'm around you."

The words were like a caress, spoken in such a sweet, reverent whisper that she turned her face into his shoulder, letting the warmth of him sweep clean through her. "I want to be with you, Cole."

"I know." His arms wrapped around her, held tight. "Me, too."

She shook her head. "You're leaving this weekend."

His hand stilled in her hair. "I can stay. If you want me…"

Even as her heart lifted, she rejected the possibility. "But you have somewhere to go. Plans…"

His lips touched her brow in a tender motion that melted her. "Nothing that can't be postponed."

As he held her in the gathering shade of dusk, she breathed him in, memorizing the feel of him, the feel of them together here in this moment. Another one of those moments she wanted to encapsulate forever.

COLE STARED at the small device in the palm of his hand. It was the size of a pen head. So small, yet so intrusive.

Just one more layer of deception.

He listened to the inn around him. The two floors above were as quiet as could be—Briar and the Josefstines were tucked in bed. No lights illuminated the ground floor where he crept about on silent feet. No headlights flashed through the windows to reveal him as he knelt behind the check-in podium and inspected the main phone line.

The one in the office was simpler than this one, but this was where she answered the bulk of her calls. It was a two-line system, but old enough not to have caller ID. Clearly, most of the inn's technology hadn't been replaced in fifteen years, which made it easier to manipulate and his job ten times quicker.

Quick, he thought, studying the bug in his hand.

Just another quick, hidden betrayal. He couldn't think about that, though—he couldn't afford to dwell on the lasting, dire effect this might have on Briar. After last night…

No. Last night was another thing he refused to think about. He focused on the task at hand. With this, he was one step closer to getting Tiffany off his back. Cursing under his breath, he unplugged the line from the back of the phone and got to work.

On the way back from his day with Gavin, Cole had thought of nothing else but the fact that he would be betraying Briar. And though he'd come to her with dark, underlying motives, as soon as she kissed him, he'd lost himself. He'd almost felt the snap of all those walls inside him break. Using the small laptop Tiffany had "donated" to his cause, he selected the software program that had come with the recording device. He switched the device on and cleaned up the area so it would look to Briar as if no one had been there but her.

Cole closed the small computer and stuffed it underneath the waistband of his jeans at the base of his spine, covering it with his leather jacket. Now whenever she made a call from either of the two lines, the computer would automatically record it and he could send the content to Tiffany's smartphone.

He glanced at the grandfather clock that ticked away the seconds. Tapping Briar's phone lines had taken less than five minutes. Quick. As he moved through the dark back up the stairs to his suite, his feet didn't feel nearly as heavy as his heart.

"I'd really rather not dwell on the numbers," Briar warned. "I kissed a man and you assume I'm going to sleep with him. Do you really think I'm that much of a hussy?"
Not? Adrian, ever the peacemaker, was projecting her own indignant scowl as though...
Olivia snorted. "Why so judgmental, wench? You—
The question about...

CHAPTER TEN

"AND THEN?" Olivia demanded the next morning over breakfast.

Briar filled the mug in front of her with black coffee and couldn't remember the last time she'd felt so smug. Lifting a shoulder, she grinned. "He helped me make dinner."

"Uh-huh," Olivia said with a knowing smirk. "Did you two get tangled up in the bed linens afterward?"

Briar rolled her eyes, heaved a short sigh but couldn't fight the smile. "No."

"And by no, of course, you mean *not yet*."

"But he kissed you again, right?" Roxie asked as she reached for another cinnamon roll.

"No." Briar beamed. "I kissed him. I can do that, you know."

"Hell, yeah, she can!" Olivia slapped a hand on the table. "Praise God! My girl's becoming a woman."

Adrian peered at her over the rim of her mug. "Don't tease her, Liv. She's been with guys before."

"Yeah, like one, maybe two."

"I'd really rather not dwell on the numbers," Briar warned. "I kiss a man and you assume I'm going to sleep with him. Do you really think I'm that much of a hussy?"

"No," Adrian put in. "She's just projecting her own hussylike tendencies onto you."

Olivia snorted. "Why so judgmental? Weren't you once a proud member of Hussies United?"

"I think the question should be," Roxie intervened as Adrian's brow sailed onto her forehead in a whip-like motion, "whether or not Briar asks him to stay."

Briar's heart pounded. She wanted to have Cole to herself for one more week, but still…even the thought of what could happen between them made her nervous. It was true; she had only been with two other men and the most recent relationship had turned out to be a fiasco of epic proportions. "I haven't really decided yet."

"Where's the man of the hour?" Olivia asked, spreading cream cheese on a poppy-seed bagel. "Usually he's the first one here for breakfast."

"He left early," she said. "I heard the bike about half an hour before I came down."

"He left without saying goodbye?"

Briar remembered the leaf of inn stationery she had found in front of the coffeemaker. "He left a note."

"Oh. My. Word. He wrote you a love note?" Roxie's eyes turned to dough as Briar took the paper from her apron pocket. "Forget you. I'm a goner."

"She saw him first. Dibs." Olivia yanked the paper from Briar's fingers. She spread it on the tabletop, wiped her hands, chewed, swallowed then cleared her throat. *"Dear Briar—"*

"Aw," Roxie cooed. "He called you *dear*."

Briar pried the note from Olivia's fingers before she could read the rest of Cole's message aloud. "We should keep it down. We might wake the Josefstines."

Olivia rolled her eyes. "Killjoy." She glanced at Adrian. "What's with you?"

Briar looked at Adrian whose tension throughout the conversation couldn't be masked. "Is something wrong?"

Adrian looked thoughtful for a moment then set her coffee down. "I haven't seen you this happy in a long time, Briar. I just don't want you to rush into anything."

"Well, aren't we Miss The-Glass-Is-Half-Empty?" Olivia muttered.

"I just want you to be careful," Adrian said, ignoring Olivia. "He's a good guy. Promise me you'll take it slow, though? I don't want you to get hurt."

"None of us wants to see her get hurt," Roxie asserted.

Briar tucked Cole's note back in her apron. "I think it's pretty clear that I'm not going to rush anything." Setting her coffee aside, she cleared her throat. "As much as I've enjoyed having breakfast with you ladies, I really should get to work."

Roxie rose, licking a small drop of icing from her thumb. "Right you are about that. I'm off to the home improvement store to buy paint."

Olivia shook her head as Roxie exited through the screen door into the dewy morning air. "She's as giddy about home improvement shopping as she is about dressing mannequins in lace and chiffon. I swear she spends her free time skipping through meadows and chasing rainbows." She patted Briar's shoulder and leaned down to kiss the top of her head. "In all seriousness, I'm happy for you, cuz."

In response, Briar simply touched a brief hand to the one Olivia had lain on her shoulder and smiled. "Come by for lunch."

"I'll try." Olivia eyed Adrian sternly. "If Debby Downer here doesn't conjure up a midsummer's storm in the meantime."

Briar waited until Olivia followed Roxie out before shifting her gaze back to Adrian's face. "She's neither an optimist nor a pessimist. I don't think she rightly knows how to appreciate one or the other."

"You don't have to tell me," Adrian said, eyeing the last bit of food on her breakfast plate.

When neither of them said a word, Briar rose from the table and began to clear it. She didn't like this unsettled feeling between her and Adrian. She didn't know how to handle it, either. Confronting tension head-on hadn't served her well with her father, had it?

"Can I help?" Adrian asked when Briar turned on the tap to rinse dishes.

"No, thanks, I've got it," she assured her.

Adrian shifted from one foot to the other, walked to the counter's edge and gripped it uncertainly. "Briar…I hope you know that I want nothing more than to see you happy."

Briar looked over and caught Adrian's earnest stare. She offered a small smile. "I know. And I hope you know that your opinion means a great deal. You're always honest with me, and I'd take brutal honesty over hearing only what I want to hear any day."

Crossing her arms across her chest, Adrian turned and settled back against the counter. The frown still pulled at her mouth as she fixed her gaze to the floor. "Twice I've gotten caught up in the idea of something—the idea of someone. Both times it brought me nothing but disaster. The only good thing that came out of either relationship was Kyle. And while he was well worth everything I had to fight through to have him in my life, the pain's still there. And so is the regret."

She pressed her lips together as she turned back to face Briar. "I'm a pessimist, it's true. But I used to be much more like you. I don't want you to go through the pain that I went through."

Briar's brows drew together as her attention strayed to the first golden fingers of light poking through the dense daybreak fog. "Thank you for caring that much, Adrian. But if life's taught me anything, it's that happiness doesn't wait in the wings."

Adrian's mouth slowly softened into a grin. "Maybe it's you who should be giving me the advice."

Briar let out a small laugh and shook her head. "No, because at the very end of all this you might be the one saying 'I told you so.'"

Adrian patted her on the back. "Trust me. Whatever happens, you'll never hear me say that."

NIGHT HAD FALLEN and the inn was already glowing with warm, homey light from within by the time Cole rolled back in on his motorcycle. Though he hadn't been able to explain everything to Briar in the note he wrote her, he'd left Hanna's at the crack of dawn so he wouldn't miss Tiffany and Gavin's departure from Ono Island.

He'd needed to say goodbye—to look into his son's eyes one more time and know that what he was doing here at Hanna's was worth it in the end. Saying goodbye to the kid had hurt just as much as returning here, realizing once again that he could never have the semblance of home the inn had come to represent for him. As much as he wanted to think that homey light within was reserved for him alone, it was an illusion, one he had to ignore as much as the hand inside him that reached for it.

As quietly as possible, he crossed the threshold, walked through the dim entryway and toward the canned noise of the television down the hall. He stopped short of entering the sitting room where the Josefstines sat on the couch watching a late-night sitcom, their daughter curled up in a chair. In the shadow of the banister, he looked beyond them to the windows that faced the bay on the sun porch beyond.

The dock where he'd kissed Briar—where she'd kissed him—was somewhere out there.

It would be another sleepless night. The war he waged with himself over what he wanted and what he had to do to get it, was growing more costly and damning with each day. He had a very real sense that even if he did get Gavin in the end, he would lose his soul in the process. Allowing Briar to look at him as the kind of man who deserved to be in her life would destroy him, sooner rather than later.

"You missed a fine meal," Mr. Josefstine commented, catching Cole's stealth movements in the corner of his eye.

"I'm sorry for that," he said, finally facing them and letting that homey light spill over him. "Meeting ran late."

Mrs. Josefstine turned her head to smile at him. "She left a plate for you in the oven."

He blinked at the thoughtfulness of it then wondered how he could be surprised. The gesture was classic Briar. "Did she go up already?"

"Preparing one of the suites for tomorrow's arrival," she told him. "I think we're about to tuck in."

"Me, too. Have a good night."

"Sleep well, dear," Mrs. Josefstine called after him as he climbed the stairs.

He was worn out, but he bypassed the bay-view suite, drawn toward the lighted door of the honeymoon suite across the hall. Pushing it open, he saw the stripped bed, gleaming floors and clean drapes over the long, narrow windows. Furniture had been polished and the metal of the wall sconces shined like new.

She'd been working hard. The scent of lemon tickled his nostrils as did the subtle tinge of fresh-cut grass. On closer inspection, he saw she'd cracked the windows to let the cool night breeze filter through the screens. It was yet another nice room with buttercream walls and light blue accents.

He heard the sound of scrubbing from the adjoining bathroom. Peering in, he found her on the floor, cleaning the tiles with a vigor some would've deemed compulsive. Her hair was pulled back in a loose braid and her face was flushed with progress. A thin line of sweat rolled unnoticed down her temple. She bit her lip as she worked briskly over the small expanse, her hand moving fast on the handle of the brush. Her T-shirt rose and fell, offering teasing glimpses of pale skin underneath.

He'd never seen her in a pair of shorts. They fell to midthigh. Come to think of it, he'd never quite realized just how long her legs were.

He rapped his knuckles on the door and watched her jerk, snapping out of her frenzied reverie. When her head lifted, he saw slight embarrassment creep into her eyes. "I didn't know I had an audience."

"Only for a moment." *More than a moment.* He shifted his feet. They felt oddly heavy.

She blew out a breath, running a hand over her damp brow before dropping the brush and standing. She winced at the quick motion, falling against the counter as her hand went to her back.

"What's wrong?" he asked, crossing to her.

"Mmm." She braced a hand against the sink and hunched her shoulders. "Wow, that hurt."

He steered her from the bathroom and ushered her carefully to the bed. "What hurts?"

She shook her head, squeezing her eyes shut tight. "Nothing. It's nothing—"

"Don't give me that, Briar. Tell me what hurts."

She hefted a weary sigh. "It's just my back."

"Here?" he asked, rubbing a hand over the base where her hand had automatically gone. Muscles knotted under his touch. He massaged them with his knuckles.

"It happens every so often," she said, biting her lip.

"How often?"

She closed her eyes. "It's nothing to worry about, Cole."

He rubbed his hand up the length of her spine. "Have you seen a doctor?"

"No. Everybody has back pain."

He frowned at the grimace that still gripped her

features as his knuckles continued to massage. Any thought of hitting the sheets early had vanished as soon as he'd seen the ache flash across her face. He could think of nothing now but salving it. "What kind of pain is it?"

"Sharp," she admitted. "Pretty acute. Sometimes it goes all the way up my spine, into my neck...."

"You need to see a chiropractor," he said. His hand moved to her neck. He watched her head lull forward as he kneaded the muscles there.

"Mmm, that's nice."

"Lie down," he said. When she frowned at him, he nudged her back onto the naked mattress. "Roll." After a short pause, she flipped to her stomach.

He positioned himself beside her, lifting her shirt until the fastening of her bra showed. Before he could do anything more than admire the glow of her skin, he placed his fingertips on the small of her back and rubbed.

A rolling purr answered his kneading. "That's... that's very nice," she said as his fingers worked up her back, inch by inch. Slowly, she relaxed and seemed to sink into the mattress. "Where'd you learn to do this?"

Her skin was hot under his fingertips as he directed them on a strict path over the pooling muscles. "I had a good doctor. He taught me a few at-home tricks to help relax. You're tense. You need to learn to let go."

The little sounds she made tormented him. He

fought to construct those walls around his heart again. They were ill-made, as most quickly constructed things were, wobbly and unsure, but he did his damnedest to make sure they held.

Once he'd worked his way to her shoulders and back down, her breathing had deepened. Her face looked lax in repose and a smile tugged at the corner of her mouth. "I'd hire you."

He laughed. A real laugh. Clearing his throat, he pulled her T-shirt back down. "It's nothing."

"You're stopping," she said, peering at him over her shoulder and pinning him with that soft, incandescent stare. The wobbly walls inside him buckled. "I thought we went through this yesterday."

He tried not to let his fingers dig into her shoulder as he leaned down slowly and touched his lips to her brow. There'd been a crease there when he came in. It was gone now, but he lingered, wanting to banish it for good. "You work too hard."

"So I've heard." Her voice lowered, vanishing into a hum as his fingers spread through her hair, unable to stop from losing themselves in her tresses.

In turn, his lips grazed to the high point of her cheekbone. "Your skin's so soft," he murmured. He'd forgotten how soft a woman could be. He craved the softness of Briar's skin. The softness of her heart. In fact, the craving worked itself into a keen ache. His heart drummed a quick cadence as he traced his fingertips lightly down her side and a shudder washed through her.

She rolled to her back. He saw the sleepy flush of her cheeks, the long, heavy sweep of her lids as the lashes lifted. His breath seized and he leaned down to her, overcome by the ache for her.

"The Josefstines," he whispered, the words barely audible.

Her breath flittered over his face, and his heart leaped as her mouth lifted to his. "The door's closed." Her warm, narrow hands rose to his face, fingers threading the hair at the nape of his neck, pulling him closer.

He dipped in, savoring every wave of heat that caressed the underside of his skin, mesmerized by every response that shuddered, sighed, hummed out of her. A quiver worked into his hands as needs clashed inside him. The ache swelled into a full-on burn.

Fighting it, he clenched his hands together on either side of her head, afraid of what they might do if he let them loose. He pulled away, watched the arch of her lashes as they swept back again. What timidity he'd seen in her before had melted into unwrapped desire. Her eyes, dense and dark, answered his need, stirred it anew. It coursed like fine, sultry wine through his blood, inciting him, frightening him.

He took a gulp of air. "Slow. I promised you we would take this slow."

"I want you to stay," she told him. "I want another week with you."

Lowering his brow to hers, he cursed himself inwardly. Yes, he would stay. A week. A month, if she asked. A year.

Knowing full well they didn't have nearly that long, he exhaled on a long rush. "I'll stay," he assured her. "As long as you need me, I'll stay."

HURRICANE BRETT CHUGGED closer and closer to the Gulf Coast with each hour, gaining wind, speed and intensity. The more organized the tropical system was at its core, the deadlier it could be. Forecasters predicted the storm to make a Category 2 landfall and the impact zone had narrowed considerably. The cone was now zeroing in on Pensacola and the Alabama and Mississippi coastlines. Mobile Bay and the Eastern Shore lay right in the center.

The Josefstines were growing visibly wary as Brett closed in. Gas prices escalated and lines at the pumps grew longer with everyone filling their tanks, anticipating a quick departure. Supermarkets prepared for the rush on batteries, jugs of water and canned goods.

Briar went about business as usual, as did Olivia at the tavern, Adrian at Flora and Roxie at work preparing Belle Brides for its grand opening. Watching the radar and seeing the monster headed straight for them, Cole began to think they were all crazy, especially when meteorologists discussed the possibility of mandatory evacuations for Gulf Shores and

Orange Beach, and closing the interstate's south-bound lane to open traffic to northbound evacuees.

"It's starting to sound serious," Mr. Josefstine muttered to Cole.

Briar's tinkering laugh made them both glance up from the television as she carried a tray of apple crisps to the coffee table. "It's normal. They're say-ing all the same for the Florida panhandle and Mis-sissippi. This storm's going to decide which direction to take within the next twelve hours. It's best to wait until there's more certainty. There'll still be plenty of leeway for driving, especially if they close I-65 South. Where're you thinking of going from here? Back to Savannah?"

"We planned to head west and see some of New Orleans before heading back home to Georgia. But you're right. It all depends on where the big bastard makes landfall."

"It's no Katrina," she assured him. "That was something to see. Her rain bands covered the en-tire Gulf."

Olivia breezed in from the kitchen. "I smell apple crisps, and I'm hungry."

Briar handed her one neatly on a napkin. "I thought you were giving Roxie a hand today."

"We broke for lunch," she explained. "Want to whip us up a couple of sandwiches?"

"Yes, of course. Anybody else want a bite?"

Before they could answer, Mrs. Josefstine walked

in, laden with shopping bags, red-faced and nearly panting. "The air's like molasses out there."

"It's the pressure rising. Here, have a seat," Briar said, taking the woman's bags. "I'll put these in your room."

"Oh, dear, you're busy. Please just leave them there for now." She shrank to the sofa cushions under the ceiling fan. "Everyone's milling about today. A few shops are taking down their awnings and boarding up."

Olivia snorted. "Premature."

As the women retreated into the kitchen, Cole's cell phone vibrated against his hip. He pulled it out of his pocket and frowned at Tiffany's number on the screen.

He scowled. She was probably calling for a progress report he wasn't ready to give. Not after the hour he and Briar had spent nestling in the honeymoon suite the night before. He hadn't even checked the computer to see whether or not Briar had made any phone calls pertaining to investors or selling. "Yeah?"

"Surprise."

He froze. "Surprise what?"

"Guess who wanted to see you before we evacuated north."

He swallowed panic. There was no way…. *"Where are you?"* he asked, walking briskly toward the entryway.

In answer, the blast of a car horn reached his ears.

He swore, clapping the phone shut as he rushed out the front door and closed it tight at his back.

If there was one thing he did not want to happen right now, this was it. As he crossed the porch to the steps, an Escalade pulled to a hasty stop in the gravel drive.

Standing his ground, he crossed his arms over his chest and frowned at Tiffany as she climbed from the driver's seat. Today's sundress was red as a horned devil. Her smile was as wide as a bus. She'd tucked her hair up into a wide-brimmed sunhat and covered most of her face with designer sunshades— probably to mask her appearance.

"This is a new level of stupid, even for you," he growled as she went around to the passenger-side backseat door.

"You really want to talk to me that way in front of Gavin?" she asked as she yanked the door open. "This is me being a good mommy."

Before he could offer up an opinion on that score, Gavin's feet dropped to the ground and Cole lost his voice.

"Dad!" Gavin said, beaming. Tiffany's hand on his shoulder was the only thing that stopped the boy from running to his father. "I asked her to let me see you one more time, and she said yes."

"That's great, chief," Cole said, unable to stop himself from smiling. The smile fled just as quickly, though, when he heard the door to the inn creak open behind him.

"Cole, is something wrong?"

Every inch of him seized up as Tiffany studied Briar. The hand that came to rest on his shoulder, soothing, made it all the worse. His voice grated low as he spoke. "You shouldn't be out here."

"Don't be ridiculous," Briar said, raising her hand to greet the newcomers. Her eyes narrowed on Tiffany. "Do I know you?"

"I want to stay with you, Daddy," Gavin begged.

"Daddy..." Briar breathed the word as her face fell into shocked lines.

Cole did his best to keep his fists from clenching. He wanted to growl, but he kept his voice as neutral as possible as he addressed Tiffany again. "There's a storm coming. You should go."

She ran a hand over Gavin's hair. "Come on, baby."

Gavin looked to him beseechingly. "I want to stay."

"You're not safe here," she said, gripping his hand and tugging him along.

"I'll see you soon, Dad?" he called back hopefully.

Cole nodded, though he wasn't certain. No, with Tiffany, you never knew what to expect. She leveled a last look at them before she helped Gavin into the car. Moments later, she peeled out of the gravel parking lot, spewing dust in her wake.

DEAR GOD. COLE had a child. A child who looked so much like him, there was no denying it.

They stood together yet so far apart. The squeal of tires faded into silence, leaving her struck dumb and him stiff as a board.

Long after the dust settled, they stayed that way. Then he turned slowly to face her, hesitant, gauging her reaction.

She didn't know what to think. Above all else, one fact kept creeping back to her.

He hadn't told her. This man she'd thought of being intimate with, this man she was falling for so quickly, hadn't thought to mention that he'd fathered a child. A child who obviously loved him. That had been all too clear by the longing expression on the boy's face.

Why?

Shaking her head, she backed away to the inn's door and fled through it, escaping the heat.

Olivia met her in the hall. "What's wrong?"

"Nothing important," she replied, sidestepping her into the kitchen.

THINGS ONLY GOT WORSE AFTER the phone call from the couple who'd reserved the suite that Briar had cleaned the night before. A cancellation in light of the decisive wobble that Brett had made toward Mobile Bay.

She'd just replaced the phone in the cradle when Mrs. Josefstine walked into the entryway. "Briar, dear—"

"You're leaving," she surmised. When Mrs. Josefstine lifted her shoulders in a helpless gesture, Briar held up a hand. "You don't have to explain. Do you need help packing?"

"I think we've got it."

"After you load everything, I'll have your bill ready."

"We do appreciate it."

As soon as she'd waved the family off, Briar went through the house, flipping on all the radios. Storm watch was under way on every local station. She listened to the coverage with half an ear as she mopped the kitchen floor, desperate to busy her hands and head.

She didn't want to think about what she was going to do about the money she'd promised the county tax office before the July due date a few weeks away. Or the investors she was supposed to be gathering to save the inn from bank foreclosure. Or Cole.

Especially Cole.

Adrian stopped by to tell her they'd hired a couple local boys to board up the tavern and shop windows and asked if she needed them to do hers, too.

As if she had anyone else to nail them up. She handed over a fifty-dollar bill for their trouble and went back to work.

Opening the screen door half an hour later, she listened to the slap of hammer on wood. The wind was picking up, whipping the trees around the inn and churning the bay surface into a white-capped frenzy.

Cole didn't bother her until she was nearly done

with her clean sweep of the lower floor. As she scrubbed the last of the baseboards, she felt him hovering behind her. "Can I do something for you, Cole?"

"Why do you do that?" Cole asked in a weary voice.

She didn't spare him a glance, only continued to work furiously. "What?"

"Why do you clean when you're mad?"

"I'm not mad. I'm prepping for the storm."

"That's bullshit, Briar."

Her eyes snapped up to his. "How would you know? You're a stranger to me."

"This is about Gavin."

"Your son."

His eyes darkened at her brusque tone. "My son," he agreed. "The only good in my life."

Her jaw tightened. She turned back to the baseboards and began to scrub again. "I see."

With a sigh, he reached down and grabbed her by the elbow. "Get up."

"Don't touch me."

"I can't stand to see you on your hands and knees working like a slave day in and day out."

"Why does it matter to *you*?" she asked. Tears spilled into her eyes. She blinked, but they didn't recede. "This is what I do! If it bothers you so much then maybe you should just leave."

The words echoed for a long, frightening moment. Then he said quietly, "Is that what you want?

You want me to leave so you can get back to your tidy life, Briar?"

Tidy life? When had her life *ever* been tidy? "Everyone around here leaves eventually." She pressed her face into her hands. "Better sooner than later, in this case. If you leave now, you'll beat the weather."

With a frown, he jerked his head in a nod. "Fine."

She fought the grief building in her throat and kept working as hard as she could, almost thrilling in the punishing soreness of her fingertips that mirrored the mounting ache in her heart.

CHAPTER ELEVEN

BRETT WAS SLATED to make landfall before dawn. Briar hated night storms. Nothing made the howling of the wind, the moan and creak of trees and the rattle of windows worse than total blackout. All it took to cut the power to the Eastern Shore was one felled branch. At Category 2 and strengthening, Brett would make sure her generator ran by midnight.

Just to be certain the front of her house was as weatherproofed as it could be, Briar staked a heavy-duty tarp over her vegetables, hoping it would hold up through the night.

Olivia offered to stay with her instead of with Adrian and Kyle in their cottage a block away. But as much as she didn't care for nightly hurricanes, with Cole gone she needed to be alone with her thoughts.

She knew he'd hit the road after glancing out the window and finding the spot under the magnolia where he parked his Harley empty.

Maybe a long, vicious storm was just what she needed with her brood.

She set candles out in her rooms on the third floor and readied a portable fan and her den couch for sleep. If the power went out, the rooms of the old inn would get hot quickly. She needed to wear something that breathed so she changed into a short, thin nightgown.

Picking at a bowl of homemade chicken noodle soup, she convinced herself she could go about her day-to-day activities just as she had every day for the past year, and not think about Cole Savitt and what she'd shared with him.

Had she really thought he was the sort of man who would want to share the burdens that came with her?

Her thoughts circled back to the uncertainty of the inn. Where would she go if everything went belly-up? She had finished culinary school before her mother's illness, but she had a feeling the head-chef job she'd been offered over a year ago in Atlanta was no longer a possibility. And one thing was for certain: there was no going back to Paris. She couldn't bear to face her history there any more than she would be able to remain in Fairhope if she lost the inn.

Never mind her—she only had herself to fend for. When the property was seized by the state, what would the other girls do? Adrian had Kyle. How would she provide for him? And Briar wasn't the only one who'd be losing a family business; Olivia doted on the tavern. It was her lifeblood. Would Roxie's dreams of owning her own business recover or would she give up after losing the shop space she'd deemed "perfect" from the get-go?

Panic seized her as she shrank back into the couch cushions. Her mother's legacy wasn't the only thing riding on the inn's dwindling success.

Branches tapped on the glass of the closest window. Their fingerlike shadows fell against the blinds, highlighted by the streetlamps below. A shudder raced through her and suddenly she wished that she'd asked Olivia to stay. No doubt, her cousin's lively company would keep her mind off the damning heaviness she felt inside.

Pulling a blanket over her legs, she curled up and listened to the quickening *tap-tap-tap* on the windowpane.

One thing she knew for sure. She wouldn't sleep a wink tonight.

It DIDN'T TAKE long for the wind to start howling. First it came as a kettle whistle. Then it strengthened into a steady, wolfish wail, interrupted only by brunt gusts that tossed limbs against the side of the house. The inn began to groan loudly, as if the storm's elements made it feel its age like never before.

Driving sheets of rain drilled the Eastern Shore in sporadic bands. One minute the wind was all that existed, the next stinging nettles of water pounded the roof.

As the night wore on, it escalated. Endless wind, endless rain coupled with several hotspots in the fast-moving clouds. Then the sky rumbled its fury and deadly bolts forked overhead, illuminating the hampered world with blinding, white light.

And finally, the hail. The clouds littered rocks of ice on the bay. As soon as Briar heard their chilling cacophony, she knew Brett was closing in.

The power lasted longer than she would've wagered, but when it shut down, it did so without a warning flicker. The house fell dead around her. There'd been no television or radio on, no noise inside the house. But without the fan spinning above her, without the drone of the air conditioner or the refrigerator, and without the comfort of light, she felt little between the storm and herself.

Lighting the line of candles she'd set on the coffee table, Briar pulled on a robe, grabbed a hurricane lamp and left her rooms.

The silence of the floors below warred with the scream of the storm, an eerie contrast. She hummed, trying to distract herself as she descended both flights of stairs, making her way to the laundry room. Through a half door in the room's exterior wall, she entered the shed where she kept the generator. Setting the lamp aside, she worked to crank it to life.

It gurgled twice but refused to ignite. On the third pull, she gritted her teeth and willed it to life. The machine growled, hesitated then roared. Lantern in hand, she waited to make sure it would keep running. Satisfied, she picked up several lengths of ready extension cord and unraveled it as she made her way toward the kitchen.

It took a minute to wrestle the refrigerator away from the wall, but once she put her back into it, it scraped across the floor with a shriek. First cord in hand, she unplugged the fridge and fit the cable into the extension. A spark from the surge between the two zapped her palm and she dropped both with a clatter, cradling her numbed hand as the fridge hummed to life.

"Are you all right?"

Heart launching into her throat, she pressed her back to the wall, blood draining from her head as she glanced up into what she thought for a moment was the face of a ghost. Then she blew out a shuddering breath. "Oh, dear God, Cole. Where did you come from?"

"Upstairs," he said, pointing toward the ceiling. At her blank look, he added, "I...never left."

"Your bike's gone," she pointed out, puzzled.

"I moved it onto the side porch. I thought that would keep it out of the worst of the storm."

As she struggled to her feet, holding her numbed hand in the other, she frowned at him. "Why didn't you leave?"

He lowered his eyes, lifted a shoulder. "I couldn't leave you here. All alone in this."

She stared at him. All this time, she'd been convinced she was alone. She'd resigned herself to it. And here he was.

Unless that zap from the power cord had done

more damage to her than she assumed, and she was hallucinating.

If anyone were likely to show up as part of her hallucinations, it would be Cole, wouldn't it?

He moved forward. "Are you okay?"

She stepped back in blatant retreat. "Yep. Just a zap." She heard the wall of hail harden and frowned. "We should put your bike in the entryway."

"You sure?"

"In another hour or two, nothing will be safe out there. We better do it now before it gets worse."

She found coats for both of them in the closet. Hood drawn in place, Briar unlocked the front door. The wind on the street side of the inn wasn't quite as brutal as the bayside, but they still had to plant their feet on the porch boards to fight it as they made their way around to the side porch where the Harley hugged the wall.

Together, they rolled it into the entryway. After the door shut, Briar got two towels from the linen closet and helped him dry the bike off and dispose of the leaves plastered against its sleek body.

"Do you need help hooking anything else up to the generator?" he asked once they were done.

She shook her head. "Not really, just a portable fan upstairs that I need to hook up. I'll get one for your room, too. It's getting stuffy in here."

"You're going back upstairs?" he asked, voice dimming.

She sensed the concern behind the query and

ignored it. In the storage closet she found the extra portable fan. "Take this. You'll need it as the night wears on. Are you hungry? You haven't eaten, have you?"

"I can find something in the fridge for myself," he said, taking the fan with a frown. "Are you sure it's safe up there?"

She brushed passed him. "I'm not Dorothy, and this house isn't going anywhere."

EVEN WITH THE fan cooling things somewhat in the bay-view suite, Cole couldn't settle. He lay on top of the sheets in T-shirt and shorts, frowning at the ceiling and listening to the low-tuned, battery-operated radio he'd found downstairs.

The DJs promised to stay up through the night with listeners, providing the latest updates on Hurricane Brett, whose slanted eye was now staring straight down the watery barrel of the bay. The treacherous east side of the storm was already pounding the Alabama and west Florida coastlines. Several tornado warnings were in effect. Early damage reports trickled in from cell phones.

One message was clear for those who'd not evacuated—*don't venture outside*. Law enforcement officers and meteorologists stated imperatively: *stay away from windows. In case of tornado, find a safe, windowless room in the lowest part of the house for cover.*

down to the first floor. Taking her hand, he led the rest of the way up to her rooms.

Briar went into her bedroom alone. He waited in her kitchen. The storm seemed far louder up here. He stared at the boarded-up window above the nook table. He couldn't see out, but the vicious animal sounds coming from the other side chilled him to the bone.

How had she stayed up here alone listening to this?

She emerged in long pajama pants and a short-sleeved T-shirt. The new clothes made her look smaller, more vulnerable.

Why the hell had he left her alone? "You need anything else?"

"Cole, I can stay here," she said, gesturing to the dark room.

"No," he said firmly. "We'll both be safer together downstairs."

A bar appeared between her eyes, but she nodded her acquiescence. He took her hand, squeezed it re-assuringly and led her away from the upper floor.

Once downstairs, he put himself to work tossing the quilt over the sofa and setting up the fan and placing the lantern on the coffee table. "We should be comfortable enough here."

She hesitated, as if she were unable to advance forward. Maybe, as with him, the idea of lying, or even sitting, on the same surface would awaken too much in her.

"Or…I could sleep in the chair," he offered.

Before she could answer, another ominous clatter broke through the silence. Her face fell, stricken. "The porch."

He reached for her. "Here, sit." Gently, he ushered her down next to him on the sofa. "Just sit. There's nothing we can do until morning."

"Right," she said, swallowing. "You're right." Another crash. "God."

His arm wrapped around her shoulders. Comforting, he told himself. Strictly comforting.

But his need to protect, to enfold, overwhelmed him. He leaned back with her hugged close at his side. Tension loosened from his chest when her head fell to his shoulder and she didn't hesitate to curl into him.

They lay in the stillness, listening to the chaos outside. Their breaths eventually slackened into relaxed, deep pulls. After a while, he realized he'd unknowingly matched his to hers—or vice versa. Though she didn't move, he knew she lay awake, alert.

Desperate to fill the lull between them, he broached the subject of the day's events. He'd have to stick to the fine points…but she deserved an explanation.

"I don't want you to think I abandoned my son," he told her. "I wanted—*want*—him with everything in me. When my ex, Tiffany, came to me for a divorce, I made it clear that I would see her in court for joint custody. That's when she began throwing accusations around. She told everyone that I'd been beating her for years. I think only her family believed her at first, but then she brought Gavin into it."

Her mouth dropped open in horror. "Your son?"

"She made him testify against me. That's all it took for the jury to grant her full custody. Since then, I feel like I've been everywhere and nowhere. I don't know where I'll end up or if I can ever try to put down roots of any kind again. Tiffany cut me off at the stump—without him, starting over feels impossible."

"How old is he?"

He swallowed. "He's six. He hates math, loves to draw and plays soccer in the spring and fall."

"You're a soccer dad."

Though the ache in him swelled, he smiled. "I never missed a game."

"You wouldn't." Her hand draped warm over his. "What she did...what I'm guessing she's still doing is too terrible for words. Why do people act out against the people who love them?"

"We'd been slipping into the cracks for a few years," he admitted. "At first, we both did our best to shield Gavin. But then she started seeing other people."

"Oh, Cole."

"I fell out of love with her a long time ago," he explained. "It's funny how you think you know someone. But then you live with them, start to peel away the layers beneath the surface that you didn't notice before—or maybe chose to ignore. I knew all along she could be selfish, but I was so determined to make it work that I convinced myself I could live with it. Until things changed."

"I wish I could meet Gavin."

He laughed. "Your cinnamon rolls would win him over in a heartbeat."

"He looks so much like you. She has to live with that every day."

"I hope she doesn't use it against him."

"You should've told me all this before," she told him. "I'm sorry I acted the way I did earlier. I was just so shocked."

"I wish I *had* told you sooner," he said. He realized he meant it.

"Will you ever try to get him back?"

"Yes. I'd do anything to have him back."

"You're a good father."

A part of him had needed that reassurance. Coming from her, he knew it was absolutely pure. Another part of him, a greater part, churned with renewed guilt. What would Briar do if she knew he'd chosen Gavin over her already?

"I understand," she said quietly. "I may not be a parent, but I do understand, more than anything, what it's like to lose something...to be willing to go to the moon and back to retrieve it."

"I know you do," he murmured. His hand tightened around her, refusing to loosen his grip even as he contemplated how hurt she would be by the end of all this if he got Tiffany what she needed. Torn, he turned his face into her hair and breathed her in.

She smelled like home.

Her brow creased as she looked down at her hands. "For a long time, I've thought my life would be different than this."

"What do you mean?" he asked, trying to read her face.

"Up until I began applying for college, I wanted to be just like my mother. I wanted to run the family business, take care of guests, plant a garden, start a family. But my father wanted me to follow in his footsteps and I didn't know how to say no. So I went off to law school. I was six weeks away from graduating when I decided to take a sabbatical and follow a group of friends to Paris."

The creases in her brow deepened and she reached up to rub the furrows with her fingertips. "I knew enough French to get a job, and I was able to extend my stay. That's when I fell in love with cooking. For the first time, I knew what it was I wanted for myself. So I applied for cooking school."

Cole thought of the man who had come to visit Briar not too long ago and the dismal mood he'd left behind. "I can't imagine your father was pleased."

She let out a mirthless laugh. "That's putting it mildly. He flew to France to drag me back home, but there was nothing he or anyone else could do at that point to stop me from pursuing my dreams. I'd stopped living off his means and was making my own way for once. I lived in a tiny flat with hardly any hot water. The walls were mostly windows so it was hot in the summer and freezing in the winter. But I loved every moment. I was in my second semester of culinary school when I met Jean-Luc."

He frowned. "A man."

The corner of her lip quirked up as she glanced at him. "This is Paris we're talking about. It was spring. Falling in love was only natural. Is it so surprising that I would?"

"No," he said, realizing how selfish it was to think that he was the only man who had ever been in her life. Especially when he pictured Briar—a younger, dreamier version of her—in Paris, a smile on her face as well as her heart. No, it wasn't at all surprising that she'd found love in that romantic place where so many people had found it before her. He had no reason to be bitter toward the man so he asked, "What was he like?"

She let out a small sigh, wistful and a bit foretelling. "He was extremely charming. All my American friends and family thought he was too old for me. I never really knew how old he was. His hairline wasn't receding, but there were sprits of gray at the temples, and there always seemed to be laughter in his eyes. He made me feel for the first time in my life like I didn't have a care in the world. Up until then, I'd been afraid of the world—of living, even—but with him I began to see it in a different light. And I thought we would forge our way into that bright, sweet light together."

On the last few words, all the hope and bright prospects of the young woman she had been then seemed to crinkle and fade from her expression like leaves at the brink of winter. Perhaps there *was* a reason to hate the man who'd stolen Briar's heart.... "What happened?"

She stared at the floor, expression wiped clean of emotion. Clearly, she had relived the experience enough times in her mind over the years that the memories didn't have the bite they once had. She spoke from an objective slant. "One morning I woke up and all my valuables and what little money I had saved was gone. If not for the missing items, I might've been able to convince myself that he'd never been there. It was ridiculous of me not to question how quickly our relationship progressed, but I was so caught up in the glorious swing of things. The best I can say about him now is that he was an incredible actor...or at least I hope he was."

Snorting out a laugh, she lifted her hands and shoulders in a helpless shrug. "I have to believe that because if I don't the alternative is that I was just blind and stupid. *L'amour est aveugle,* I suppose." At his lifted brow, she translated, "Love is blind."

The bitterness he had initially felt toward Jean-Luc had been right on target. However, it tasted too much like the bitterness he felt toward himself. Hadn't he conned Briar into believing that he was just a guest here at Hanna's? And hadn't he used the attraction he felt between them to his advantage?

"You weren't stupid," Cole told her. "You were hopeful. In life, most people start out that way. Until someone comes along and makes you believe the world's a lot dirtier and edgier than you thought it was." He squeezed her shoulder.

"Anyway, my love-spun dreams of French life and becoming this century's Julia Child were pretty well dashed," she admitted. "I no longer had the tuition money for culinary school, and I was hardly scholarship material. So I limped back home. My father made sure I realized how deeply I'd let him down. I still haven't lived down my so-called failures in Paris as far as he's concerned. But my mother took a stand. She offered to give me the tuition money for another culinary school in Atlanta, but my father was determined to see me back in law school. I'd never seen them so divided before. And by choosing to go to Georgia and continue pursuit of my dreams, I drove the final rift between them that lasted until the day she died."

"Your father sounds like a stubborn ass. *That's* what drove the rift between your parents, not you."

"Whatever it was, her cancer might not have progressed as quickly if I'd been here to share the load of the inn."

"I bet you made her happy by doing what you wanted to do." He thought about Gavin—that was what he hoped for him one day.

Her smile was short but true. "I hope so. It was what she wanted at the time. As soon as I heard that she was sick, though, I dropped out and came back home. I did my best to make her comfortable—that was all there was left to do at that point. And I could see what a relief it was to her that I was capable of taking Hanna's as my own. That was her dream, for me to take over from her one day." Briar hesitated, frowning over her next words, then said what had obviously been weighing on her for some time. "I still think of it all as hers—not mine. As much as I *had* wanted Hanna's Inn, I don't know if I still do."

Cole nodded. "If you had the choice…" He felt her brace and rubbed her arm to ease her. "Put aside your parents' expectations, your mom's legacy… Would you go back to culinary school or stay here?"

She shook her head, lifting an empty hand. "I don't know. I don't know what I want anymore." Glancing at him, she asked, "What about you? If you had your son, and your ex-wife was out of the picture, where would you go? What would you do?"

He hadn't thought that far ahead. Her question opened up a world of possibilities that seemed too risky to explore.

Mostly because one of those possibilities was staring him right in the face in the form of Briar Browning herself.

Who was he kidding? After all this was said and done, even if Tiffany kept her word and let him have time with Gavin, Briar wouldn't be part of the picture. The light of hope still shined in her eyes, despite all she had been through. It was faded—perhaps a bit jaded—but there. It took everything in him not to reach out and grasp it…because he would be the one to destroy that light. He had already set things in motion to ensure that what dreams Briar had would be dashed all over again.

"I…" He cleared his throat, looked away from her. "I don't know."

The words hung heavy between them in the thick, humid air until the sound of hail and a gust of wind made the aged walls of the inn emit a pained groan. "It's coming ashore," she whispered.

He shifted carefully. "We should try and get some sleep."

Briar wrapped her arm over his waist as her head fell against his shoulder. Their legs tangled together as the silence drifted once again and the storm rattled the walls around them.

CHAPTER TWELVE

BY MORNING, Brett hobbled north, drenching the Eastern Shore in ten inches of salty rain.

Briar walked out to gauge the destruction in a hooded coat and rain boots. The vegetables were gone. She'd known they were doomed the night before when she'd discovered the heavy arm of the tree that had toppled over the garden patch and clawed its way through the porch roof. Damp leaves covered the lawn in a dying carpet. The jasmine and annuals had suffered, but other than that, damage to the inn and the shops was minimal.

Just after noon, the last of the rain bands gave way to blue sky and hot sun. Without power and climate control, the day became oppressive.

An eerie calm always followed hurricanes. The system inhaled every breeze within hundreds of miles around its tunneling ranks, dragging them along for the ride. Though the pressure of the air lifted, without a stir, misery became the order of the day.

As soon as the gray shroud lifted, though, all four ladies of Hanna's, Flora, Tavern of the Graces and Belle Brides went to work, with Cole helping take down the storm shutters. Sweat trickled down Cole's bare back as he sawed fallen limbs into transferable pieces then hauled or rolled each of them to the street for pickup.

Briar swept the porch and gathered the leaves into garbage bags. She trimmed back the jasmine and pulled up drowned petunias. Thankfully, she managed to harvest all the daffodil bulbs—they could be replanted in dryer conditions.

The vegetables, on the other hand, were ruined. Everything had crumbled and lay flattened under the tarp Cole and his chainsaw finally uncovered. She mourned the squash, peppers and the big round tomatoes she and her mother had planted together. Digging up dead stalks and vines, she stuffed them, too, in garbage bags and took them to the street.

Afterward, she went into the muggy inn, putting the portable fans to work in the kitchen as she squeezed lemons and tried to take her mind off the loss. She was lucky—they were all lucky. It could have been worse. No use mourning and brooding when there was so much more to be done.

Through the open windows and the screen door, she heard the thwack of a hammer high above. After finding an extension ladder, Cole had offered to check for structural damage and replace the shingles that had been blown off.

She prayed there was no roof damage. Already, she had to get the porch to rights. She'd have to hire someone, of course. Construction was about as good for business as tropical storms.

A porch could be fixed quickly, though. An entire roof? She'd have to shut the inn down for a couple of weeks at least.

By the time she finished making lemonade, Cole was climbing down the ladder, hammer hooked through his belt loop. She carried out a tray full of finger sandwiches and the lemonade jug with two ice-filled glasses. A fine sheen of sweat coated every inch of his skin. His hair was slicked back from his beaded brow. His shorts were dirty. Specks of mud and dirt dotted his chest and shoulders.

She set the tray on the porch rail and filled him a glass, trying hard not to stare. "Starving?"

"Hot," he muttered, tipping the glass back and gulping its contents all but for the cubes of ice. He pressed the cool surface to the side of his face and closed his eyes. "No damage as far as I can tell."

She sighed. "That's a relief."

"Thanks," he said when she handed him a sandwich.

"You should sit," she said, gesturing to one of the porch rockers. "You've been working for hours."

Without argument, he dropped onto the nearest cushion and downed his sandwich in three bites. Sitting next to him, she gave him a few more and shoveled down one herself. Brushing crumbs from her shirt, she said, "I hope you don't mind. I invited the girls over for dinner. Kyle, too—Adrian's son."

"Sounds like a party," he said. "Am I invited?"

"After all you've done today, you can be the guest of honor."

"I hope I get to shower first," he told her, glancing over his arms and chest. "Some guest of honor I'd make as is."

"Liv talked to the power company. They're slowly getting everyone back online. It'll be several more hours, I'm sure. But you can shower, if you don't mind cold water."

"A cold shower sounds great," he said, leaning back in the rocker.

She tried not to think about him under the running water. Even more bare than he was now. She certainly wouldn't mind being the one to lather his skin in soap and wash the grime of work away.

Must be the heat. She could all but feel his slick skin beneath her hands.... She refocused her attention on the naked grove where the vegetables had been.

"You couldn't save any of them?" Cole asked.

She shook her head. "They were too far gone."

"Will you start over?"

An icy chill rippled through her, panic on its heels. She thought of all there was to do with what little she had. When it came time to replant, would Hanna's even be here anymore? Would she?

"I don't know," she whispered. Because she suddenly couldn't breathe, she stood and gathered the napkins and glasses. "I'll make some more lemonade."

"Three glasses were enough." Before she could veer past him, he reached out and touched her arm. "The vegetables can be replanted. I'm just glad you're still here."

Looking into his face, she felt every hour she hadn't slept wash away and every worry on her mind sink to the backburner. Though worrying and planning would probably be smarter, the escape of him was too irresistible.

He'd stayed. Through the storm, through the unease between them, he not only stayed with her—he comforted her. He stood as a buffer between her and the storm.

And she was dangerously close to relying on his shoulder.

She let her fingers fall against his, linking them for a moment before she wordlessly walked to the screen door.

VOICES CLAMORED THROUGH the inn, filling it with life and warming Briar's heart. All the more because they were the voices of the people she loved most.

Olivia lifted her tea glass as they settled around the dining room table. "A toast?"

As the others mirrored the move, Briar frowned. "If I'd known we would be toasting, I'd have taken down champagne and flutes."

"Oh, hush," Olivia chided through a beaming smile. "A toast to Cole."

"Me?" he asked, puzzled.

"Yeah, you," she said as the others fell silent. "It's been a while since we've had a decent man around here to help. Thank you for all you did to get this place halfway back to rights and asking nothing in return."

"Cheers to that," Adrian echoed, shooting Briar a look over the rim of her glass. After sipping, she set it aside and reached for the nearest bowl—leftover potato salad. "This looks wonderful, Briar."

"I'll say," Roxie cheered as dressed down as any of them had seen her to date in blue-jean cutoffs, a thin, sleeveless, button-up blouse and a bright bandana tied around her head. "It definitely beats another night of Jell-O and bananas."

"I love Jell-O," Kyle piped up, mouth already full of potato salad.

"This is hardly a scale up," Briar muttered. "I just pulled it out of the fridge."

"You really need to learn how to take a compliment, Briar," Roxie advised.

Olivia groaned. "That's the understatement of the century."

"It is good," Cole added, lifting his eyes to hers.

She smiled, feeling warmed again at his praise. "Thank you." Shifting her gaze to the others, she saw the winged looks shooting between them. Reaching for another bowl, she lifted the spoon. "Here, Kyle. You need green beans."

"Blah." When Adrian nudged him with a telling elbow, he straightened, pouting. "Fine. I'll eat them."

"Just a few," Briar promised, spooning them onto his plate. "Did you enjoy the storm?"

"Oh, yeah. It sounded like *Twister*. You know, the movie *Twister?*"

"I think I've seen it. I bet you're ready for school to start back up."

"Double blah."

Cole chuckled. "Typical boy."

Adrian rolled her eyes. "Let me tell you. In a perfect world, summer would last forever."

"If only," Kyle grumbled. Looking to Cole, his freckle-dotted expression lightened several degrees. "Were you really a cop?"

Alarmed, Briar looked to Cole to gauge his reaction. His smile didn't waver. "A detective, actually."

"Like *CSI?*"

"Not quite. I worked in Narcotics. Do you know what that is?"

"The drug guys came to our school last year," Kyle admitted, nodding sagely. "They brought the dogs. They were pretty cool. Did you ever work with canines?"

"Sure," he replied. "Plenty of times."

"What about undercover?"

"I did a bit of undercover work," he said with a laugh at Kyle's undeniable curiosity. "It's probably not as cool as what you see on TV, though."

"Did you ever shoot anybody?"

"All right, that's enough," Adrian warned. "Eat your greens."

"I was just asking."

"It's okay," Cole assured her. "It's the question kids ask the most these days."

"It's all violence for them," Olivia noted.

Adrian slanted her a scrutinizing look. "Didn't you tell me once that John McClane is your idea of the perfect mate?"

"I'm a grown-up," Olivia retorted, stuffing half a buttered roll into her mouth. "With needs."

"And video games," Briar intervened, sensing that the conversation was headed south. "Kids are so into video games."

"The Kinect is my favorite gaming system," Kyle told them. He turned to Cole again. "Have you ever played?"

"No, can't say I have," Cole admitted.

"Maybe you could come over sometime. I'll take it easy on you, at first."

Adrian sighed. "Mr. Savitt has more important things to do than duel controllers with you. If you're not going to eat the rest of that, why don't you take it to the kitchen?"

"I'll take it," Briar said, scooting her chair back.

Kyle was already on his feet. "I've got it. Is there any ice cream, Briar?"

She beamed, settling back into the chair. "You know there is. It's homemade, too, just the way you like it. Want me to get it for you?"

"I know where it is," he said, carrying his plate through the swinging door and flashing Briar a grin.

"Bowls are in the second cupboard." She shook her head and looked to Adrian. "He's growing so fast. How do you not just weep over him?"

"I have my moments," she admitted. "He's only being chivalrous because he still has a mad crush on you. And Cole, please forgive him. He's desperate for another Y chromosome around here. It's from growing up without a real father figure."

"It doesn't bother me at all," he told her. "He seems like a good kid."

"Father figure or no, it looks like you're doing a spectacular job," Roxie agreed. "He's wonderful."

"Thank you," Adrian said, glowing a bit. "I like to think he's mostly me."

"I wish you'd bring him over more often," Briar told her. "Would anyone else like ice cream?"

"I'm stuffed," Olivia said. She held up a halting hand when Briar began to rise again. "No, no, you sit. You've fed us. We do the dishes. Fair trade."

"Don't be silly. This is my home."

"And we're all family," Olivia argued. "There'll be no waiting on us, at least until the air-conditioning's back on."

Resigned, Briar sank back down. "Whatever you say, Liv."

Olivia dropped a kiss to her head. "That's right, cuz." She winked at Cole as she carried her dishes out. "Whatever I say."

It didn't take long after dishes were dry and put away for Olivia to pull Briar aside. The others said their good-nights to Cole, distracting him long enough for her to ask, "Did you pounce him?"

Briar blew out a laugh. "Don't be ridiculous—"

"Wait a minute, wait a minute. You were stuck together all night long in an empty house with half a dozen beds and *nothing happened?*"

"How many times do I have to tell you it's not like that?"

"No, no, no!" Olivia squealed, raising both hands to halt the rational explanation. "For heaven's sake, Briar! Didn't you see the way he was looking at you over dinner? He's all over you. Like something warm and gooey."

Briar winced. "That's so not sexy."

"So *you* say. Stop using your head and start thinking with that thing the rest of us recognize as our libido!"

"Now you're just being crude."

Olivia gripped her arm. "It's obvious that he wants you. And you need this. Admit it."

Nerves began to shred her composure. "I guess I could go upstairs and change really quick."

"When I leave with the girls, I'll tell him that you need him for...I don't know...some fixer-upper emergency," Olivia contemplated. "He'll haul ass upstairs to the rescue. You'll open the door looking all sexified and voilà." Olivia folded her arms, looking very satisfied with her new plan. "What do you think?"

Briar gaped at her. "He's seen me under the sink

with tools. You really think he's going to fall for that?" Better yet, did she really think she wouldn't chicken out before he got halfway up the stairs to *help?*

Olivia grinned. "I doubt he'll be thinking about anything but what you two will be doing later." She gave Briar a push. "Now go."

"But what if he——"

"No," Olivia intervened, raising her hands and backing away. "Don't think. Just go. Be a temptress."

In her T-shirt and shorts, she hardly fit the bill. As she turned and numbly climbed the stairs, she fought to get back her vital hold on composure. But now that she knew there was a possibility she could be... well, *not sleeping* in a matter of minutes, it made her nerves recharge.

Closing her eyes, she stopped to catch her breath and steady herself on the landing. Cole's face instantly filled her thoughts. Over dinner, he'd been quicker to smile. The grin had complemented his narrow face so well. The creases were wearing into the corners of his eyes again. A shadow of stubble had cloaked the lower half of his face. He was more a man than anyone else she'd known before him.

She might not fit the sexy bill, but he certainly did.

Damn it, if she was going to be a temptress, she had to make a better effort. After ascending the stairs to the third level, she closed the door and, safe in the confines of her bedroom with the hurricane lamp glowing at the bedside, she stripped to her skin. Catching a glimpse of herself in the mirror, she frowned at her appearance.

She hadn't put any sunscreen on before going out under the blazing rays today. Her arms, shoulders and cheeks were tinged bright red. The rest of her looked far too pale. How could she live on the water and not have some semblance of a tan?

She put on the closest thing she had to lingerie—a pair of skimming silk underwear, and a thin nightgown. Not at all comfortable with the hem floating around her upper thighs, she pulled on her robe and tied it tight.

She heard the knock on the door and her hands fumbled. Trying to remember how to breathe, she smoothed her hands over the skirt of her robe and made her way slowly to the door.

As she closed her hand over the knob, something buzzed along her nerve endings. Excitement. A straight shot of thrill that wove its way into her blood and heightened her anticipation.

Pulling in another steadying breath, she yanked open the door.

It snaked out in an unstable rush at the sight of him. The candlelight complemented his features as well as a smile did. Her lips tingled, eager to cruise along the rough surface of his jaw.

His eyes, dark and knowing, skimmed from her made-up face over her cloaked shoulders and down to her bare calves, ankles and toes. "You almost look ready for bed."

Not even close. "Come in," she said, stepping aside so he could cross the threshold before she changed her mind and shut the door in his face.

His hands slid into his pockets when she slowly turned to face him. "Liv said you needed something?"

"Er…yes." She brushed a hand over her hair, looking around. Her eyes latched on to the kitchen sink and she gestured him that way. "It's clogged."

He walked to the kitchenette on the far end of the living area. Following him, she crossed her fluttering hands over her chest.

"Do you have any Drano?" he asked as he inspected the sink.

"Nope. No Drano." *What now?* she thought frantically. Where was that little devil when she needed it?

"It seems to be draining just fine," he deduced, running water into the sink. "Are you sure it's clogged?"

"I guess not." When he turned off the water and held his hand over the sink to drip-dry, she automatically reached for the dishcloth next to the stovetop. "Sorry."

"It's no trouble. Sinks can be tricky. Particularly when they're old." He turned to her. With the table at her back, she was suddenly very aware of the few inches between them. As he finished drying his hands with the checkered dishcloth, his eyes locked on hers, darkened as they took a journey over her face.

Feeling as if she were standing over a pit of fire, she swallowed. "Are you hot?"

His eyes took their time roaming her face, the line between his brows deepening. Finally, he said, "Yeah. I am."

Knowing very well he meant something else entirely, she felt the answering boil in her blood. By God, she needed him, much more than she had originally thought. Olivia was right. She *did* need this, and she refused to think anymore. Nodding her decision, she closed the little bit of distance between them, fingers lifting to fumble with the buttons of his shirt.

She heard the quick snag of his breath. Lifting her eyes to his, she gauged his reaction. Clearly speechless, he watched her with conflicting levels of need and something else she couldn't quite define. Determined to vanquish whatever else it was, she raised herself on tiptoe and met his mouth with hers. The clash was hot. It felt like a brand. Claiming him. She was claiming him for herself. It was about time.

Just as her hands began to skim over the hot, chiseled expanse of his chest and the taut, smooth skin that stretched over it all, she felt his fingers close around her wrists. He tugged her away, making a noise deep in the back of his throat caught between longing and frustration. "No," he said. "No, Briar. We can't. I can't."

The air shuddered out of her as his rejection hit her like a punch to the stomach. "I'm sorry. I thought… Olivia said you…" Raising her eyes to search his face again, she didn't expect to find the pain she saw in his eyes. She raised a hand to his cheek. "Cole, what's wrong?"

He hissed out a breath, lifting his hand to the back of hers. "This isn't right. I shouldn't."

She remembered that night in the downstairs kitchen not so long ago when he had pulled away. The same look had haunted his expression. The same pain had lurked like phantoms in his eyes. She'd assumed he'd pulled away out of some maddening form of chivalry. Not now, she determined. She'd felt his searing need in his kiss. He wanted to be with her as much as she wanted him. "There're two of us here. And, I'm sorry, but you don't get to decide for me this time."

"Briar—"

"No," she said. "You're trying to be the honorable man. I get it. And it wasn't very long ago that that would've won me over. But not tonight."

"Easy," he said, steadying her with a hand on her waist.

"You stayed. You stayed through the storm. For me." She watched his eyes clear and focus on hers, the doubt washing away as he looked at her, really looked at her. Something there in his deep, dark gaze answered back, acknowledged her words. His grip on her wrist loosened, no longer restraining, and his thumb smoothed over the hammering pulse point just beneath the surface of her skin.

She surged forward. "I know you care for me and you don't want to hurt me."

He sighed, lowering his brow to hers so the tip of his nose brushed hers. "I don't."

"Cole, it's been a long time since I've believed in something. Really believed. But I believe in you now. I believe in us."

"Briar…"

She kissed him, deep but soft. When she pulled back, she looked at him, hoping she'd vanquished some of that phantom pain. His lids remained closed over his eyes, but the muscles of his face were no longer taut. Lifting her mouth to his again, she took it deeper, a bit darker. "Touch me."

He answered, shooting straight past tenderness as the restraint she sensed beneath his skin broke in two. His body pressed against her fully as his tongue finally answered the longing flick of hers. He jumped to the pace she set without question, his touch sliding across the planes of her shoulders and up the column of her throat to frame her jaw.

The ache welled up and seared her. Desperate to appease it, she arched against him, only managing to break open a whole new chain of emotions. Ravenous need squeezed so tight around her, she shook. She wanted every piece of him. Despite timidity, despite everything, she wanted the hard, driving length she felt under his jeans inside her. "Touch me," she begged again.

A trembling sigh answered the touch of his hand on her thigh. It crept up, warm, steady, strong, lifting the hem of her gown, revealing the skin of her hip. He nipped her lower lip before trailing along her jaw to her ear. A gentle nibble of his teeth on the lobe had her melting against him, her eyes rolling back to a close.

Her breath came in fast, shallow bursts as his fingertips coursed up the outer edge of her thigh. He touched her hip, fingered the scalloped edge of her underwear, tracing the hem around the band to her belly. His knuckles caressed the fabric just above the snug, foreign fire that blazed at the cusp of her legs.

Her hands balled into fists at his back when he spread openmouthed kisses over her shoulder.

"You okay?" he asked after he'd traced his way back to her mouth. "Do you want me to stop?"

"No." She sighed, leaning into him. Her lips parted in invitation.

He tipped his mouth away from hers, teasing. "Thank God." Watching her, he delved under the fabric, fingertips traveling leisurely over skin as alive with needs as the rest of her.

As his hands wandered, she couldn't draw a deep enough breath. The ache grew to a peak as Cole wrapped his fingers underneath the heat to daub the product of her arousal. The flush in her cheeks spread down her neck and dipped between her breasts. All the while, he watched her with deep, knowing eyes and she couldn't breathe. His fingers turned up, parting the petals of her sex to find some sweet, explosive spot nestled underneath.

Her head fell back in shock as he manipulated her in slow, steady strokes. A gasp launched from her mouth, her hands clutching fistfuls of his shirt. Her hips bumped the doorjamb as she moved against his caress. A fine sheen of mist had popped out onto her skin.

He stopped as every muscle in her body seized, tightening as she loomed on the edge of a hot, stormy, turbulent sea. She stood limp, falling away from that dizzying precipice he'd held her over for one startling moment. His hands nudged the garment over her hips and let it fall to the floor. He wrapped his arms around her waist and lifted her, spinning around the jamb and into the bedroom.

Setting her on the bed's edge, he pushed the skirt of her gown up, baring both thighs. He stepped into the vee of her legs to press his denim-clad arousal to hers. Propping her hands on the bed behind her, she arched to him. His gruff groan thrilled her. She undid the remaining buttons along the front of his shirt. Answering her thirst for skin, he rolled his shoulders and shrugged free of the fabric.

It fell to the floor and she lowered her hands, unlatching the fly of his jeans. She strained forth so she could touch her mouth to the taut, candle-licked skin of his abdomen, feel it glide underneath her lips. The sinuous wrench of arousal leading, she pressed openmouthed kisses over the heated expanse. The muscles in his jaw flared, his sinewy shoulders and rib cage rising and falling rapidly with resonant pants.

Courage leading, she let her hands roam over the strong line of his back, tracing the lines of him down to the hips and the jeans now loose around his waist. He jerked in surprise when she moved them under the denim, molding the shape of his flank. Lifting her chin, she looked into his dark eyes as she nudged the material down and away.

He toed the jeans off before taking her down to the mattress. The weight of him made her moan even as his hand trekked between them, over her. She lifted her knee, turning her leg out so he could circle the sweet spot he'd found before.

He went one step further, plunging. Touching a tender kiss to her brow, he stroked the taut walls inside her. Wrapping his free arm under her waist, he pushed her up to the spinning edge again, this time refusing to back down.

She panted as he drove her to the brink. Quivered, nails biting into his shoulder.

"Let it go," he murmured in a rough, roused voice. "Let go. I'm right here."

She plummeted on a gasp, a small cry following the choked sound. He held her to him, murmuring words of assurance as his head tilted, trailing over the smooth terrain of her throat. His lips came to rest briefly on the pulse before he nipped his way down to her collarbone.

Urging him on, she lay her head back and cupped the nape of his neck. His lips journeyed down to the bodice of her gown. For a moment, he stopped to indulge in the spot between her breasts, nuzzling and making the muscles of her thighs shiver and burn. Her breath quavered out as he teased her nipple through the paper-thin fabric. When the hot, damp cloak of his mouth soaked through, she let out the first moan, arching against him in a surprising burst of need.

His head lifted and she blurted, "Sorry."

He shook his head, lowering his lips to glide over her other breast. "Do it again."

The heat built and she bowed again, harder this time, fisting his hair. "Please," she begged.

He stopped, reared up and pulled the gown hem up, baring her inch by colorless inch. His mouth followed, first brushing over her navel then her sternum, lingering for a moment again between her breasts. Finally, she lifted her arms and he dropped to her, skin to skin.

The heat of him seared. His kiss blazed with tension and needs yet to be fulfilled. No turning back now. She knew it. What he'd already manipulated under her skin, the charge that surged through her blood, demanded it. He knew it, she sensed as the kiss built and she began to tremble.

Arching underneath him again, she felt the iron

length of him against her inner thigh. She bent her knees and wrapped her legs around his waist, watching him as she moved beneath him. He hissed, a guttural sound stirring in his chest and vibrating through her.

"Now," she murmured, sliding her arms around him, too, so she enfolded him just as he'd already enfolded her.

His hips moved against hers. As he breached, it sent a teasing electrical pulse along her nerve endings, sparking another climax. Her body went from stiff, bracing, to relaxed and she curled into him, touching her brow to his just as he had to hers at the beginning, closing her eyes to savor as he stopped, panting.

His eyelids hovered to a half-close as if he savored the rush of being inside her. "Hold on to me," he said. His fingers threaded through hers and he raised her arms overhead, keeping them linked and squeezing in quiet assurance. When she gripped him tight in return, he moved and they took sharp, twin pulls of air.

Her head ascended into the clouds, but her body remained grounded, churning right along with him, falling quickly into the age-old rhythm. The heat swelled between them. The outside humidity rose from their joined forms, and friction built to an unbelievable brink as he drove her up again.

Her legs gave out, sliding limp to the sheets, but he didn't stop. Not when sweat trickled down the side of his face and over his rigid jaw. Not when she squealed as those cataclysmic sensations collided and washed around her again in a warm, bubbling pool. Not until every inch of him seized and he groaned, lowering his face to the curve of her neck as he shuddered and his erection kicked.

When he, too, was spent, they both lay unmoving. Exhausted. Sated. Briar felt comfortable despite the exposure, despite the fact that he remained firmly rooted between her thighs. She lifted a hand and raked it through his mussed black hair, lips curving slowly, warmly. The afterglow eclipsed everything that had come before it. Humming. Blissful. Perfect. He was perfect, the haunted man who was so much more than a stranger to her now.

He was her lover. With him lying close, warm, his fingers still entwined with hers against the turned-down sheet, she didn't feel alone.

She felt changed. Renewed. Buoyant. Loved.

A wonderful stillness fell over her mind and she sank with him into the hazy cradle of sleep, not at all worried about tomorrow.

CHAPTER THIRTEEN

BRIAR USUALLY WASN'T one to pull the covers over her head and ignore the light creeping through the curtains.

Sometime in the early morning hours the power had come back on. Air streamed, blessedly cool, from the vents over the bed. It kissed her skin and made her smile as she roused from sleep. For once she let the clock on her bedside tick by without remorse. Cole's upper body was curled against her back and his arms were banded around her. And there was no way she was waking him up.

His sleeping breaths fluttered light over her ear, stirring the hair lying over the nape of her neck. The inn sounded so peaceful around them. The walls seemed to be breathing a contented sigh with the return of central cooling. The only sound she could hear was the very faint cry of seagulls returning to the battered shoreline. Other than that, she and Cole could have been alone in the world.

Not so long ago, the silence of Hanna's had served as a reminder of all her failures. With Cole in her bed, for once it didn't give Briar unrest, and that dependency on him no longer gave her pause.

She loved him, so very much. As the hour hand struck six and the first sliver of sunlight slanted through the curtains onto her face, she basked in the certainty that she could love again. That she did.

The telephone next to the bed broke the silence, the ring jolting them both. She ran a hand over her hair, pushing herself up onto her elbow as she reached out to lift the receiver from the cradle. Cole rolled to his back, arms raised over his head. She cleared her throat and answered, "Hanna's Inn."

"So, did ya get some?"

A wide grin bloomed, along with a quiet laugh. Briar pressed her lips together, glancing over her shoulder to make sure Cole was sleeping. Lowering her voice, she said, "I'm starting to think you have a one-track mind."

"Nuh-uh," Olivia replied. "No evasion. Just deets."

"It's early."

"Like you weren't up at the crack."

A hand, wide and warm, slid over her hip. She closed her eyes, melting at his touch. "I have to go."

"Second wind?"

Briar rolled her eyes. "Later." Hanging up on Olivia's protest, she shook her head. "Sorry. I was hoping you'd sleep awhile longer."

"Mmm." His hand cruised its way into the dip of her waist, right at home.

Rolling to her back, she let his fingers splay over her bare belly. She'd fallen asleep before she could think to reach for her nightgown. Her breasts met cool air, and her arm came up automatically to shield them from view.

He grunted a sleepy protest, threading his fingers through hers and tugging it down. Eyes still closed, he rubbed his whiskered cheek over them.

The rasp brought out a laughing gasp. As his stubble chafed, the peaks drew up and a long tongue of melting-pot lust swept clean through her. She wriggled away. "I have to make breakfast."

"Mmm," he growled again, knee rising and tugging the sheet with it. His abs looked taut even in repose and, because she knew *exactly* where it led, she forced herself to look away from the trim line of dark hair that disappeared under the covers. "Coffee?" he muttered.

"That, too," she promised, pulling her robe over her shoulders. "Rest." After brushing her lips across his brow, she regrettably left the sexy, sleep-rumpled man in the rumpled sheets. The tantalizing image and the pinching flush on her cheeks stayed with her as she crossed from the bedroom door to the kitchenette.

It was such a simple, everyday thing—making breakfast. But today the chore was significant. She was cooking breakfast for the man she loved. As she arranged two places at the small nook table, her eyes shifted to the windows at right and the long sweep of blue bay. The sun shined off the pinpricks of water.

Magic, she thought. There was magic in the air

this morning. The kind of magic she'd begun to doubt existed.

Cole joined her moments later, wearing the jeans from the night before and nothing else. "Coffee's on the burner," she greeted, trying not to stare too much.

He made a beeline for the counter and took a mug from a hook. "Smells good."

"Breakfast is cooling," she explained. "You have impeccable timing."

"Mmm." The small spoon she'd set out for stirring tinkered against the inside of his mug as he splashed in a bit of creamer. "Anybody joining us?"

"Not that I'm aware of," she replied. "But you never know who might pop in at the last minute around here. I think it's safe to say, though, that we'll be dining alone today." She glanced at him and her smile dimmed at the contemplative frown on his face. "Something wrong?"

His head lifted from the task, his lids heavy from sleep. Despite that, his dark gaze held a conflicted glint. "I've never been more afraid of anything than I am of hurting you."

"You didn't hurt me," she said, thrown off track by his admission. It was just like that moment on the dock when she'd first kissed him. He'd spoken of hurting her then, too. And, like now, it had been hard to discern if he was talking about what was between them in the moment or something else. "If you don't have enough faith in yourself, know that I have it in you."

"I'm not sure I deserve it."

She wove her arms around him and held tight. "Then I'd say you need more convincing." Lifting herself onto her toes, she moved into his embrace, her hands sliding around his neck as she raised her mouth to his.

She took the languid kiss deep. In reaction, he maneuvered her around until the back of her hips rested against the counter's edge. Losing herself against him, she threaded her fingers into the hair at the back of his head.

The afterglow shimmered over her again, a gilded, silver-edged thrill that drowned out everything else. Her tongue danced in slow cadence with his. Tilting her head into his open palm, she hummed, arousal coiling sinuously up through her, blazing in all its smoldering intensity.

His groan echoed her sound of assent and he lowered his hands, flat and possessive over her shoulder blades, down into the dip of her spine. She gasped in savory delight as they moved between the counter's edge to mold her flank. Instinctively, her hips bowed into his. The hard ridge of his excitement amplified hers until she was all but drowned by the need for reckless abandonment.

As if sensing that need, he gripped the backs of her legs and raised her onto the counter.

Dear Lord, here? On her prepping counter?

His touch was already sliding up the skirt of her robe. *Oh, thank goodness*...

He drew back abruptly, dropping his hands to the counter, trying to catch his breath. "Hell." He lowered his head to her shoulder as he steadied himself. "I swear you make me crazy."

Consumed by heat, she scrubbed the heel of her hand over her hammering heart.

After a moment, he lifted his face to hers. He rubbed his hands up her arms then down them before backing away. "We have to be more prepared before I can let this happen again."

She scanned his face. Suddenly, what he'd said before began to make sense. "You don't have to worry about being prepared." When he frowned at her, she smiled and lowered her voice. "I've got that covered."

He blinked. "Right." Scrubbing a hand over the five o'clock shadow on his chin, he cleared his throat. "We probably should've talked about this before...but like I said. I lose my mind around you."

She grinned. "I kind of like it that way."

Warmth flooded his eyes as a smile softened the lower half of his face. He lowered his lips to hers, lingered for a moment as he inhaled then pulled back, taking her hand in his and interlocking their fingers. "I was thinking about taking a ride around town to see if anyone took any serious damage. Do you want to come with me?"

"I would love that, but there're still things for

me to do around here." Sliding her feet back to the floor, she addressed the Danish that had cooled long enough.

"I can stay and help."

"No, you did more than enough yesterday. But I refuse to let you go until you've had some breakfast."

"Trust me. I wasn't planning on passing that up." As she sliced and transferred pieces onto their respective plates, he leaned over her. Though he kept his hands to himself, his sexuality shimmied along her skin.

How was she supposed to go about her day-to-day activities without taking Olivia's advice and jumping his wicked-hot bones again…and again?

IT WAS OFFICIAL. Cole had lost his mind.

From the moment he saw Briar Browning, something in him had snapped. Self-control, maybe. Or better judgment.

His biggest fear digging into Briar's past had been that he would lose himself. After the night he'd spent with her and the current, deluded state of his jumbled mind, it was clear that he had.

It was hard to regret what had happened between him and Briar. Sure, upon waking he'd gone into a tailspin after recalling that there'd been no protection involved. When he'd gone up to her rooms, he hadn't expected her to seduce him—protection had been the last thing on his mind.

As he dressed in the bay-view suite for a ride into town, he sighed heavily. The half hour he'd spent under the stinging spray of the showerhead had done little to clear his mind. Despite all the damning details, he couldn't get beyond the fact that last night had been incredible. Briar had blossomed beneath his touch like a bud already on the verge of bursting forth. He'd been helpless at her sweet urging to do anything but follow, to do as he'd wanted to do to her—with her—since the very beginning. To enfold. Covet.

He'd lost his mind, it was true. Never in his life had he lost sight of his intentions so completely, so easily. Certainly not when he fell in love the first time. Not even when he'd lost everything.

Therein lay his problem, he thought as he grabbed his helmet and keys off the dresser. He'd lost everything. His whole purpose in coming to Briar's doorstep had been to get his life back. Now he had managed to complicate things further by damn near falling head over heels in love with Briar and forgetting that his son hung in the balance.

He wanted Gavin back in his life. Nothing had changed that. But now, in addition, he wanted Briar. Worse, he feared he wanted both in equal measure.

The two lives he could envision for himself—one with Gavin, one with Briar—could never mix, could they? In order to gain visitation rights with Gavin, he had betrayed Briar—there was no going back from that. And even if she could somehow find it in her heart to forgive him, he doubted Tiffany would. If he chose Briar, he had to give up any hope of ever being a part of Gavin's life.

His temples pounded. The knot he'd managed to bind himself in wasn't going to give until he thought things through. He had to get back to that place in his mind where everything made sense, where he knew exactly what needed to be done.

Where was the stone-cold detective's instinct when he needed it? It had disappeared amidst the storm debris littering the streets.

He was going for a ride, and he wouldn't stop until he'd cleared some of the debris from his brain. Until his thoughts weren't a tangle of *what-ifs*. There was no way he could do his thinking here—Briar was here. And when Briar was around, he couldn't trust himself to think about anything but wanting her. Loving her.

Halfway down the stairs to the first floor, his steps slowed. The whistle was low, a small whine that barely penetrated the silence of the bottom floor. Instinct that had gone missing teased the small hairs on the back of his neck to attention. Gripping the banister, he listened carefully. Through the open kitchen door, he saw the stove was empty. No kettle. He would have heard Briar come downstairs. She hadn't. The floor was vacant.

He caught himself reaching for his belt where, as an officer, his gun had once rested. Slowly, silently, he crept the rest of the way down the stairs.

The whistle was coming from the right, down the hall toward the entryway. Edging along the wall, he listened for the telltale sounds of intrusion—soft footsteps, faint rustling—and heard nothing but that strange whistle.

As he rounded the corner carefully into the entryway, the whistling noise drew him to the door behind the podium—the one he had broken into not long ago. He'd had to pick the lock because Briar always kept it closed and bolted. Every nerve in his body stood on end when he saw that the door was open.

Stepping across the office threshold, a slight breeze hit his face, smelling strongly of wet earth and magnolia leaves. His eyes trekked quickly over the papers strewn about the room, the open drawers and filing cabinet. Nights ago, Briar's records had been meticulously organized. Now they were completely destroyed. Her computer had been taken, but the printer, fax machine and phone remained.

He touched his fingers to the broken windowpane, and the muscles in his jaw bunched as rage overcame him.

This was no robbery.

Knowing exactly who was behind this, he curled his fist into a ball and fought the urge to smash through the rest of the broken pane of glass.

"Cole, what are you…"

He turned just in time to see the warm smile vanish from Briar's face. Her color vanished, too, as her face fell, distressed. Her hand fumbled for the doorjamb as she swayed. "What—what happened here?" she breathed, the words trembling out of her as she raised a hand to her mouth.

He crossed to her quickly because she looked damn near faint. "A break-in. No one's here. I checked. But we need to call the police."

"The police," she muttered. Seeming to come back to herself, she shook her head hard and closed her eyes. "Yes, you're right. The police. I'll call them."

Because she still looked alarmingly pale, he touched her face. "It's all right, Briar. Everything's going to be all right."

As her eyes searched his wildly for answers, she nodded slowly before backtracking into the entryway.

Glancing back at the wreckage of the office, he listened to Briar's quavering voice speak to the dispatcher. The clarity he'd been looking for from the moment he woke up in her bed was suddenly right in front of him.

Tiffany had crossed the line, and now he would do what he had once done best.

Justice was about to be served.

"IT LOOKS LIKE the desktop computer was the only thing taken," the officer told her, echoing what Cole had explained to her and what she'd already surmised herself.

"But why?" Briar asked. She, Cole, Olivia and

the detective doing the questioning were sitting around the kitchen table. Her nails were biting into her forearms as she searched for answers and fought the helpless trembling that threatened to assault her body. She couldn't let it. She couldn't afford to be fragile. She wouldn't be weak. Not now. "The modem's outdated and has needed to be replaced for some time now. Why wouldn't they have taken something more valuable, like the printer? I bought it six months ago...."

"Looting is, unfortunately, sometimes a by-product of hurricanes," the detective explained. "Usually, we see it with bigger storms, the kind that do a lot more damage than this last one. But if the looter thought that the inn was empty, as many homes around the area have been over the past week, they would've seen it as an easy target. Also, the perpetrator might've started to clean house but heard a noise and realized that he wasn't alone. Can you tell me if there were any lights on in the downstairs area overnight?"

"No." The shock was turning her numb. It lured her into a kind of numbness she recognized—it was both comforting and distressing.

She'd felt the same numbness for months after her mother's death. It had helped her get through the grieving process, but there had been a period several months long where she'd feared she wouldn't be able to break out of it—to go on living a normal life with all the necessary emotional stimuli. Shaking off the niggling voices in her head, Briar cleared her throat and forced herself to go on. "The power was out until sometime early this morning. I didn't leave any lamps or candles burning."

The detective—she couldn't quite place his name amidst the chaos in her head—nodded as he made notes on his pad. "And what time did you go to bed?"

She did her best not to look at Cole. Or Olivia, for that matter. "It was around…nine. Maybe nine-thirty. The girls were here to keep Mr. Savitt and me company over dinner. I'm not sure when they left exactly, but I went up to bed shortly after that."

"I was the last to leave," Olivia said, reaching over to place a supportive hand over Briar's. "It was right around eight forty-five. I locked up behind me."

"This is just a routine question, but do either you, Ms. Browning, or Ms. Lewis, know of any enemies you might have? Any reason why someone would want your computer files?"

"No," Briar said at once. "There's no one."

"No one who would wish you harm?"

Briar shook her head. "No one," she repeated, at a loss. When Olivia said the same, she knotted her hands together. "Detective…if you think it was just a looter, why would you ask these questions?"

"Like I said, Ms. Browning. They're just routine." The officer turned to Cole for the first time.

"You went to bed around the same time Ms. Browning did?"

"Yes," Cole replied. "As soon as I heard Olivia here lock up, I went upstairs. To my room."

"Your suite is on the second floor," the detective stated.

"Yes, it is."

"But you didn't hear anything?"

"No, I didn't," Cole replied.

Briar watched a muscle in his jaw tighten and quickly spoke up for him. "Mr. Savitt was kind enough to help us take care of the debris and repairs around the inn and shops yesterday. He worked very hard to get everything cleared up. It's no wonder he didn't hear anything. He was exhausted, I'm sure."

Cole's eyes rose to hers briefly. They'd been hard since the police had arrived. Since they had discovered the break-in, in fact. Now, facing her, they softened by a fraction. It was her heart that trembled and broke through the numbness she'd dreaded, warming her cold limbs inch by welcome inch.

The police didn't take up much more of her time. The detective that had spoken to them assured her they would get back to her with any leads, but Briar couldn't help but notice that the words sounded hollow, routine.

"I have to clean up…." she told the others after they watched the police depart.

Olivia tucked an arm around her waist. "I'll help."

Cole cleared his throat. His voice grated, raw against his throat. "I would, too…but I have some business in town I need to take care of."

Briar looked to him. The knot in his jaw was working hard against the bone. She wanted to reach up to touch him, soothe him. "Thank you. Both of you. I hardly know what to make of all this."

Olivia smiled in reassurance. "We'll get it cleaned up. I'll call the window repair people. And if they don't catch whoever did this, if it was looters like they say, they're long gone."

"I hope you're right," Briar nodded. She took a cleansing breath, gathering confidence from the both of them standing strong around her. "No, I *know* you're right." She patted her hands over the apron she had put on as she came downstairs. Before the day that had started out so perfectly took a long slide downhill. "I didn't get to make lunch."

"Don't worry about that." Cole's hand found hers as his eyes once again latched on to her face and softened several degrees. "I'll get something in town."

"Will you be back in time for dinner?" she asked, hearing the hopeful lilt of the words for herself.

He hesitated, searching her face. Then he whispered, "Count on it." He touched his lips to her cheek. "Liv," he said with a nod to her before he walked down the porch steps, helmet in hand. "Take care of her."

"Will do. Come on, cuz," Olivia said, guiding her back to the door. "Let's do this."

CHAPTER FOURTEEN

BRIAR KNEW THAT it was mostly to get her mind off the break-in, but as soon as she and Olivia finished cleaning the office and piecing together what was left of her files, her cousin walked her over to the shops. Adrian and Roxie both offered her what would have been sure distraction on any other day. She found it hard, however, to think of anything but that broken pane of glass and her missing computer.

"It doesn't make any sense," she muttered to herself as she sat on a stool in Roxie's boutique folding delicate swatches of satin and silk. She'd asked Roxie if she needed a hand preparing the shop, as desperate to distract herself as her friends were determined to keep her mind off the morning's events. Each swatch was different, ranging from spring pastels to deeper hues more suited to autumn. They would go in the bridesmaids' design portfolio Roxie was putting together.

The wedding coordinator's voice echoed from the open changing stalls toward the back of the boutique. "I know it doesn't make sense, Briar, but there's no use getting your thoughts more tangled up than they need to be. The police will do their job. During Ivan, my neighbors two doors down were looted."

"Were the looters ever caught?" Briar asked curiously, folding a delicate, salmon-pink swatch over one of burgundy.

"They were," Roxie replied. "They actually ran into one of the National Guard patrols. The idiots were the only ones out after the county-wide curfew that was enforced in the storm's wake. Looters aren't generally the smartest members of the herd."

"Right," Briar said. "You're right." She glanced toward the changing stalls. "Are you sure you don't need a hand? I feel pretty useless."

"No, you just keep folding, honey," Roxie called back in a reassuring voice. "Trust me. There's nothing like folding, or any other mundane task, for that matter, to get you back in the right mind-set."

The boutique smelled of the newness of fresh paint and possibilities. Briar found herself looking again at the mannequins bedecked in profusions of white fabric. "Your work is exquisite."

The hardworking lady peered out of a dressing room, paint roller in hand and a long handkerchief tied from her brow to the nape of her neck to protect her coif. "That's the gown I designed for my eldest sister's wedding. It took everything but a loaded gun to convince her to let me add it to my collection."

"Why wouldn't she want you to?" Briar asked, fingering the long Irish lace train. "It's your design."

Roxie lifted a shoulder and disappeared again, voice echoing once more. "My sisters are all creatures of selfishness and vanity. My mother, too. You get used to it."

"Were you adopted?"

"Sometimes I dream." Roxie backed out of the dressing room, gauging her paint job. "The Honeycutt women don't settle for anything but the very best, so don't get me wrong—the fact that both of my wedded sisters came directly to me for their gowns pleases me to no end. I guess I'm partly a creature of selfishness and vanity myself."

"You're no such thing." Briar eyed the dress again wistfully. "I bet she looked absolutely stunning."

"The wedding was alfresco in the middle of a field with a backdrop of wildflowers. I was going for nostalgic whimsy." Roxie dried her hands on a wet rag as she approached Briar. "Though it is one of my best, I'd have to do up something completely different for you."

"Really?" Briar narrowed her eyes. "You've thought about me...in a wedding gown?"

Roxie laughed, delighted by the perplexed look on Briar's face. "Honey, it's the first thing I think about when I meet a prospective customer. Or friend. Or simple acquaintance. I'm somewhat obsessed, and I'm not afraid to admit it. Tea?" she asked as she walked behind the glass display checkout counter and lifted a teapot inlaid with pink and yellow pansies.

"Sure."

Roxie poured both of them a cup. Steam billowed from each, infusing the air with a soothing, herbal blend. She passed one to Briar then took out a sketch pad as she made herself cozy on the high-backed stool behind her. While her tea cooled, Roxie picked up a pencil and began to draw. "First I'd go with a sweetheart neckline. And linen. You'd look sublime in virgin-white linen."

Briar lifted the delicate cup to her lips and blew the steam off the surface of the tea. "Not that I've dwelled on it overly much…" She cleared her throat carefully. "But I always kind of pictured a garden wedding. At Hanna's."

"Yes, yes!" Roxie's pencil hand drew in quicker, surer strokes. "With a mixed, cascade bouquet. And white blossoms in your hair in lieu of a veil. Lily of the valley, perhaps."

Briar closed her eyes, trying to see it more clearly. "On the north side of the house. Summertime would be best, preferably before it's too hot."

"Late April or early May," Roxie suggested. "I love a late-spring, early summer wedding. And, you're right, we wouldn't want the guests to drop like flies in the heat. The vows could be exchanged under that charming jasmine arbor."

"Mmm." Briar beamed. She could smell the jasmine's torrid perfume. Her heart picked up pace as she imagined walking through the shrubbery and blooms her mother had planted…the ones she'd nurtured and sustained…walking toward…

Her pulse leaped. *Cole.* She could see Cole standing under the arbor, waiting.

"This is it."

Briar's eyes popped open. She stared at the drawing of a faceless model of herself. The gown was simple, empire-waisted. The skirt tapered down in a soft flair. Roxie's clever vision had added a chapel train. She let out a breath. "That's it," she agreed in a whisper. She shook her head, reaching out to take the pad and admiring the details more closely. "You're a visionary, Roxie." She could practically feel the linen, the weight of the gown around her. Her heart gave another thrilled leap when again Cole appeared under the flowered arch, hand outstretched, eyes warm.

With a sigh, Briar edged the pad onto the counter, clasping her hands tight over her knee. "Oh, Roxie. What are you doing?"

"Making you a princess," Roxie replied in an airy voice as she tucked the pencil behind her ear. "It's my job."

"Yes, well." Briar forced her eyes away from the drawing. "I'm not getting married."

"You don't know that."

When Briar's mouth fumbled open, Roxie offered her an encouraging grin and reached out to pat her hands. "Here's reality, the way I see it. You're beautiful, sane, stable. What man wouldn't want you?"

Briar shook her head. She'd set aside dreams of wedded bliss when Jean-Luc had left her high and dry in her Paris loft. "No one's ever..." She fumbled as Roxie gauged her reaction. "There hasn't been time to..."

"You seem to be making plenty of time with sexy Mr. Savitt."

She took a steadying breath. "Cole... He's not looking for marriage."

"Have you asked him that?"

"This soon? Of course not—I'd run him off."

Roxie chuckled, sipped her tea. "It took some time for my Richard to come around to it—four years to be exact. But at the end of the day we love each other and want to continue to be together. It'll happen, if you both feel it for one another."

Briar's heart rapped against her breastbone, and she couldn't quite meet Roxie's eyes. "I haven't known you all that long. But there's something delicate I need to say to *someone*."

"I'm your friend, Briar," Roxie assured her. "Lay anything you want on me. It doesn't go outside that door."

Briar eyed it, uncertain. "Last night... Well, he and I..."

"Tangled? I thought so."

Seeing the amused gleam in Roxie's eyes, she couldn't stop the corners of her lips from twitching up. "How did you know?"

"Well, for one, you've got the twinkle. And the

worried crease between your eyes has mysteriously disappeared. Two and two. So…how was it?"

She hadn't expected the outright question from anyone but Olivia. Yet as she eyed Roxie, she realized she'd been dying to brag. "Unbelievable. He's unbelievable."

Roxie cupped her chin in her hand, expression smug. "Mmm, yeah. I sensed that." As Briar lapsed into silence, Roxie considered her again. "You have every right to dance a jig right there on that stool, if you want to. I wouldn't stop you for a minute. Hell, if Liv were here, she'd video it just to commemorate the occasion then post it on YouTube and proudly invite all her internet devotees to watch. I suspect those are legion."

Briar laughed despite herself. "She would…and they are."

Roxie lifted a brow and said, "You know, I think I might have something for you.…"

Briar watched as her friend rose to poke through some of the moving boxes crowded around the boutique. "What are you doing?"

"On the sly, I design more than gowns. Recently, I started doing lingerie. The good stuff—negligees, baby dolls.… Victoria's going to get a run for her secret once I start marketing it. Somewhere around here I've got one of the finished prototypes."

"Prototypes?" Briar blinked, hands gripping her teacup. "Are we still talking about lingerie?"

"Indeed. Ah, there she is." She lifted something

slinky and held it up by the straps for Briar to observe. "Ta-da!"

She gaped. "Oh. My word."

Roxie beamed. "Briar Browning, meet Carmela. What do you think of her?"

"She's…kind of wicked."

"Damn right she is. And she'll look magnificent on you."

"Me?" Briar blanched. "You're joking. I can't take that."

"Yes, you can. Consider it a gift. I'll wrap her up for you. Or you could try her on, see if she needs adjusting."

"You're crazy." Briar laughed.

"No, hon." Roxie thrust the garment into Briar's hands and winked. "I'm helping you give that fine member of the male species you'll be tangling with again soon a kick in the ass he won't soon forget. You both can thank me later."

"IT'S BEEN A long time, tumbleweed."

Cole grinned. He hadn't thought it was possible after the morning's events at Hanna's, but hearing his older brother's voice again did just that. "Tad. It's been a long time."

"Too long," Tad asserted. "Where're you calling from, brother? The Keys? Costa Rica?"

Glancing around, he tucked his phone between his ear and shoulder. Cole was sitting on a bench high up on a bluff overlooking the Fairhope Pier. He was alone, but for the rustling of the wind through the trees around him and the twitter of songbirds. Indeed, his surroundings did sound a lot like paradise. "No. But I'm not far from it."

"Did you call to brag?" Tad asked wryly.

"No," he said, leaning forward to brace his elbows on his knees. "I'm actually calling for a favor."

"Haven't seen you in eight months and all you want is a favor. How 'bout you come over for dinner? That would make both me and Maddie happy."

"Maddie." Guilt swamped him. Tad, a lawyer, had battled on Cole's behalf in the courtroom, while his sister-in-law had taken care of him—since he hadn't been in much shape to do so himself. She'd fed him, encouraged him. If it hadn't been for Tad and his wife, he wasn't sure what he would have done a year ago. "How is she?"

"She misses you. We both do."

Cole closed his eyes as a tidal wave of grief hit him. "I miss you, too."

"So what's this favor?"

He cleared his throat. "It's Tiffany."

Tad sighed. "Are you kidding me? What's she done now? Murder? Grand larceny?"

Cole snorted out a bitter laugh. "She's making waves again, but it's not your legal services I need. Do you remember her old man?"

"Douglas? Sure. Who could forget a nasty old barnacle like him?"

"Something she said…" Cole ran it through his

mind. "I was wondering if you could do some digging for me. You still have that PI contact? The one you used to follow Tiffany around the time of the divorce?"

"Yeah, Smithson. Saw him last week. What do you need?"

"I want to know about some of Douglas's real-estate interests, particularly in east Baldwin County. I know it's been a long time, but I figure someone with as many substantial land holdings as Douglas Howard wouldn't be too hard to look into, dead or alive."

"You're right about that, especially considering what he lost when several people he'd taken land from sued him. It was pretty ugly. Apparently, he made one too many bad threats. Fraud and blackmail cost him almost everything. Any interests in particular you want Smithson to look into?"

"Yeah, a little bed-and-breakfast on the Eastern Shore of Mobile Bay called Hanna's Inn."

A pause wavered over the line. "Would that in any way be related to a woman named Hanna Browning?"

Cole's heart turned over. "She's the founder, deceased. Her daughter owns it now. How do you know her by name?"

"Because she's the one who initially took him to court," Tad said. "He tried blackmailing her. She didn't stand for it. Hell of a lady. Hate to hear of her passing."

"It was a year ago, from what I understand," Cole explained. "Cancer. What was it about Hanna's that Douglas was willing to go to such criminal lengths to obtain?"

"Location. He'd bought up several properties along the shore, and the Brownings' was smack-dab in the middle. It was his greatest wish to level every building along that stretch of shore and build an impressive bayside resort—the A-lister kind. He had blueprints drawn up and everything."

"I'll be damned," Cole muttered. "All this for a resort?" He couldn't believe he hadn't thought of it before. This was right up Tiffany's alley. He could practically see her lounging poolside, her father's monstrosity situated behind her where Hanna's should have been.

"Hanna Browning's case against Douglas was the first in a long line of court battles that eventually led to his professional demise. Her winning was the battling cry for everyone else he'd bullied over the years."

"Never mind about Smithson, Tad," Cole said, standing up to pace to the edge of the bluff and back. "You've given me all I need to nail Tiffany's ass to the fan."

"What does all this have to do with you? How do you know anything about the Brownings?"

"Ah…" He cleared his throat. *Tread carefully here, Savitt.* "I'm staying there. For the time being."

"Uh-huh. Did you say Hanna had a daughter?"

"I don't know. Did I?"

"She'd be about eight years younger than you, right?"

Tad was too smart. Cole combed a hand through his hair as his lips twitched. "It's complicated."

"It always is. I take it Tiffany's taking up Douglas's mantle."

"Seems so."

"You want my advice?"

"I know—I'm gonna need a good lawyer? I believe I already have one."

"That didn't work too well for you the last time."

"You weren't the reason we lost. And that was family law—you're a real-estate lawyer and a damn good one."

"You only have to ask and I'm there for you, brother."

Cole sighed. When it came to Tad and Maddie, he'd never had to explain himself. They were the only ones who hadn't believed Tiffany's lies from the start. Their support had never wavered. It had been difficult leaving them behind in Huntsville. But he'd known if he had any chance of starting over, it would have to be far from where he began. "Thanks, Tad. I mean it. I'm sorry I won't make it for dinner today. Tell Maddie I love her."

"Will do. And Cole? Be careful."

HOURS AFTER HE left the inn, Cole finally nailed down a meeting with Tiffany. She claimed to still be staying at the house on Ono Island. After he threatened to drive out to Orange Beach and drop in uninvited, she finally agreed to his terms. A public place, somewhere they could converse privately.

The place was located outside of Fairhope. Probably wise, since she had a history in the small town and obviously didn't want to be recognized.

And Cole knew now just how dark that history was.

It had been hours since the initial fury had set in, and he was still fuming over the break-in. Remembering how Briar had looked when she'd realized what had happened, he felt everything he'd felt that morning—the fury, bitterness and clarity—swamp him again.

They would be playing by his rules from now on.

Tiffany sat down, frowning at him behind designer shades. Today's immaculate outfit was crafted from a pressed white silk suit. The pleat in the pants was razor-sharp. All businesswoman with a bit of an edge.

The edge of a woman who was so desperate to get what she wanted, she was willing to go to criminal lengths.

"I don't appreciate being ordered around," she said as she raised her hand to a waiter. "Glass of water," she snapped when the young man approached. As he walked away, she turned her frown to the window beside their back booth. "It's hot as hell outside."

"I thought that'd make you more comfortable," Cole told her. "Being the devil that you are."

"Did you bring me here just to insult me? That's not going to make me look too kindly on your charity case."

"You crossed the line," he growled.

She sniffed. "I haven't the slightest idea what you're talking about."

"No, you know damn well what I'm talking about." He trailed off when the young man set Tiffany's ice water on the table. "We're not ready to order just yet."

"Whenever you are, just let me know," the waiter said. Sensing tension, he shot one cautious look between them before making a quick escape.

Cole waited until the man was out of earshot before beginning again. "The break-in at Hanna's last night. It's got your fingerprints all over it."

"I'm sure the police will disagree. You, in fact, wouldn't find my fingerprints anywhere near it. And I believe I have an alibi for the time in question."

"Fine, you got one of your boy toys to do the work for you. Maybe this guy Gavin tells me you've been seeing—what's his name? Chad?"

Her frown deepened. "He's in Huntsville. Where he belongs."

"Oh, yeah? Well, when I came to say goodbye to Gavin the other day, who's four-by-four was that next to yours in the driveway?"

She pursed her lips. "You think this gives you the upper hand?"

"I think it gives me enough right to tell you to go straight to hell. I'm done cooperating with this scheme of yours."

She leaned back, crossing her arms over her chest and looking a shade too smug. "Is that right? Well, well. Look who's grown a pair." She reached up to remove her sunglasses. "So you've decided that Gavin isn't what you want anymore."

"No. The arrangement is simply changing," Cole told her. "I'm out, Tiff."

She let out a scathing laugh. "If you're out, Cole, then what are you still doing booked at Hanna's Inn?"

"That has nothing to do with it."

"Oh, I think that has everything to do with it. I know for a fact that you're involved with Briar Browning. And knowing you, Cole—knowing how you lose all focus when there's a bleeding-heart, innocent woman thrown into the mix—that's why I took matters into my own hands with the break-in. So I'll ask you one more time—are you ready to lose Gavin over her?"

"I get visitation," Cole said through clenched teeth.

"Oh, really. Or what?"

"I go to the police, tell them who exactly was the one to break in last night. Only I think I'll leave your boy toy out of it and tell them it was you. I doubt seriously your alibi is *that* tight."

"And my motive would be…?"

Here he had her. Leaning forward, he braced his hands on the table's edge. "I did my digging. You want to finish what your old man started. An A-list resort on the Eastern Shore of Mobile Bay would be a lucrative venture." As her expression froze in blank surprise, Cole grinned in satisfaction. Yes, he had her. "That sounds like motive enough for me. Just one question, though. Do you want it for profit alone or is it the thrill of the hunt, the kill? Because that would truly make you your father's daughter."

She stared at him, formulating her response carefully behind her cool composure. "If you tell the police about my involvement, you realize that means revealing everything to your doe-eyed innkeeper?"

His jaw tightened. "I'm prepared for that."

The motion of her mouth was as sharp as a blade as she found a smile once more. "I'll make you a deal."

"I'm done taking your deals."

"If you refrain from telling the cops I'm involved, I'll loosen your visitation restrictions." When his face fell, her smile strengthened. "What do you say to that?"

"You'll just…let me see him? Regularly. After everything that's happened. All the threats, all the lies. All the effort you took to make sure I never saw him again?"

"Yes," she said. "I'll even have my lawyers draw up a new settlement and sign it myself."

He scowled. "Assuming that's true…you'll also agree to leave Briar Browning and Hanna's Inn alone?"

"No, I can't promise that," she told him. "You know that. But there will be no more break-ins. Now that I have the inn's financials, I won't need to."

He couldn't take her word for it. He knew that all too well. But he had leverage now, and he knew that police involvement was the last thing she wanted or needed. She was offering him a trade, an even one. One he would be stupid to resist. He shook his head, looking down at the menu closed under his hands. "One more question."

"What's that?"

"You hated your old man," he reminded her. "Why are you so determined to be like him?"

"Not *like* him," she snapped, eyes firing at the suggestion. "Better than him! I never wanted anything to do with my father. He tainted the Howard name. I'll never forgive him for that. And I'll never have closure until I rebuild it. One brick at a time, if that's what it takes."

"Or, in your case, one resort at a time."

She lifted a shoulder. "Sure, if you will."

"If you're so unlike him, why were you so determined to hurt me a year ago?"

"That has nothing to do with this."

"Oh, yeah? How so? Tiff, it's hard for me to distinguish you then and the you I'm facing now."

"You still don't see it, do you, Cole?" She sighed. "I wanted Gavin. But with a name like Douglas Howard casting a pall over me, the only way I was going to win against you and your law-abiding brother was to ruin you."

Cole scrubbed his hands over his face in frustration. "But if you'd just come to me we could have worked something out. I would have done anything to keep Gavin from having to go through what he did when we battled it out in court. No, it was about more than just getting Gavin—you hated me."

The grin melted from Tiffany's face slowly but surely. "You don't get it—"

"What could I have possibly done to make you hate me that much?" Cole demanded to know.

"I hated who *I* was," she snapped back. The rare show of temper cracked the exterior polish Tiffany had donned since her father's fortune had passed to her. "I hated who I became after I married you. While you were out in the world solving crime and doing what you thought was worthwhile, all I did was wait for you to come home and act like everything was picture-perfect whenever the other wives in the neighborhood came over for tea. Do you know why I married you, Cole? It was to get away from Douglas Howard, the Howard name in general. I wanted to get as far out from under his shadow as I could."

He gaped at her. "Ten years. We were together ten years, Tiff. I thought we were happy."

"Yeah, well, you thought wrong. And why? Because you were happy. You were perfectly content. You worked long hours. Even when you were a beat cop on traffic duty, you were consumed by work, by other people's problems. And when you came home, you didn't take the time to look. If you would've looked, you would have seen that I was miserable."

"Gavin..."

"I thought I could change. I thought I could be someone else so I had a baby. I thought he would change me, but you know what, Cole? I guess the apple doesn't fall very far from the tree after all. I still hated my life, and that's when I started to hate you."

He couldn't believe what he was hearing. All that time, he'd thought it was him she was discontent with, angry at. But she'd been angry at herself above everyone else. And she'd taken it out on him. "You couldn't have just told me all this? You couldn't have gone to therapy? You had to drag it out in court, ruin my life and a good part of our child's so that you could gain some sense of self again?"

She lifted a shoulder. "It was the only way I knew how." Seeming to pull herself back together, Tiffany brushed a strand of perfectly straight blond hair behind her ear. With steady fingers, she unrolled her utensils from the linen napkin. "So what will it be, love? Does visitation sound like a good enough reward for keeping quiet, or do we need to go another round? I'm just dying to know." She unfolded her menu and began to read it with cool eyes. "And where's that waiter? I'm famished."

THE THOUGHT OF squeezing herself into something as wicked and tiny as the lingerie prototype Roxie had given her was distracting enough. Olivia, however, knew her a bit better.

"You're trying to make me tipsy," Briar surmised as Olivia laid another round of drinks in front of them both at the tavern that evening.

"Wouldn't be the first time," Olivia admitted. "Only this time it's going to work. You're going to drink everything I pour you and you're going to like it."

"Sadly, you really do seem to think so." When Olivia turned her back, Briar fingered the salt on the rim of the margarita glass. She did love Olivia's margaritas. "I've decided to hire an accountant."

Olivia spun around and eyed her balefully.

Briar raised her hands. "This has nothing to do with the break-in. This is me focused completely on something else."

Frowning, Olivia exchanged a drink for singles with a paying customer on the other side of the bar. "Are you still thinking happy thoughts?"

"The happiest," Briar lied.

Unconvinced but out of ammo, Olivia sat down

next to Briar, knocked back another shot then sighed. "Tell me more."

"I think it's the best way to line up investors," she said. "People in accounting generally know people who want to invest, especially locally, right?"

"As long as you use someone locally, you might be right on the money," Olivia agreed. "Good thinking, cuz."

"I'm ready to get this tax business off my back," Briar said, taking a sip of her margarita. She had to squint as the salt mingled with the lethal Lewis mix. "Along with everything else. Even if it means putting someone else's name on the inn."

"Someone else's money," Olivia corrected her. "Investors invest. They don't run the place. That's your job."

"They run the books." Briar sighed. "I think that's why I've been hesitant to take the final step toward the investor route. We've always run the books at Hanna's—it's a family business. The thought of bringing people in who aren't family and might not understand it scares me."

"Anyone who'll want to invest in Hanna's for the right reasons, will understand what family is," Olivia assured her. "The inn all but breathes it."

"Even if it's just me now?"

"Yes." She nudged the glass toward Briar. "Finish that. I'll make you another."

"You're going to have to cart me home."

"I have full-grown men to do that for me."

Briar looked around at the near-empty bar. "Yeah, I see they're just lining up to do your handiwork."

Brow arched, Olivia braced a hand on the bar. "Hey, that's sarcasm."

"Yeah, so?"

"So for twenty-seven years, you've been the pretty one, I've been the smartass. Do I get to be the pretty one now?"

Briar shook her head, passing a jigger into a tavern customer's hand. While she was here, she might as well put herself to work. "I can make petty jokes. I learned from the best."

"Whoa." Olivia backed up a step. "Briar Browning just made a dig at me." Her hands clasped over her heart and she tilted her head, eyeing her cousin whimsically. "I think this is the happiest day of my life."

Briar let out a laugh, despite herself. "Sorry. I don't know what's gotten into me."

"Don't apologize. Never apologize. And I know *exactly* what's gotten into you."

"Oh, geez," Briar said with a shake of her head, depositing a damp dollar bill from a customer into Olivia's tip jar. "You're not going to be crude, are you?"

"Honestly, I wasn't even going to go there. But the fact that you did just proves this day should be marked."

"As what, exactly?"

Olivia spread her hands and looked dreamily into the distance. "As Briar's Independence Day."

"For heaven's sake," Briar groaned. "I've been independent for as long as I can remember."

"Briar's Independence From Inhibition Day."

"In other words, it should be lauded by all who enter here as the day I slept with Cole Savitt."

"Not just that," Olivia pointed out, talking over the blender as she mixed another margarita. "Though I celebrate the date I first slept with a sexy, scruffy man every year in bed with a bottle of wine and, if I'm lucky, more sexy, scruffy man candy." As the jukebox segued smoothly from The Rolling Stones to The Who, Olivia wet and then dipped an upended cocktail glass into a widemouthed container of crystallized salt. "For you, it's so much more. It's like you've finally molted."

Briar spared her a bland look. "Yes, the day one transitions from crab to woman is remarkable, indeed."

Olivia clapped her hands and hopped gleefully up and down. "It's playful banter. She's making playful banter."

Briar raised one hand and pressed the other to her temples. "Wait a minute. I'm trying to figure out how you moved this conversation from taxes to playful banter."

"The next step is dirty talk. But you need to save that for *your* man candy." Olivia reached for a bottle and held it up. "Tequila. Straight tequila goes great with dirty talk."

"I don't think so," Briar said, pushing the bottle away. "I'll have one more margarita. Then I'll be stumbling off to bed like the lush you apparently think I am."

"Off to bed…where something sexy and scruffy will be waiting."

Briar shook her head and realized that Olivia and her margaritas had done the impossible and had managed to distract her from her worries. She raised her glass. "To you, Liv."

"Why's that?" Olivia asked, raising the tequila bottle.

"Because with you, life is never dull."

Olivia tipped her bottle to Briar's glass and smiled. "I live to serve. Now drink that down so you can go get some and I can get back to my envy."

"Deal," Briar agreed and tipped the margarita back.

COLE FROWNED AS he entered Hanna's. The lights were off. The whistling noise from the broken pane was gone. He'd noticed that the window had been covered until repairs could be made.

It was late. Much later than he'd anticipated returning. He'd needed time to get his thoughts together. She deserved that. As much as she deserved the truth.

He had to tell her the truth. If any of this was going to work out like he hoped it might, he had to be honest with Briar. He had to tell her why he'd come here. And what had led him to stop doing Tiffany's dirty work.

It wasn't just the break-in. True, that had given him the edge he'd needed to get Gavin back in his life. But as mixed up as he'd been all morning, he'd known that his heart would lead him back here—to Hanna's. Back home. To his innkeeper.

Walking toward the den, he called her name. Nothing stirred. No noise from above. When the instinct at the back of his neck didn't prickle in alarm, he reached over to turn on one of the lamps next to the sofa. "Briar?" he called again, peering into the kitchen. Silence.

He was about to go upstairs to check her rooms when he saw toes. Veering toward the sun porch, he rounded the corner and saw her laid out in one of the chaise longues, fast asleep. There was a glass in her hand. He crouched, laying his hand over hers, and bent his head to sniff the substance.

His head sailed back at the sharp tang of Olivia's margarita mix. Smiling, he gauged Briar's face. She was deep in her cups and looked so peaceful there amidst the bright yellow cushions, he hesitated to wake her.

Sitting on the edge of the longue, he leaned forward and touched his lips to her brow. "Hey. Sleeping Beauty."

"Mmm." Her eyelids flickered but didn't quite open.

He chuckled, brushing the hair back from her face. "Hey. If you sleep here, you're gonna wake up with a crick in your neck."

She sighed, nestling farther into the cushions by turning onto her side and curling into a ball.

He didn't have the heart to move her. Not when she looked so cozy. Reaching for one of the blankets she'd folded carefully for guests, he covered her with it up to her chin. Taking the glass, he set it aside. "Sweet dreams."

"Mmm-hmm." She reached for him in the dark, her hand coming to rest on his thigh. "Stay with me," she murmured in a sleep-drenched voice.

How could he resist her? It didn't take much urging for him to remove his shoes and crawl onto the chaise. She curled into him, laying her head in the crook of his arm. He pulled her close, burying his face in her hair. Breathing her in until she became a part of him. Smoothing a hand over her back, he listened as her breaths deepened and she drifted off to sleep again.

He'd stay with her. If she asked him to, if she forgave him, he would stay with her forever.

CHAPTER FIFTEEN

THE FIRST THING Briar saw when she opened her eyes the following morning was an inordinate amount of sunshine. Bolting upright, she winced at the headache gnawing at her temples and pressed a hand to her head. Blinking, she frowned. Why was she sleeping on the sun porch? And what time was it?

She hadn't slept past 6:00 a.m. in years. With the sun beaming high and bright over the water's surface, it had to be near midmorning.

"Morning."

Tilting her head, she got her first dose of embarrassment when she found Cole leaning against the archway that led into the den. He was smiling at her in a way that told her he knew very well she had slept on the sun porch...and why. She ran a hand over her hair and hoped she didn't look as disheveled—or hungover—as she felt. "Um...hi?"

"I made breakfast," he told her, jerking a thumb back toward the kitchen. "You up for a bite?"

"You..." She shook her head to clear away the fuzziness. It did little but give her a case of the dizzies. Gripping the edge of the chaise longue, she shifted her feet to the floor. "You made breakfast."

He lifted a shoulder in a modest shrug. "It's not much. I just heated up some of the things you had in the refrigerator."

"You didn't have to do that."

One corner of his mouth lifted into another half smile. "I had a feeling you wouldn't be up to it."

She cleared her throat and stared at her bare toes, not quite ready to wobble to her feet just yet. "Thank you, Cole. That was very nice of you."

"It's my pleasure, Ms. Browning." He pushed off the jamb and offered her a hand. "Olivia's a bad influence."

She felt her cheeks color. Yep, he knew very well she was hungover. With a sigh, she placed her hand in his. "Yes. She is. But I love her."

Lifting Briar from the chaise, Cole tucked an arm around her waist and paused in order for her to gain her balance. "Head clear?"

"Mmm-hmm." It was only a small lie. She placed one foot in front of the other, directing them on the path to the kitchen she knew all too well. Thank goodness they were cooperating, even if her whirling head wasn't.

As soon as she sat down at the table, he handed her a mug of steaming black coffee. She could've wept with gratitude. "Thank you," she said, looking up at him reverently before tipping the mug to her lips. On the table there was a plate filled with sausages and another piled with toast. Though her stomach began to protest, she took a breath and prepared herself a plate. "I can't remember the last time someone made me breakfast," she mused as she spread a light layer of strawberry jam on a piece of toast. "It must have been before my mother passed away."

He forked a few pieces of sausage onto her plate then his. "Tell me more about her."

"My mother?"

"Do you mind?"

She smiled. "Not at all. She was a hard worker, but you would never have known it. She loved inn-keeping so much, I don't think she thought of it as work. Not until she began to slow down, which wasn't long before she died. I think there were other signs, but she ignored them…until one day I saw her give out. From then on, it was a slew of doctor's visits and tests, all of which only brought more and more bad news. She went quickly, once she decided she wanted to come home and stay. She wanted to be here, facing the windows and watching the bay."

"I don't blame her," he said in a quiet voice. "And when you were younger, you knew you wanted to do what she did."

Briar nodded as she finished off the toast and washed it down with another sip of coffee. "For a long time, I thought we would work side by side, until she got sick…." Picking a crumb from the tablecloth and depositing it on her napkin, Briar frowned. "Life never asks you what the order of things should be, though, does it? You have to take it as it comes, figure out what's right—for you and those around you. And sometimes you have to do it alone."

As her eyes rose back to his face, Cole's smile was gentle and his gaze was warm. "You're not alone," he told her.

She grinned. "I know. I have Liv. And Adrian. And Roxie, too, apparently."

"You have me," he added, reaching for the hand she'd laid on her knee.

Her lips parted in surprise. His expression was so earnest, how could she not believe him? Somewhere beneath her ribs, her heart swelled. She looked away quickly, denying herself the certainty she saw there in his eyes. "Cole...I'm sure if you could have asked life for what you wanted, it wouldn't be to share the kind of burdens that I have."

"Briar," he said just as firmly as she had spoken. His fingers tightened around hers and his thumb caressed her palm. "For the first time in a long time, I know exactly what it is that I want."

Her breath hitched, and she tried to look away from his sincere face. She couldn't quite manage it. "There are things that you don't know about the inn, Cole. I could lose it. There's no guarantee in a month that I'll still have it."

"I'm willing to do whatever it takes to make sure that doesn't happen."

"I..." She blinked at tears. "You don't know what you're giving me."

"Yes, I do. I intend to stay here, in Fairhope, with you—if you want me."

She let out a quavering laugh. "You're serious," she realized.

"Of course I'm serious," he said with a beaming smile. "I'm here. Whatever you ask of me, that's what I'll do—what I'll be for you. I don't have much to offer you other than what I feel...."

"What do you feel?" The question came out on a rush, and she caught herself. "I'm sorry."

"It's a fair question," he admitted. "One that I'm eager to get to the bottom of myself. Know this, though, Briar. I haven't felt this way about anyone. And I'm determined to do right by you."

It wasn't a proposal. Neither was it a declaration of love. What it was, however, was a pledge of loyalty and devotion. Her heart pounded at the thought of where such things could lead to down the road. "This is the first time in a long time I've been excited for what's to come."

He leaned forward and touched his mouth to hers. "Me, too."

Taking a breath, she brought herself off the high, fine, silver-edged cloud his words had left her floating on. "Oh, look at me. I'm a mess all over again."

"You're beautiful," he said, reaching up and brushing a loose strand of hair behind her ear.

"As much as I'd love to believe you, I have to get

washed up. My appointment with my new accountant is in an hour or so, and I can't go looking like this."

"Okay, then. You go get ready and I'll do the washing up."

"Oh, no. I can't ask you to do that—"

He rose, picking up plates. "You didn't."

As he transferred dishes to the sink, she raised her hands in defeat. "If my cousin caught me arguing with that, she'd slap me silly." Rising, Briar wiped her hands on her napkin. She touched a hand to his shoulder then rested her head against his back for one long, stolen moment, breathing him in. "Thank you for this. For everything."

"This is just the beginning," he promised. "Do you have a mower?"

She blinked, surprised. "Yes. In the shed where I keep the generator. Why?"

"All that rain made the grass spring up fast," he said, jerking his chin toward the window overlooking the lawn that sloped down to the bay. "You don't mind if I tackle the lawn today, do you?"

"Do I mind?" She let out a laugh. "I'd pay for somebody else to do it if I could."

"By the time you get back, it'll be done."

She sighed, pressing her lips to his cheek. "You might be the best thing that ever happened to me." As she turned and walked toward the stairs, she couldn't help but smile.

Scratch that. She *knew* Cole Savitt was the best thing that had ever happened to her.

LAWN MOWING IN late June was dirty work. By the time he'd finished half the yard down to the sandy strip of shore in front of Hanna's, Cole's shirt was soaked clean through. The humidity felt akin to molasses and made ordinary things like breathing difficult. Still, the work was rewarding. It felt good to get a full-body workout the way he used to when he mowed his own yard during summers in Huntsville, or every other day in his home gym.

It felt good, too, doing something productive—something besides snooping into innocent people's lives and business.

He hadn't been able to bring up his work for Tiffany over breakfast with Briar. He'd seen the headache nibbling under the surface of her temple, the shadows under her eyes, and he could focus on nothing other than caring for her, making sure she ate a full meal before she busied herself as she always did with something concerning the inn or running errands in town.

Her business in Mobile today meant he would have a while to think, to string his thoughts together. Find the best possible way to tell her about his reasons for coming to Fairhope.

Growing up in Huntsville, his father had instilled in him a strong work ethic. It had all started with mowing their lawn…then the lawns of neighbors and relatives. He could have opened his own lawn service if he hadn't decided soon after high school that becoming a police officer was what he wanted to do with his life. Maybe it was because he hadn't worked—well, *really* worked—in so long, that this simple chore felt great. Even better that he was doing something useful for Briar and taking a load off her shoulders.

He wanted to tell her he had changed, he realized as the yard became more and more trim. He wanted to tell her how she had brought about that change— that she was the reason why he could no longer do Tiffany's dirty work.

He was in love with Briar. The golden bliss of that moment at the table this morning had called for such a declaration.

However, there was no way he could tell her that he loved her until he shared everything else with her. Until she knew all of him, the dark and the light.

Funny that both the shadows and the bright spots featured the two women who had turned his life up- side down—Tiffany being the dark, and Briar the light. But there was Gavin, too. If he'd never fallen in love with Tiffany way back when, there never would have been Gavin. His son was the best part of him.

Hopefully, if he could find the right way to re- veal all these bright and shady aspects of himself in equal measure, both Gavin and Briar would be a part of his new life. A life he now foresaw on the Eastern Shore.

If she accepted his apology, he'd find his own place in town. He had no doubt there were other guests who would choose to stay in the bay-view suite. There would soon be other people she had to tend to. And if mowing her lawn taught him anything, it was that he missed having a purpose. He missed being useful.

A job. He didn't think he could go back to working for the police, even in this different locale, but there was always security.

He cleaned the mower and pushed it back into its corner of the shed. Then he gassed up the weed eater and carried it to the back of the house to trim the grass the mower hadn't been able to reach. The hairs on the back of his neck rippled with warning. Letting them lead, he turned his head in the direction of the kitchen door.

A suited figure stood there amongst the azaleas, looking like a shadow himself in Briar's sunny alcove of the world. Cole frowned. He didn't recognize the man, not from this distance. He was distinctly tall, slim for his height. His hair was thin and gray and he was staring out at Cole curiously, briefcase in hand.

Because the man looked expectant and clearly out of place in a perfectly plain, dark-toned suit and gray tie, Cole set aside the weed eater and headed over. "Can I help you, sir?" he asked as he approached.

"Who's asking?" the man barked, shading a pair of flinty eyes with the brunt of his hand.

"Name's Savitt, sir. I'm a guest here at Hanna's."

"A guest?" The man scowled. Up close, grim lines furrowed his brow and the sides of his mouth. "She has guests doing the work around here now?"

It didn't take but a second for the man's presence to sink in. He bore no resemblance to Briar, but Cole had a good sense that this was her father. He shifted his stance. "You must be Mr. Browning."

"I'm looking for my daughter." The words should have formed a request, an inquiry at the very least. But they were clipped, commanding and set Cole's teeth on edge. "It's urgent that I speak to her."

"She's out." When the man's scowl deepened, Cole crossed his arms over his chest. The urge to protect Briar and her whereabouts surged through him, originating around the prickle at the base of his neck—that raw instinct he'd never had a reason not to trust. Remembering the way Briar had behaved after her father's last visit, he'd have wagered instinct was right on the money again. That this man was about as welcome here at Hanna's as another Category 2 hurricane. "I think she said she had a meeting with her accountant."

"Accountant," the man echoed. His lips pursed. "Hmm. Well, at least she's taking some responsibility."

Cole felt the muscles in his jaw tighten. "Is there anything I can help you with, Mr. Browning?"

His brows winged up, eyes hardening further with suspicion. "If I didn't know any better, I'd say by your tone you are more to my daughter than a tourist."

"I don't see why it would matter to you if I were."

"Leave it to her to overstep her bounds."

Maybe it was the swamping humidity or the blistering heat of the noonday sun beating down on his head, but Cole heated up like a live wire in an instant, advancing toward the man in three long, impending strides. "She hasn't overstepped anything. Your daughter is the most decent person I've ever known. She works harder than anyone I've ever met. And I'm ready to personally take issue with *anyone* who thinks he has the right to say anything to the contrary."

"Savitt, is it?" Mr. Browning sneered, his flinty stare now acerbic enough to cut stone. "Let me tell you something about my daughter. She's never known what's right for her. By investing everything she has into this godforsaken place, she's made a mistake she can't unwind, a mistake that will cost her dearly. And if she's not careful, and I'm right about who you are and what you're doing here, she'll get herself into more trouble in the meantime."

"Where do you come off, old man?" Cole asked, squaring off with the bastard. "She's dedicated her life to something good and all you seem to want to do is tear her down for it. Did it ever occur to you that your support, however marginal, is all she's ever wanted from you?"

"You've gone too far," Browning growled low in his throat, stepping off the stoop to loom in Cole's face. "You don't know anything about my relationship with my daughter, such as it is. And I can guarantee that you won't be around long enough to make a difference to either of us."

"I daresay I've made more of a difference than you've bothered to," Cole asserted, refusing to draw back. "You know, my father passed away before my son had a chance to really get to know him. But he was more a man than any other I've ever met, and I was lucky to have him. No matter what I did or where I ventured, he never lost faith in me. I wouldn't be anyone without that kind of unconditional support, and I hope I can offer the same to my son. Now, think of what you've deprived Briar of all these years. She's starved for even the barest trace of appreciation or praise from you. And despite all she is, all she's done and made here, you hold back. You punish her for being who she is. Frankly, I don't know how you sleep at night."

Browning held his stare, a chilling showdown, for what felt like a small lifetime. The muscles in his jaw quivered with wrath. "You're going to regret ever walking into her life."

"We'll see about that."

"Try to make yourself useful, Mr. Savitt, and tell my daughter I came looking for her." The man turned on his heel and stalked out of Briar's garden. Cole watched until he disappeared before relaxing his stance. He wiped the sweat from his brow and braced his hands on his hips. Collecting his breath, he worked to cool the simmer in his blood.

Maybe he had butted into something that wasn't any of his business, he thought as he made his way back to the weed eater. But there was no doubt Briar's father had hurt her, and that he would continue hurting her if he got the chance. It was time somebody stepped up to the plate for her and made it clear to the old man that his brand of crap would no longer be tolerated.

Storm clouds rumbled in the east yet the sun wasn't giving up its reign of the early afternoon. He was finishing up on the far side of the property when he caught sight of Olivia as she walked out onto the tavern terrace. Judging by her white tank, cotton shorts and the microfiber cloth hooked through the shorts' side belt loop, she'd been in the midst of cleaning. He shut off the mower and reached up to wipe his brow with what he hoped was a clean forearm.

Olivia pulled her cloth loose and tossed it his way. "Dry off, why don't you?"

"Thanks," he said, scrubbing it over his face and around to the back of his neck. "So, how much did you hear?"

When he glanced at her, she lifted a shoulder, gazing at him with eyes too wise. Leaning against the railing, she crossed one ankle over the other in a casual stance. "You ever replace a car battery?"

His mouth fumbled open. As always, he hadn't known what to expect Olivia to say—this, least of all. "Sure. There's not much to it."

She pushed herself off the railing, propelling down the steps to the trim lawn. "This way."

He watched her walk away for a moment then shrugged and followed. They wound up in the tavern parking lot, which was only a narrow lot of gravel on the far side of the tavern. Cole sensed the placement was strategic on the part of Hanna's. None of the tavern bustle would be visible from any of the inn's sprawling windows.

There was one lone vehicle in the lot, a burnt-orange 1980s model Ford pickup parked under the shade of an overhanging oak tree. "This yours?" he asked in disbelief.

She shot him a winged look over her shoulder as she popped the hood. "You saying a girl can't drive a truck?"

"Would you call me a chauvinist if I did?" His lips twitched when she turned to him, propping a hand on her hip. "Kidding. Where I grew up, everybody has a four-by. I just didn't expect it of you."

"Because I'm so feckless and dainty."

"Dainty, maybe. But hardly feckless."

"Why, thanks, sugar." She walked around to the driver's door and leaned in through the open window. "This here's Chuck."

Cole's lips twitched. "Chuck the truck?"

"Yep. He was my father's till he and my mother took the college money I was never going to use and invested it in an RV. Three months later, they took off on the road and haven't been back but once a year since, leaving Chuck here and the tavern in my care." Carrying a new battery, she joined him again at the hood. "I bought this because Chuck's been having some trouble starting."

"You sure it's the battery?" he asked, knowing he risked a valued appendage by voicing the cautionary question.

As expected, she sent him a bland look. "The damn thing doesn't start. It's a battery problem."

"Could be," he granted. Stepping around her, he took a long gander at Chuck's restored engine. "Or the alternator might be going out."

"If that were the case, would it be turning over?"

"Probably not."

"Okay then, grease monkey. Here's the deal." She patted the new battery. "I don't like anybody's paws except mine on my ride. Despite your delusions of grandeur, I'm willing to trust you. And I'll pay you for the trouble."

He swiped the battery from her grasp and disconnected the old battery cables. "If it is a battery problem, this'll take me all of five minutes—if that. You're not paying me."

"It *is* a battery problem, and I *will* pay you. If you won't take money then you can quit digging your heels in the mud and tell me what you and my uncle Hud were discussing so heatedly a while ago."

His jaw tensed before he realized there was no reason to jump on the defensive. No getting around the fact that Olivia was Briar's cousin and they were close. He respected the link and its importance to Briar. Careful not to lean his midsection against the truck's hot grille, he frowned thoughtfully as he worked and she hovered like a hawk.

It wasn't until the thunderhead to the east rumbled, announcing its descent on the Eastern Shore, that he spoke again. "These cables are corroding. You'll need to replace them soon, too."

"New battery cables, check." Leaning against the hood, she eyed him expectantly.

Cole sighed. "Your uncle's a jackass."

"Agreed."

When he gaped at her, she lifted her shoulders, expression sober. "He's hard on Briar for all the wrong reasons. He won't admit it's because he sees Hanna when he looks at her and it hurts something awful. But he's gone too long taking his grief out on the most convenient person around."

Maneuvering the new battery into place, Cole secured it, scowling over the work and Olivia's words. "It's been a year and nobody ever stepped in?" Standing back, he rubbed the grease from his hands and turned the fierce stare on her. "*You* never stepped in?"

"I tried," she tossed back. "Lord knows I tried

so many times to bash some sense into that stubborn fool's head. But one reason he hasn't retired from law is that he loves sticking to his guns and he doesn't back down when he's convinced he's in the right. If Briar inherited anything from Hud, it's that damned stubbornness. Not that I can say much. The Lewis side of the family is just as bad...."

Finished with the task at hand, Cole closed the hood and turned slowly, mirroring Olivia's stance by leaning against the truck, the cleaning cloth slung around his shoulders and his arms locked over his chest. "She's like her mother, right?" At her nod, he added, "Hmm, I don't see someone like her going for a man as hard as he is."

Something softened the contours of Olivia's face as she gazed off toward the bay, squinting at the glare off the water. "The thing with Hanna was that she had what we used to call 'X-ray vision.' She could see through the toughest armor, right into the heart of the hardest person and she knew how to draw that side of them out. It's part of the reason why she was such a great innkeeper. And Hud was different with her—up until Briar went off to college. Then whenever I came over for dinner and guests weren't around, I'd often hear the tail end of heated arguments. Tension hung in the air, like some sick cat walked in and died there on the table but nobody cared to talk about it. By the time Hanna died, maybe even before, Hud had regressed back fully into that tough old rhino skin you rammed your head against this afternoon."

Cole shook his head sadly. "He really never did make his peace with it, did he?"

"That would require some semblance of feeling. He hasn't felt a stir in so long, I'm shocked somebody hasn't taken him for a zombie and popped him one with a .308 Winchester."

His lips quirked up briefly at the image. "It's crazy how different things would be…"

The small, drawn lines around Olivia's mouth eased. "If she hadn't died? Yeah. Life would be a helluva lot easier for Briar, that's for sure. But trust me. Hud would still be riding her to do something else with her life, even if she'd gone to Atlanta for culinary school."

Cole considered the situation carefully. Hudson Browning's feud with his daughter was far from over.

The telltale sound of tires crunching gravel in the inn parking lot distracted them both.

"That'll be her," he murmured.

"Are you going to tell her about this?"

"I have to," he said, pulling the cloth down from around his neck and handing it back to Olivia.

She took it, scrutinizing him closely as she folded it in half and tucked it back into her shorts. Then she surprised him by taking his face in her hands and giving him a short, noisy kiss on the lips. "My cousin's found herself a damn good man. Men around here have proven to be disappointing in the past, so I don't say that lightly." With a firm pat on his cheek, she added, "Go get her," and walked off.

It took him a moment to find his feet and stroll back to Hanna's to fess up to his innkeeper—in more ways than one.

CHAPTER SIXTEEN

BRIAR WATCHED THE two charcoal thunderheads come together like stern brows overhead and threaten the sunny outlook on her side of the bay.

Typical, she thought as the sun evaded the first grasp of cumulonimbus. The morning's headache had finally vanished—and, if Byron Strong was right, the inn's troubles would soon be over, too. And now the weather had decided not to cooperate with what promised to be a fine, cheerful mood.

She scooped fingers through her hair so pins tumbled from the professional updo she'd fashioned to meet the accountant who'd spoken to her so kindly after her father's visit a week ago—not that her father knew about any of this. The folder on the small nook table in front of her held the names of several potential investors, ones Byron had promised would jump at the chance to plunk a finger down in Hanna's deep, historical pie.

They had agreed it was best at this time not to tip their hand to her father who'd been so sure Byron was her only chance to get out from under the inn's burden of debts unscathed. Byron had even chosen to meet her away from her father's Mobile practice, at a far less intrusive location, the university library.

She would review the investors again and make arrangements to meet them over the course of the week—and take the first real jab in this fight for what was hers. Especially now that it looked like a battle she could very well win.

And yes, she acknowledged as a smile warmed her lips, the inn was hers. As Byron had laid everything on the table and gone through it bit by bit, the rush had swept through her blood and for the first time in a long time she had let it.

Hanna's not only could be hers, but it was. She wanted to fight for it not just for her mother's sake but for her own.

She wasn't sure what had brought about the shift. A few days ago, she hadn't been able to think of the inn as anything but her mother's domain. The fight to save it had been Hanna's—Briar had only picked up the gauntlet.

Byron had helped her find her own gauntlet, though, and she hadn't hesitated to throw it into the midst of the contest.

Taking his business card from her sweater pocket, she placed it on top of the folder. Her father had been right about one thing—Byron Strong was what she needed to get her affairs in order. Only Hudson wouldn't be at all pleased to find out that his business partner had decided to go rogue, aiding his daughter in her fight instead of shutting it all down.

Suddenly, everything from the inn's financial straits to her relationship with Cole seemed to be taking a turn for the better.

She picked up the hairpins, veering back toward her bedroom to change into more comfortable shoes. Despite the dimming light from the windows, she was determined to throw off the afternoon gloom.

Before she could do more than deposit the pins in the seashell-shaped dish on her bathroom vanity, the phone rang. She had only to think of her near-empty guest book to propel herself back into the den of her third-floor living quarters and snatch it up on the fifth ring.

The call lasted little more than three minutes. By the time she replaced the phone in the cradle, she felt as if the earth had shifted beneath her feet. As raindrops broke apart on the window above her, she stared at the phone's receiver, lips parted in shock.

Then she heard the voice shouting from the floor below, the sound of her name. On her bare feet, she walked briskly to the door to the stairs and down to the second level.

As soon as she tore through the door to the hall of guest suites, she saw him standing opposite the door to his room on the landing. Relief waged against guilt for claim of his expression. She let the door creak to a close behind her as thunder rolled over-head and didn't give him a chance to speak first. "Did you speak to my father?"

He frowned. Shifting his stance from one foot to

the other, he considered her. "Speaking isn't exactly how it went."

"So it's true," she said, pulse picking up pace. "Everything he said you said…"

He nodded cautiously. "Yeah, I probably said it." When she only continued to stare, he lifted his hands. "Look, maybe it was the heat. I don't know. But I can't apologize."

"Don't," she blurted. At his stunned look, she followed the towering impulse tugging her down the hall toward him. Without another word, she flung her arms around him and pressed her mouth hotly to his.

His sound of surprise died in his throat as she delved into his mouth, tongue seeking his as heat and triumph and reckless waves of raw desire consumed her in a flash. She felt his hands on her, returning the blistering hold, cruising over her as freely as hers roamed his body. For a moment, she felt the bite of his doorknob at her back before he threw open the door and they stumbled into his room.

Faint, watery shadows fell over the bay-view suite from the wide, undraped pane. She walked backward toward the bed, trusting him to lead the way as her hands tore at his damp T-shirt. The sound of cotton ripping made her fumble. Their mouths parted and she panted, looking down at the tear she'd made in the material from his collar to his sternum.

As his dark eyes veered from the rip back to her face, she saw that the blaze in his eyes was unhindered and barked out a laugh. "I'm not sorry," she said breathlessly and pushed him back against the bed. He toppled to the spread and she straddled him, holding him back by the shoulders and taking his mouth again.

He moaned, a virile noise like a growl that caught her breath as much as the play of his strong, molding hands down her sides to her hips and back farther over her rear. The heat clawed at her last barren shred of control, pushing her beyond the brink of desperation. She wanted him. God, did she want him.

She arched back, tugging the tails of her button-up blouse from the pleated skirt she'd worn to the meeting. Locking her gaze on the dark fathoms of his, enjoying the play of his thumbs over her navel underneath the hem of the blouse, she unbuttoned the pearl clasps one by one.

She wouldn't have thought it possible but his gaze darkened, mouth dropping open. His breath spilled out. "Oh, hell," he groaned, his hold tightening around her waist.

Smiling, she shrugged the shirt from her shoulders. God bless Roxie Honeycutt and her new line of lingerie. Judging by the look on Cole's face, struggling into the wicked black-lace bustier this morning had been so worth it.

Before she could shift over him, he stopped her with, "Wait a minute, wait a minute."

She halted. Rain trickled in rivulets down the

glass over his head, chasing shadows across his reverent face as his eyes licked over her in heated strokes. His hand sought hers and he tugged it toward his chest until her palm blanketed his heart and he held it there, watching her face as she measured his pulse.

It was pounding. His heart was pounding, a hard, heavy artillery. The sweetness of it sang. She searched his face, feeling not just the burn of unbridled lust but the silken slide of tenderness. A million silent words passed between them as she held his stare then slowly lowered into his embrace, sighing blissfully as he rolled her beneath him.

Their lovemaking was fervid in its intensity. They left nothing unsaid with either hands or mouths, bodies leaving inhibition at the door. She thought she would break in two, emotions straining, sensation bowing her up to climax until she feared she'd never come down, never crash back to earth.

She didn't. Instead, she slid, loose, limber, lost. Her head lolled back on her shoulders as she gloried in the gilded edge of satisfaction.

Lowering to the bed, he tucked her into him. The rain continued to patter gently against the window. The world remained dim, hazy and cloudy. She didn't give a thought to their slick bodies or the disheveled state of her hair or the sheets. His lips brushed her temple, lingered, his breath falling hot on her skin.

She was naked, pressed to the brazen heat of him.

She'd never felt so comfortable in her own skin. It was the middle of the day, there were a thousand things to do, rain or no rain...and she didn't give a damn.

For the first time in her memory, she felt unburdened. Both by her lover and the purpose she had found that morning in the inn's skirmish. Beaming wide, she snuggled farther into the heat of his solid frame. "We should have done this sooner."

He chuckled, the mirthful noise wheezing a bit. He still hadn't quite caught his breath. "It's hard to argue with that."

"I'll buy you a new shirt."

"Forget the shirt." He traced her bottom lip with the rough pad of his thumb. "I'll be damn sure to stand up for you more often."

She hadn't thought it was possible, but her grin widened. "I'm not going to apologize for jumping you...even if I did frighten you for a moment there in the beginning."

"Don't," he murmured, the mirth in his eyes fading into sweet tenderness as he lowered his mouth fully to hers.

She pillowed her head on his shoulder and decided to indulge herself a little longer. "I've never slept in a guest bed before." She sighed as sleep rushed up to meet her. "It's nice."

"Good." His fingers sank into her hair and his head came to rest against hers. "'Cause we're not going anywhere for a long while."

OVER THE NEXT few days, workers congregated around the inn. Before she would allow any investors to tour Hanna's, Briar wanted to make sure the building was in perfect shape.

Olivia found a way to convince a contractor friend of hers to give Briar a quote on the porch roof and railing. Since contractors were in high demand after the damage the Alabama coast had sustained from Brett, this was an impressive feat on Olivia's part.

Soon the contractor had his team out at Hanna's doing repairs. Briar also found someone to replace the broken window in her office and called the building inspector to ask if he could give Hanna's a walk-through. A positive report on his part would certainly build investors' confidence.

When Cole wasn't helping the carpenters with the repairs or giving Briar a helping hand while she scrubbed the inn from top to bottom, she suspected he was out looking for an apartment or condo he could rent until he found something a little more permanent.

Everything was coming together, she thought, happily cleaning the sprawling windows of the sun porch. Despite the noise of power saws and hammering from outside, she couldn't help but hum as she worked. Guests had been calling over the past few days to confirm that their suites would be available in the coming weeks and to make sure the inn and the shore hadn't sustained enough damage to deter their stay in Fairhope. Briar had been all too happy to reassure them as well as book a few new names toward the end of the summer.

As she finished cleaning the windows and their sills, she glanced out and saw Adrian traipsing through the garden toward the screen door. She raised her hand in greeting before grabbing her cleaning supplies and stepladder to meet her friend in the kitchen. "Come in," she said, opening the door and ushering Adrian in. "It's hot enough to bake cookies out there."

"July's coming on quick," Adrian said, mopping her bangs back from her brow. "Oh, you should know Olivia's entertaining the construction crew. As she's wearing little more than a sports bra and shorty-shorts, I'm not sure how much work they're getting done."

Briar shook her head. "I'm more worried about them than her. They're harmless—we can't say the same for Liv."

"No, we can't," Adrian agreed, amused. "I've been in the greenhouse most of the morning, which is why I'm sweating like a pig. New shipment of ferns. I remember you saying a week ago that you'll be ordering more for the entrance."

"Oh, yes," Briar remembered as she poured Adrian a glass of iced tea. She added a sprig of mint for the sake of the heat. "The storm ruined the ones I had hanging on the porch."

"How many do you need?" Adrian asked as she took a load off in one of the chairs. "I'll bring them over this afternoon."

"Four. And thank you for thinking of me first. They'll look lovely for the tours Byron Strong and I will be giving investors within the next week."

"Oh, right, Byron."

"You know him?" Briar asked.

"Family friend," Adrian said with a wave of her hand. "He does the books for my parents' nursery off and on. You know Mom—she doesn't sit down long enough to do anything but write checks to suppliers. She used to ride Dad's ass to do the books, although she knows full well he can't add or subtract to save his life. Byron has saved their marriage on more than one occasion, which is no easy deed." She rolled her eyes. "Mom even tried to hook us up, being that I'm so single and alone. We went out on a few dates, that's it."

"How was he?" Briar asked, knowing full well the question was probably more suited to Olivia but couldn't curb her curiosity.

"Oh, he's definitely hot," Adrian recalled, eyes widening to reveal just how much. "Sexy without even breaking a sweat. And still single, I believe. *Somebody* should've snatched him up by now. He's even nice, a miracle given my dating and marriage track record. I think he just lost interest in me. Not that I blame him. Single mother and sole business owner doesn't exactly scream 'Take me, man hunk, I'm yours.'" She glanced around. "Speaking of, is there anything else you need from the shop before then?"

"Not that I know of off the top of my head," Briar said. "But I'll let you know if I do think of something. The new arrangement in the entryway looks beautiful. You really outdid yourself."

Adrian sat back, tipping her head to let the cool air from the vent above wash over her face. "Anything I can do? You've been busy."

"It's nothing I haven't enjoyed," Briar admitted, taking a seat across from Adrian. There were piles of silverware arranged on the table. She had started polishing them this morning before the team had arrived. "Cole does all the real labor. I'm thrilled that I have someone I can call on for plumbing now."

Raising a brow, Adrian tilted her head. "Though I doubt you pay him—not with money, anyway."

Briar couldn't fight a grin. "No, I don't pay him money."

"Mmm-hmm. Just as I thought."

"What?" she asked when Adrian continued to study her face.

"You look like morning sex."

"I do not!" Briar shrieked, raking a telling hand through her hair. She flushed when Adrian only pursed her lips. "Is it really that obvious?"

Adrian chuckled. "It's one hundred degrees and humid as all hell outside, and you've done nothing but smile since I got here. From what Olivia oh-so-proudly has been telling me, you and Cole are now sexually involved. There's nothing wrong with my math skills." She raised a finger. "The only thing I can't figure out is why you could discuss it with Olivia and Roxie but you didn't think you could tell me."

For the first time since Adrian had arrived, Briar's smile fell a bit. "I'm sorry. I'm not sure why."

"Maybe because I haven't been as supportive as the others?"

"It's not that," Briar said quickly and meant it. "I have no excuse, really. Your friendship means the world to me. I hope you know that."

Adrian nodded, understanding. "And vice versa. I'm thrilled that everything's working out for you and Cole and that he's everything you thought he was."

Briar smiled. "He is." Sighing, she picked a small bit of lint off the place mat in front of her. "He's talking about making things more permanent."

"That's wonderful," Adrian replied. "So he's staying?"

"Yes, but he wants to rent a place of his own in town," she explained. "A part of me wishes he would just stay here. In my bed."

"I don't blame you, but I think his decision to rent elsewhere says a lot about him and the way he feels about you," Adrian told her. "The way he respects you. And mutual respect is vital in any relationship."

"You're right," she said, nodding. "Would you like another glass of tea?"

"No, thanks. I don't have much time. I've got to finish the arrangements for the ceremony tomorrow morning."

"Remind me about that one."

"Catholic wedding," Adrian explained. "Ten bridesmaids, ten groomsmen, a junior bridesmaid, a junior groomsman. And don't get me started on the flowers for the church itself. The bride's bouquet is the largest cascade I've ever made. It's a masterpiece. I just hope she doesn't trip on it."

"I wish I could see it."

"Come by when you get a moment and take a peek," Adrian invited. "Most of the bridesmaids' bouquets are done. It's down to boutonnieres and corsages. When it's all over tomorrow night, I'm going to put my feet up on the tavern terrace with a big margarita and toast myself on a job well done."

The swinging door opened and Cole walked into the kitchen, fresh from his morning shower and dressed in riding clothes—boots, comfortable jeans and a T-shirt. He carried a helmet and his riding jacket and beamed at Briar on sight. "Adrian. How're you doing?"

"Like hell till I had a sip of Briar's sweet tea," she said, lifting the ice-filled glass in toast. "It still tastes like it did when Hanna made it. I swear she used to put sunbeams in it."

"That she did," Briar acknowledged. She turned to Cole. "Join us for a glass?"

"I'd love to, but I've got an appointment with a Realtor. I'm looking at a small rental house a few blocks from here. Pretty close to where your cottage is, Adrian."

"Oh, the old fruit and nut section, huh?" Adrian nodded. "Good neighborhood."

"I hate to run," Cole said. "I'm gonna pick up some new battery cables for Olivia's truck, too."

Briar rose. "Well, go on then, I won't keep you."

He grinned, pulling her in with little more than an arm around her waist. Her body fit to his and her arm hooked around his hips as his fingertips splayed over the small of her back. "You can keep me as long as you want." His head bent to hers for a stirring kiss that made Briar forget momentarily that she had company at the table.

Lingering, he touched his nose to hers. "I'll miss you."

"Me, too," Briar managed in a thick voice.

"See you, Adrian," he shot over his shoulder. Then he took off through the screen door.

A moment passed in his absence. Then Adrian blew out a surprised breath. "Wow."

"You all right?" Briar asked, blinking away moonlight and magnolias to study her friend.

"If the man isn't in love with you, I'll eat that cascade bouquet, lilies and all."

Briar blinked in surprise, heart lifting at the thought. "You...you think so?"

"Are you kidding me? If he dropped his pants right now, you'd see the heart-shaped bandage he rigged to cover the wound from the well-tuned arrow Cupid shot him in the ass with."

"He hasn't said anything yet," Briar admitted.

"I may never have been on the receiving end of that level of deep, abiding affection, but I know it when I see it, and I swear that the guy that just walked out of here *loves* you."

"Wow," Briar said, dropping to her chair again. She clasped a hand over her heart and allowed the grin to spread. "Oh, wow."

"Yeah," Adrian concurred as she cupped her chin in her hand. "To hell with tea. Bring on the mimosas."

Briar rose to sift through her liquor cabinet to see if she had any champagne left when the screen door opened again. Her pulse pattered for an instant because she thought it might be Cole coming back to give her one more goodbye kiss. She tried not to look too disappointed when she saw that it was Byron Strong, instead.

"Briar," he greeted.

"Byron," she said, stepping forward. "This is a surprise. I wasn't expecting anyone until Monday."

"That's part of the reason why I'm here," Byron told her. From all her meetings with him over that past week, she knew him to be a very amiable man as well as an amusing and compassionate one who never failed to make her feel comfortable.

Today, though, his smile stretched taut against the lower half of his face and didn't quite reach his eyes. "I'm sorry to barge in, but I have some news I don't think can wait."

When he glanced apologetically Adrian's way, she rose. "I'll leave you to it. Good to see you, Byron."

He blinked in surprise. "Adrian. I didn't see you there."

"No worries," she replied, touching his wrist. "I was just on my way out."

"How are Van and Edith doing these days?" he asked.

"Oh, just peachy," she muttered, voice laden with irony. "They'll likely be dropping in on you soon."

He cleared his throat, nodded to her. "Thanks for the warning."

As Adrian exited, Briar gestured Byron to the table. "Have a seat."

He glanced over the silverware and place mats. "I'll make this quick, but it's probably best that you sit, too."

"Oh? That can't be good." She obliged him, dropping to a chair.

Byron sat down in the chair next to her that Adrian had vacated. For a moment, he couldn't quite meet her eyes. They rose to hers finally and he took a breath. "I'm sorry to have to tell you this, Briar...but I've been on the phone with all five of your potential investors this morning. Most of them wouldn't tell me why, but they've all decided to look elsewhere for investment opportunities."

Her mouth fumbled open. Dread, cold and heavy, culled to life within her bosom. "All of them?"

"It's something neither of us could have anticipated," he assured her as gently as he could. "But yes. They're all gone."

She shook her head to clear it when her ears began to ring. Panic began to rear its ugly head. "I don't understand."

"I don't, either, to be honest," he said. "Though one of them was a little more forthcoming than the others about his reasons for leaving Hanna's."

Here he hesitated again, and she braced herself. "What is it?"

An awkward expression crossed Byron's handsome face. "He claimed to have information, personal information, about you and an…intimate relationship you've entered into with someone by the name of Cole Savitt."

"What about Cole?" she asked, baffled.

Byron frowned. "By involving yourself that way with another potential investor, you can see why the others would feel cheated. By entering into a relationship with him of any kind, you've given Mr. Savitt an advantage."

She held up a hand. "Wait. Cole isn't an investor. Other than his relationship with me, he's never shown any interest in the inn."

The frown deepened. "He hasn't?"

"No," she said. "I can't imagine where anyone would get the idea that he has. Only a handful of people know about our relationship, and I know none of them would be capable of sabotaging..."

Byron's eyes narrowed as she trailed off and her face cleared slowly of everything but shock. "Not all of them, I take it."

She firmed her lips together as they began to numb. Locking her hands together, she watched her knuckles whiten. "No." Glancing up at his face, she jerked her head in a nod. "There's one who I think would like very much to see us both fail at this."

She watched it sink in. Byron took a breath and eased back in the chair, running his hands thoughtfully over the thighs of his slacks. "Yes, that would make sense."

"He brought you here to help me close down the inn," she reminded him. "He's the only one around me who never supported my decision to keep Hanna's open. He makes it a point to regularly tell me that I should rid myself of it. And a few days ago, he told me that my relationship with Mr. Savitt was indecent and that I'll regret involving myself with him."

"He said that exactly?"

Thinking back over the blistering words her father had spoken to her over the phone that rainy afternoon, she nodded. "Word for word."

Byron looked thoughtful for a moment. "I may

be able to find some other investors for you. I'll do my best. But if your father continues to sabotage our efforts, I can't say we'll be able to lock anyone in before the county tax deadline."

She swallowed. "What should I do?"

"If he's this determined to make sure the business doesn't survive then I'm not sure what confronting him would achieve. I don't think I can recommend it. Unless, of course, you think he'll listen to you."

She let out a bitter laugh. "I've been fighting him on this for a long time. My mother fought him for years prior to that. I even begged at one point to make him listen. I can't do that anymore. Especially if it's come to this...." Spreading her hands help-lessly, she looked down again at her lap, determined to hide the emotions she knew were visible on her face. Grief warred with anger and betrayal for higher ground. She shook her head when he offered her a handkerchief. She wasn't going to cry, damn it. Not over this.

She was blindsided. As much as he'd discouraged her throughout the past year, she hadn't thought her father capable of this kind of treachery. One of the chief reasons she'd fought so hard and so long to keep Hanna's open was to prove to him that she could. That she could succeed, choose her own path. Maybe even achieve the impossible and make him proud.

Disgusted with herself as much as him, she gath-ered herself carefully. That feeling she'd been all too familiar with after her mother's death—like she was a pane of splintered glass a hairbreadth away from shattering—hovered close around her. But she wouldn't shatter—that at least she knew for sure.

Facing Byron again, she said in a quiet but steady voice, "Thank you, Byron. Thank you so much for coming all this way to tell me this."

"Of course. And I mean it, Briar. I will do everything in my power to get you the investors you need before July."

She pasted the best smile she could manage on her face. It felt false, but she kept it in place as she walked Byron to his car. For a long time after the gravel dust settled, she stared after him, feeling the storm rise and churn inside her.

Her father had some serious explaining to do. And while she didn't think confronting him would do her much good, she needed to have the last word in the long, bitter conflict between them.

CHAPTER SEVENTEEN

BRIAR WAS HALF tempted to ask Olivia to join her on her jaunt to Mobile. As far as meetings with her father were concerned, backup and extra ammunition were always appreciated. But she realized that she was too angry and conflicted to explain everything. The drive across the Bayway would give her time to compose herself and marshal exactly what she wanted to say.

Another afternoon storm was brewing, thanks to the building humidity. It would be a rainy drive. She should probably put it off to tomorrow, but she couldn't possibly—not with her emotions tangling under the surface like this.

She was in the mood for a good, loud thunderstorm. *Bring it on,* she thought, as she slung her purse over her shoulder and glared out her bedroom window at the darkening clouds.

Her brood was interrupted by the sound of a high voice echoing through the lower floor. "Hello? Anybody there?"

She'd been so distracted, she hadn't heard the bells over the entry door chime. The workers had departed for lunch, leaving the inn empty of activity and noise. She doubted it was any of the girls. Olivia, Adrian and Roxie all knew to enter through the kitchen.

Wandering out into the den, Briar glanced into the hall leading to the entryway.

The woman standing in front of the podium studying the pictures on the wall behind it was leggy and blonde. She had moved her sunshades from the bridge of her nose to the top of her head. She carried a large Brahmin bag and wore a black silk pantsuit that Briar would have deemed too hot and expensive for the baking heat of late June on the Gulf. The matching slingbacks on her feet made Briar's arches ache with pity. "Ma'am, can I help you?"

The stranger's head turned sharply toward her voice. The eyes narrowed in a stunning face. As the woman walked down the hall, recognition slowly buzzed along the cusp of Briar's memory.

"You must be Ms. Browning. Or do guests get to call you Briar?"

Wondering just where she'd seen that face before, Briar pressed her lips together thoughtfully. "Call me whatever you like. Are you here to make a reservation?"

"Briar," the woman decided with a nod, breezing over the question. "It's such a lovely name and unusual, too—which is more than the rest of us can say."

"Would you mind me asking your name, Ms...?"

She smiled. The movement of her lips wasn't the least bit friendly. Much coarser and more self-satisfied. "You don't recognize me? I was here a week or so ago."

It had taken a moment for it to click, but the self-assured smile had done the trick. Memories of that horrible afternoon before Brett hit, when she had found Cole outside in the midst of a heated debate with the same leggy blonde in front of her. "You're Tiffany," she said finally. Clearing her throat, she added, "Mr. Savitt's ex-wife."

"Oh, you can call him Cole," the woman said in lieu of confirmation. "We both know your relationship has skipped far beyond the silly bounds of *mister* and *miss*. And don't be shy. You can call me by my name—one he's cursed on several occasions in your presence, I'm sure."

Briar stared at the woman's outstretched hand. Instead of shaking it, she tucked both of her own in the pockets of the apron she had forgotten to discard in her rush to depart for Mobile. "May I ask what you're doing here?"

"Hmm." Tiffany scanned her from head to toe. The sweep was critical and approving in equal measure, though Briar couldn't have said how. She then turned her unnerving attention to the room at large and its arrangements, roaming comfortably on those pricey high-heeled shoes. "You're a polite one. But you've got spine. I'm sorry to say I didn't expect that. Your mother was the same, you know—or so I've been told."

"How do you know my mother?"

"Oh, my father used to rail about her. Fifteen years back, he did everything in his power to get her to sell the inn. But she wouldn't give an inch. Even when he resorted to threats of violence. My father liked threats, you see. Hanna Browning was one tough cookie, though. He couldn't crack her. He was always disappointed that he didn't get the prize. It *is* a prize. I can see that now for myself."

Briar shook her head, confused by the cryptic information. "I'm sorry. Who did you say your father was?"

"Howard. Douglas Howard." She nodded when Briar's eyes rounded. "That's right. My dear old daddy was once a terror for the private residents of the Eastern Shore. Those he couldn't buy out, he cheated out of their holdings. Only a select few were wise enough to know exactly how far he would go to get what he wanted. Your mother was one of them, despite your own father's best efforts to convince her to give in to old Douglas's demands."

"Douglas Howard…was your father?" Briar asked, still trying to stitch the puzzle together. She remembered her parents speaking of the man, her mother in the most heated of terms, her father in the most fearful. Their spouts about him had begun to fray the latter years of what she'd been sure was a shatterproof marriage. "But he was a local. I thought you lived in Huntsville...."

"Oh, once I hit eighteen, I lit out of my father's house as fast as I could. He and I never spoke much after that. I moved on, made my own life. And then he died. It was a shock when his attorney informed me he left what remained of the family fortune in my hands. I thought the mean bastard hated me. But then again, he hated everybody and had to leave the money and holdings to someone." She lifted a complacent shoulder, nearly simpered. "I'm grateful, though. It gave me a new outlook on life. I no longer had to be the lonely housewife of an overworked police officer. I could be a titan of real estate, just like my father."

Briar was beginning to understand, slowly but surely. "So you've come back to gain what he lost."

"More or less," Tiffany admitted, easing a hip onto the arm of the sofa. Her long legs crossed. "More to get what he couldn't. Wouldn't it be a laugh if I got my hands on the deed to Hanna's Inn? Things are different now, with Hanna gone. But I didn't count on her daughter to be as iron-willed as the previous innkeeper."

"You thought wrong," Briar stated.

Tiffany nodded. "I'll grant you that." She smiled that acerbic smile again. "But still, things *are* different. You've managed, despite your admirable efforts, to lose all your investors, haven't you? And I know for a fact that the county tax office will come knocking on the door with their foreclosure notice any day now."

Briar's lips parted in surprise. "You…you were the one who told them…"

"About your indecent relationship with another potential investor?" Tiffany laughed. "No, that was your father. Though I admit, it was my idea. I simply planted a little bug in Hudson's ear and made him think it was his idea. He doesn't think too much of your new boyfriend."

"You've been working with my father? For how long?"

Tiffany waved a dismissive hand. "A week or so. He heard the name Howard and became very cooperative. He's been much more helpful than my other informant."

As Tiffany's voice lowered and her eyes sharpened, the dark light in them was more noted than ever. They had come to it—the point Briar sensed the woman had wanted to drive home since she had walked through those doors.

Briar's gut churned and she shook her head. "No. I won't believe you."

She let out another tinkering laugh. "Love. It blinds, my dear. I have no doubt that you love him… and that you have some hold over him. He became very uncooperative after only a few weeks under your roof. But Cole came to Hanna's for one reason and one reason only—because I needed him to. As Douglas Howard's daughter, I couldn't afford to take the chance that I would be recognized. But Cole was a stranger and a former investigator. The perfect inside man."

"You can't make me believe he would've done that for you," Briar told her. She wanted to pace, to press a hand over her heart, which had begun to pound against her sternum like a battering ram. But she couldn't move. She could hardly breathe....

"You're right about that. He didn't do it for me. He did it for his son."

Briar's mouth fumbled, the protest dwindling before she could give it voice.

Gavin.

I'd do anything to have him back...

She sucked in a staggered breath and had to fight not to reach out for something to catch her balance. Her head was spinning. But even as her world spun itself off its axis and fell at her feet, she knew she couldn't show weakness. Not to this adversary. "You're not going to stop," she said, instead. "Whatever I do…however long I fight…you're never going to go away, are you, Tiffany?"

"Now at least we're beginning to understand one another." Clucking her tongue, Tiffany rose and walked to Briar, patting her arm. "You're pale. Maybe you should sit down."

"No," she said firmly. She lifted her gaze to Tiffany's face. "I think you should leave. Now."

Tiffany regarded her for a moment then nodded. "Very well. My job's all but done here, anyway. I'll give you a generous price for Hanna's—even if you wait until the foreclosure notice is delivered. I'm much more fair-minded than my old man."

"I would rather see the inn and everything in it broken up and auctioned off than in your hands."

"Sleep on it," Tiffany suggested as she veered toward the exit. "When you're facing true ruin, you'll come knocking on my door. I'm sure of it." Back in the entryway, she set a card on the podium and turned back to Briar with that Cheshire-cat grin. "It was a pleasure meeting you, Briar."

Briar turned away, facing the bay. She watched it blur as the bells chimed and the entry door closed at Tiffany's back.

Cole's horrible ex-wife was wrong about one thing at least—Briar would never be closer to true ruin than she was at this very moment.

COLE FELT GOOD about the changes he was making in his life. He'd found a place to live. He would sign the papers tomorrow morning and move in within the next week. Over the past few days, he had also gone job hunting. He knew his ten years of police credentials and referrals from former captains and partners were enough to get him through the door of the jobs he would prefer to have in the security field.

So, as long as he was looking at the big picture, within a month he would have what he needed in place to ensure that Gavin could live comfortably with him whenever Tiffany allowed visitation.

She *would* be generous—because he was damned sure she didn't want to do jail time. That wouldn't fit into her grand scheme. And whatever she had planned for the inn, he would figure it out. Together, he and Briar would make certain that her mother's legacy had the legs and stability to make it through the long haul.

And he would make sure that what he and Briar had built would do the same.

Once he settled into his new place and steady paychecks began rolling in, he would look into buying a new vehicle, even if he had to sell the Harley. The motorcycle had served him well, but it would be smart to have something safer for Gavin's sake.

He couldn't wait to introduce Gavin to Fairhope. To introduce Gavin to Briar. And for them to start a life together, as a family.

A life and family, he thought, with a shake of his head. Who would've thought he would have a chance at either again? After long last and longer unhappiness, he would have the kind of life he wanted. Needed. The kind of life he had lost all hope of ever having after Tiffany's accusations had sent them to court, and he'd watched everything fall through the cracks.

Briar had given him so much. She'd given him the strength to hope again. To wish. And the confidence to build, grow, love.

Tonight he would tell her so, over dinner. Before guests began trickling in over the next week, he wanted to have one more night with her alone. An intimate dinner with a hint of romance. There he would pour his heart and soul out to her. And hopefully, they could continue to grow.

One thing he hadn't anticipated was this afternoon shower. Drops fell on his head, back and shoulders as he steered the Harley into the gravel lot. He braked under the magnolia. The thick branches and leaves didn't do much to keep him from getting wet. Quickly, he dismounted, cut the engine and climbed the steps to the door.

The inn was quiet. He frowned when he didn't see any lights on down the hall. Maybe Briar had stepped out. Reaching over, he switched on the overhead light then pulled his helmet off and listened for her.

Nothing. Only the patter of rain on the exterior walls. Unease began to nip at his scalp. He displaced it, moving toward the hall that led into the den. "Briar?"

The door to the kitchen was open. Through the afternoon gloom, he caught sight of her. She was sitting in one of the chairs around the table. The image wouldn't have struck him as off if she had been doing something.

Busy. She was always busy, but not now. Her hands laid still on the place mat. With her back to him, she was staring out the screen door at the rain breaking apart on the stoop.

"Briar?" he said again, stepping into the kitchen.

His breath snagged when she didn't respond. Something was wrong. Very wrong. Thunder rumbled, a distant but no less ominous sound, as he approached.

He placed his hand on her shoulder to rub, but she flinched and he let it fall away. "What's going on?"

He heard the audible click of her swallow before she said in a voice almost too low to interpret over the dribble of rain, "Get out."

The words froze him in place. "What?"

"I said get out," she replied, her voice strengthening, though it was still quiet and unsteady enough to chill him. "I want you out of the inn. Out of my home. Out of my life."

"Briar—"

She turned in the chair and looked up at him. The knuckles of the hand that gripped the back of the chair were as white as her face. The shadows under her eyes were nothing compared to the grave light in them. Her mouth was tucked into a firm, flat line, much like her father's had been days ago. But those eyes. They bore into him, and he knew where the change had come from.

"When was she here?" he asked, setting his helmet carefully on the table.

"Don't sit," she demanded. "I don't want you to sit."

"All right," he said, holding up his hands. He had to fight not to reach for her again. "Briar...when was she here?"

"Why should it matter when she was here or that

she was here at all?" she asked. "The only thing that matters is that you lied to me."

He lowered his head. "Yes. Yes, I did."

She let out a shaky breath and looked away, but not before he saw the tears crest into her eyes. "I want the truth. Why did you do it? I need to hear it from you. And, please, no more lies."

"Truth," he agreed. "It was for Gavin." At her discerning nod, he should have felt relieved. Still, the space between them felt like a thousand empty miles he hadn't the first clue how to cross. "Whatever I did, I did it for Gavin. I had nothing. So I let her blackmail me into doing what she wanted just so I could be a part of his life again."

"And what did you do, exactly?" she asked. When he hesitated, those grave eyes veered back to his face. "Tell me. Everything."

He gripped the edge of the counter. That hollow stare cleaved him like an ax. The worst part of it wasn't the accusing gleam behind it; instead, it was the hurt he saw lurking there. He had hurt her, and *that* he could not stand. "All she wanted was for me to gather information. She needed to know who your investors were. If you didn't have any, she wanted me to find out what you were planning to do to save the inn."

"And you did these things?"

"I tapped your phone lines. Looked into your files."

Her face fell completely, hand coming halfway

up to shield her mouth before it fell away in shock. "The break-in…"

"No," he argued, dropping into the chair next to hers, unable to stop himself from reaching out and taking her cool hand. "No, Briar. That had *nothing* to do with me."

"How am I supposed to trust you?"

"I was with you," he assured her. "Remember? We were together."

"Oh, God." She pressed her free hand to her brow. "Was that part of it? Does what's between us now have anything to do with this?"

"Briar, please believe me, it wasn't long after I got here and met you that I started questioning everything," he explained. "That I started wondering if hurting you was worth it. And it wasn't. I couldn't do it."

"That day…on the pier…you said you wouldn't hurt me."

He sighed, remembering the words well. "I said I didn't want to. And I didn't, Briar, but at that point I didn't think I had a choice."

She blinked, breathed out a sob and turned away from him even as he reached for her again. Tearing her arm from his grasp, she paced to the screen door and back, fingers raking the hair from her brow. With the room between them, she faced him again. "It was all based on lies."

"No. Not all of it," he told her. Above all, he had to make her understand that.

"You let me invite you into my bed."

"At that point, it wasn't about anything other than you and me. I had already gone to Tiffany. I told her I wasn't going to do her dirty work anymore."

"You've already lied to me," she pointed out. "What could you possibly have to say for yourself to make me believe you aren't lying now?"

He fell silent, unable to see a way through the fact that she'd lost faith in him.

Briar lifted a hand to her head again. "Oh, God, my father was right."

"Your father's a jackass."

"It's funny. He said the same thing about you," she said on a sobbing laugh. "Only now I'm inclined to believe him. He said I would end up alone. And what do you know? As it turns out, I'm better off that way, aren't I? I'm better off moving on, just like he did."

Cole rose, walked to her in two long, swift strides. "Briar, whatever has happened here, whatever he or Tiffany have ever said to you, you cannot give up on the inn."

"What's the point?" she shrieked, her voice rising for the first time. "I wanted to keep it in the family. But there's no family here anymore, Cole, and there never will be again. Not as long as I'm around."

"You can't think like that, Briar. I won't let you!"

"I don't have a choice." Dropping her face into both of her hands, she shook with repressed sobs. "I don't. Just like I have no choice but to ask you to leave."

No, not like this. He wanted to beg the words. Plead with her. "I can't leave you here like this."

"Everybody leaves," she said, eyes dead, glassy now as they rose back to his. "Why should you be any different?"

"I love you."

She released a breath, closed her eyes against him. "The sad thing is, Cole, a few hours ago I could have taken you at your word. You'll understand now why I can't."

"Briar...don't," he said, the hopelessness he saw in her and felt sinking into his bones tearing him apart. "Please don't."

"Get out," she said again. "If you ever had any regard for me whatsoever...you'll leave. Now. Without another word."

He'd lost her. He'd known it from the moment he stepped foot in her kitchen. Tiffany had won, and they had both lost.

He stood gazing at her, drinking her in. He began to raise his hand to touch her once more but curled his fingers into his fist and made himself turn away.

Gripping the strap of the helmet, Cole lifted it from the table. Without another word, he moved away from her. Though it wrenched him in two, he picked up the backpack he had dropped in the entryway, took one last look toward the kitchen and felt his heart reach for her with every ounce of its strength.

Again, he made himself turn away. The bells over the door chimed and he left Hanna's Inn and its innkeeper, empty-handed.

Again, he made himself turn away. The bells over the door chimed and the fall dawn's fog and its inn-keeper simply faded.

CHAPTER EIGHTEEN

THE DAY AFTER Cole left, Briar told herself she was strong enough to rid herself of him completely. She stalled most of the morning, going about her regular duties, though there was no one to tend to. His absence echoed around her as she threw herself into mopping floors that weren't dirty, scrubbing surfaces that were already clean.

Finally, she braced herself and carried a laundry basket to the door of the bay-view suite.

It was closed. She fumbled in her pocket for the key he had left on the podium. It might have been her imagination, but when she'd touched it that morning, it had still felt warm from his hand.

It was a key—cold metal. It meant nothing more than access into a room that had never really belonged to him. Not that it would belong to her for much longer, either.

She pushed that dismal thought away. With her heart hurting like it was, it would be a while before she could contemplate the inn's uncertain future again. One heartache at a time—that was all she could handle. Unlocking the door, Briar tucked the key back in her pocket and stepped across the threshold.

Her breath shuddered. She leaned into the laundry basket at her hip. The room was perfectly ordered, empty, but she could smell him. Just that barest trace of him on the air. Her eyes filled and she bent at the hips, unable to hold back the sobs for another moment.

It was some time later when she heard a voice calling up the stairs. She heard it again, closer this time, but couldn't bring herself to answer. Knuckles rapped against the door of the suite. "Briar, you in here?"

It was Olivia's voice. Footsteps came around the bed and stopped.

Briar didn't make a move to get up from the floor or lift her head from her knees. She didn't quite know how she'd gotten this way, curled up on the far side of the bed. She remembered abandoning the laundry basket by the door and then walking around, tracing her hands over the edge of the furniture, the quilt. When it had come to stripping the bed and removing any trace of him that was left in the room, she'd curled up and wept.

Olivia's next words echoed the ones Briar had felt when the dam broke and the pain in all its towering glory came gushing through in full force.

"Oh, hell."

Olivia crouched next to her, placing a hand on

Briar's head. There was no asking if he was gone. Some things were just intuitive.

And, because they'd been through so much, both having lost people they loved whether to death or departure, Olivia seemed to inherently know that sometimes there were no words of comfort. There was just presence, steadfastness. Being there.

As Briar's shoulders shook with more sobs, Olivia pulled her into her arms and rocked.

THE FOURTH OF July blazed in with its characteristic lurid heat and scores of tourists. The inn came alive again with people and Briar had no choice but to put the events of the past week behind her as she went about her duties. She ignored the fact that she didn't put near as much heart into the routine and activities around Hanna's Inn leading up to the city's grand holiday finale as she usually did.

The fireworks show thundered and flashed, lighting the faces of people in chairs on the inn lawn and those who had poured out of the tavern. Hundreds of them gathered on the Eastern Shore to watch in awed silence.

Briar watched them from behind the windows of the sun porch, far apart from the noise and companionship.

She spotted Adrian, Kyle, Roxie and Richard Levy grouped together near the greenhouse and hoped they wouldn't come looking for her. The only reason Olivia hadn't already was because she was busy manning the tavern.

It had been only days before last year's Fourth of July when the doctors confirmed her worst fears: that her mother's cancer had taken a turn for the worst. The night of the Fourth, she and her mother and father had huddled together here in this spot, apart from the patriotic revelers. Then, too, she'd felt disconnected from the jubilation.

The disconnect had terrified her. For a while, particularly after her mother's death, she'd feared that she would go on feeling detached for the rest of her life.

Now she faced that same fear again. This time she didn't have the energy to push it away. Her guests were outside with the tavern crowd—she didn't have to paste on an artificial smile. She felt bone tired, worn thin. Yesterday she had marginally been able to assure herself that this feeling of helplessness would pass with time and she would move on. Tonight she wasn't so sure.

Cole's departure was no longer her sole reason for feeling so helpless. Her taxes were overdue again. The deadline had come and gone. Foreclosure was imminent. She was so tired of struggling, fighting. Byron Strong hadn't found any new leads on investors. Her world was truly crumbling and she didn't have the heart or, she feared, the will to fight it.

Though there was no chill in the air, she crossed her arms over her middle and rubbed her hands over them. The movement did nothing to assuage the perilous track of her thoughts. She turned toward the light of the kitchen. Keeping busy. That was the way to stop dwelling on how far she'd let herself fall.

She reached up to switch on the radio mounted to the underside of the cabinets and turned the dial until Ray Charles drowned out the reverberating bang of fireworks. The counters were clean. The dishes had all been done and put away. She pulled open the silver drawer, eyeing the patterned handles of her mother's favorite set of flatware. They could use a polish....

The knock came at the screen door. Frowning, she turned to see who it was. She stopped short when she saw Byron Strong. The man was dressed in shorts and a red polo shirt. He was wearing brown leather flip-flops and he hadn't strung his long dark hair up at the base of his neck as he usually did during working hours.

She was struck both by his casual appearance and the fact that he was grinning from ear to ear. It was fortunate he hadn't run into Olivia yet. Briar's cousin would have been all over him in two seconds tops.

Walking over, she opened the screen door and ushered him in. "Byron," she greeted, "I wasn't expecting to see you around here today."

"Hanna's does have one of the best views," he said as he stepped into her kitchen and seemed to fill it with his long, tall frame. "We wanted to see the fireworks from here."

"We?" she asked, glancing over his shoulder. The stoop was empty.

"Me and my parents," he said, pointing out to the people sitting on blankets along the shoreline. "They're new to the area, moved down just in time for the big holiday show."

"You should invite them in," she said. "I've got plenty of barbecue and watermelon left over from this afternoon's feast."

"I'm sure they would love that. But I wanted to run a couple of things by you first."

"Oh?" She shrank into a chair. Whenever Byron visited, memories of the day he had told her of her father's betrayal came lurking back. Though his face still beamed light, she couldn't help but brace herself. "What about?"

"It's business," he admitted and, true to form, took the seat beside her.

"Oh, boy," she breathed, laying her hands carefully on her lap.

He grinned. "It's good news. First of all, I wanted you to be the first to know that I quit my job at your father's firm."

She blinked in surprise. "You did?"

"I've decided to open my own accounting business," he explained. "It's what I've wanted for a long time, but I didn't know how to do it. That is until I walked into the inn that day with your father and saw you stand up for your dreams. You inspired me, Briar. And now I'm striking out on my own."

"Byron." Placing a hand over his, she smiled a real smile for the first time in days. "That's wonderful news."

He chuckled. "I was hoping you'd say that. As it stands, you're my only client."

"I'd be happy to recommend your services any day."

"That's good to know." He paused for effect. Then the words spilled out as if he'd been waiting for the right moment to say them and had finally found it. "I think I've found a pair of investors who would be happy to do business with Hanna's."

Her heart did a small leap. Pressing the heel of her hand to the center of her chest, she fought hope. There would be no hoping this time. Not until the deal was done. "Really? Would I know who they are?"

"Not personally," he said, the grin becoming almost boyish as it spread farther across his cheeks. "But they're here. Tonight."

"Where?" she asked, glancing out the window again as her pulse picked up pace.

"They're with me," he added for emphasis.

Looking back at that pensive grin, she narrowed her eyes. "You don't mean your parents."

His face fell slightly at her tone. "As a matter of fact…"

She sighed, brushed the hair back from her brow and shook her head. "I'm sorry, but that's not an option."

"What are you talking about?" he asked. "They love what they've seen of the inn so far. I told them about its history—they *love* a good history. They have the money. They want to invest in local business. And I can't vouch for anyone's investment portfolio more than I can vouch for theirs. I practically built it, for Christ's sake. It's the perfect arrangement."

"It's too convenient," she argued. "Did you really think I wouldn't see straight through it? My family has never taken charity, Byron, and I'm not about to start now."

"Whoa, whoa, hold it," he said, stopping her with raised hands. "Who said anything about charity? Both of them are retired, they have extra cash lying around. They want to invest in real estate. Hell, my father made his living in real estate for forty years. And my mother ran her own bakery in northern Georgia, so they love small business. Trust me. You're not going to find two people more perfect for this." He stopped her again, reading her thoroughly. "And I didn't give them a nudge. They came to me about investing. The first person I thought about, of course, was you. But if you can't see this as a win-win all the way around, I'm at a loss."

She scrutinized his face for a moment. Several

moments. When she found no crack in the exterior and couldn't bring herself not to trust what she saw beaming through his eyes, she found a smile curving slowly, warmly across her lips. "This is too good to be true. You realize that, right?"

He shrugged, leaning back in his chair with that boyish grin again and reaching for one of the nectarines in the bowl at the center of the table. "I'd say it was meant to be."

"Meant to be," she repeated as she watched him bite into a perfectly round red nectarine. She threw her hands up in surrender. "Well, what are you waiting for? Bring them in. I'll make coffee. We'll talk business."

CHAPTER NINETEEN

She needed a distraction. The winds of change were blowing at her back. Tomorrow she would be signing papers with the Strongs and solidifying their investment agreement.

Hanna's would be saved. It might no longer be hers in the grand scheme of things, and she would have to work for years to ensure she paid back every penny to Byron's family, but it was saved.

The night air was heavy and tepid. The humidity had reached its climax and would remain that way, suffocating the residents of the Eastern Shore without mercy well into August. Her flowers still hadn't recovered from Brett's wrath so there was nothing between her and the fresh, briny scent of the bay. Moonlight dappled on the restless rise and fall of the water. Any other evening, she would have stopped to watch—to meditate and remember.

Tonight, however, she headed for the refuge of sound and light. Distraction. The music pounded out of the tavern. Somebody had Skynyrd's "Call Me the Breeze" rocking on the jukebox.

Olivia worked with Monica Slayer behind the

counter, pulling tap beer and mixing drinks, exchanging monies and chatting up customers.

Watching her cousin work brought Briar some clarity and the momentary calm she'd desperately been seeking tonight.

She would keep Hanna's. Olivia would keep the tavern. And her friends Adrian and Roxie would keep their businesses. The county, state and any future debt collectors wouldn't be able to touch any part of her friends' businesses. Aside from her mother's legacy, *that* would be the most rewarding thing about signing the papers tomorrow.

Removing the light sweater she'd worn around the inn, Briar stepped into Olivia's peripheral vision. "Hey. Put me to work."

Olivia's grin fell when she found her cousin behind the bar. "You sure? You've been working your tail off to keep the inn spick-and-span for the Strongs' visits."

"I'm fine," she said. The assurance was practically becoming her litany. "You're full up and both you and Monica are working double-time. Give me a job, Liv."

"If you say so." Olivia jerked her thumb toward the sink. "We need clean glasses for rotation."

"I'm on it." She rolled up her sleeves and got to work.

The mindless task coupled with the thumping speakers did her well. As she, Olivia and Monica moved around behind the bar, she barely noticed when the jukebox segued into Elton then Journey. Then a little bit of Green Day before The Beatles' "Come Together." By this point, she was clearing tables, filling orders and had managed to let her troubles slip to the back of her mind.

"What the hell is he doing here?"

The hostility in Olivia's voice made Briar's head swivel toward the entry doors. When she saw the man standing just inside them, her mouth dropped. "Daddy? He never comes here." She looked at Olivia. "Does he?"

She shook her head. "If he's here to make waves, I'll be happy to have Freddie and Ty haul his ass out."

Briar firmed her mouth as her father's eyes found hers and his feet began moving toward the bar. "I can handle him."

"The last thing you need is someone upsetting you," Olivia muttered. "Briar, let me take care of the old buzzard while you get me three draft Miller Lites and two Yuenglings."

Reluctantly moving to the tap, Briar kept an eye on her father as she went about filling the orders. He chose an empty stool on the far side of the bar, and Olivia crossed her arms as she faced off with him. "Howdy, stranger. Haven't seen you around these parts in a while."

He flicked her a terse glance. "Could I get a shot, please?"

With a shrug, Olivia reached under the bar. "If I remember, it's a shot of Jack, right?"

"That's what I said, isn't it?"

Olivia raised a brow at his tone and placed a jigger on the bar, flipping a bottle of Jack Daniel's upside down. "You all right, unc?"

"I'm fine." When Olivia passed the shot glass over the bar, he tossed it back quickly. "Another."

Briar met Olivia's pointed look with a perplexed frown. She didn't know her father drank—and she didn't like where this scene was heading. Olivia, however, reached for the Jack Daniel's again and filled another jigger for him.

"Get me a couple more."

"Don't overdo it now," Olivia warned.

"Just do your job."

Briar took a step forward. Monica placed a hand on her arm before she could intervene. "She's got him," Monica said simply. "Don't you worry, hon."

Olivia's glare could've sheared glass. Hudson's was no less forbidding, but Briar knew him well enough to see the telling glint of sadness under the stern veneer. Pity welled within her, but as he tipped back another shot, she squelched it. After all he'd done, how could she feel anything but cool resentment toward him?

The entry bells drew her attention to the door again. This time her mouth fell open in shock as Cole Savitt walked in, eyes combing the crowd and servers.

"You've got to be kidding me," she heard Olivia say.

Despite the immediate tension that entered her body at the sight of him, Briar felt her heart drum as his gaze locked on her and stayed there. It went from narrowed and searching, to round and full of plea.

She balled a dishcloth in her hand and frowned deeply. It was going to be a longer night than she'd anticipated.

A WHOLE PLAYLIST of songs later, Cole was still there, along with Briar and, puzzlingly enough, her old man. Cole had chosen a spot out of the way, a table in the corner. Monica had taken it upon herself to serve him while Olivia was tied up with Briar's father, Hudson, whose presence itched like a burr between Cole's shoulder blades. Briar had done her best throughout the night to pretend neither of them were there, sticking to one side of the bar, her eyes never trekking farther than the few seated tavern-goers on the stools in front of her.

Cole couldn't help but watch her. It'd been foolish coming here tonight. He'd known it even as his Harley roared down the familiar path to the inn and tavern. He hadn't gone far since leaving Hanna's—a motel a respectable distance from Briar and the others, but still close enough to be considered within Fairhope city limits. He hadn't been able to go farther away from Briar or the town. Whether he'd wanted to or not, it was all home to him now and he didn't know how to let it go.

But he'd come to the tavern tonight for a good reason—to try and talk to Olivia. She likely wanted to give him a piece of her mind, and he was prepared to take it—he deserved it. But maybe, just maybe, after it was all done she would lend him her ears long enough for him to reason with her. He planned to win Briar back, in a big way. And with all the bad he'd done, a grand gesture was the only way to prove his love for her.

He didn't have the money to get the inn out of debt. That was the most obvious plan of action. There had to be some other way…. He'd come to Olivia for ideas.

It was just a bonus and pure luck that Briar had chosen tonight to help Olivia behind the bar. Not that the tavern was particularly busy. Olivia and Monica seemed to have everything under control—minus the crusty old crab on the other side of the bar.

It seemed to be a night of heavy drinking for Hudson. The strong line of the man's back had slowly deteriorated over the past half hour of inebriation, and he'd loosened his tie. As he glared down at his own hands spread before him on the countertop, Cole thought that somehow the man looked older. Brittle.

Another hour passed and closing loomed. Cole watched as Monica counted her tips as the last customers trickled out one by one into the humid night, leaving behind the subdued tune of Neil Young's

"Heart of Gold." He still hadn't found a chance to pull Olivia aside. And Briar still hovered, wiping tabletops and avoiding his gaze. Maybe he should try talking to *her* now....

As if knowing the train of his thoughts, Olivia caught his eye and gave him a sharp look. He felt his back straighten, thoroughly scolded, and lifted his beer to finish off the last swig in the bottom of the amber bottle.

"I'll drive him home," he heard Olivia say to Briar as she edged closer, leaning on the handle of her broom as she put her back to Cole and considered Hudson.

"No," Briar said, her voice low and almost out of Cole's earshot. "He can sleep at the inn."

"You told him he was no longer welcome there," Olivia reminded her. "And for a good reason."

"Yeah, well, you've got a bar to close, and he can't stay here all night." She wiped her hands on the washcloth and folded it into her back pocket. "I'll get him out of your hair."

"Be careful, cuz," Olivia cautioned grimly.

Cole swallowed as Briar approached her father's bent frame. He didn't like this situation at all. It took everything he had to remain rooted to his chair. He edged to the end of his seat to better hear the words exchanged between father and daughter.

Briar hesitated only for a moment before lifting her hand to her dad's back. "Hey, I think it's time you come home."

Hudson slowly lifted his head from his folded arms. When his gaze found hers, a deep furrow formed between his brows. Then Cole saw his red-rimmed eyes clear and a hopeful light glimmer to life in his eyes. Briar's mouth dropped open in shock when his hand lifted to her face.

His voice scraped raw against his throat as he murmured, "Hanna, honey. I knew you'd come tonight."

She shrank back from his touch. "Daddy, what—"

He shifted unsteadily to his feet, making Cole rise from his seat and cross the bar. Hudson gripped the back of his stool with one hand to hold himself up. The pain and hope conjoined in his watery stare as he lumbered toward Briar. "Let me hold you. I've missed you."

"Oh, God, Daddy," she said, a sob working through her as her eyes filled with tears. "Don't do this. Please."

"Come here," he murmured. He tripped on a stool leg and lost his balance. Cole sprinted the last couple of feet and took the man's weight before Hudson could hit the floor. "Whoa there, old man."

Olivia barreled toward them. "Come on, Uncle Hud. Let's get you out of here."

"I've got him," Cole said, meeting Briar's dismayed gaze. Her face was streaked with tears. His heart wrenched at the sight. "I'll take care of him," he vowed.

She pressed her lips together as if holding something back and gave a single nod.

He turned to Olivia. "Where?"

Her eyes combed his for ulterior motives. After a long hesitation, she jerked her chin upward. "Upstairs to my place. Go down the hall, take the second door on the right. Here, take the key. I'll be up later."

He grasped it in his free hand and tugged Hudson's arm around his shoulders so he could more easily support him. With one last look at Briar, Cole made his way behind the bar and through the swinging doors.

HUDSON LOOKED EVEN worse for wear the next morning when Cole brought him coffee. His clothes were rumpled, his eyes were bloodshot and the furrows on his face were still firmly entrenched there. He sat at the table in his niece's kitchen, brooding shoulders heavily slumped.

Olivia herself had let Cole in with a warning. "You've got five minutes," she'd said, looking from the two thermoses full of coffee in his hands to the determined set of his face. Cole was glad she hadn't tried to stop him from talking what sense he could into Briar's father.

Hudson's eyes narrowed on Cole's face as he approached the table. "What're you doing here?"

"I caught the show last night," Cole informed him, crossing the room.

A new line appeared between Hudson's eyes as

his gaze fell away in shame. He said nothing as Cole pulled out a chair and lowered into it. "Coffee," he said, pushing the thermos toward him. When Hudson didn't touch it, he shifted in his chair. "Drink it. It'll help."

"Why are you here?" Hudson asked in a gruff voice. "I don't owe you anything."

"No? Well, maybe you owe Briar something," Cole said, his brow raised in question.

"What I did was in my daughter's best interest."

"I don't think she'd agree."

Hudson lifted his shoulder. "She left law school for Paris and got robbed. She took up her mother's mantle and what happened? She lost it all." His flinty stare found Cole's. "She entered into an inappropriate relationship with one of her guests who turned out to be in league with the very person who could destroy her. My daughter has the soul of a gambler, Mr. Savitt. Forgive me if I choose to remove a bad bet from her life."

Cole's frown deepened. "Well, there I guess you have me. I am a bad bet. I think even she knew that from the beginning."

Hudson lifted a hand. "You're starting to see things from my perspective."

"The thing is, Hudson, it wasn't the shady parts of who I was that she chose to see," Cole went on, thinking back to the beginning and all that had transpired since. "Under it all, Briar saw the possibilities of life left in me. I thought I'd lost that. She

let me know they were still there, even before anything romantic happened between us. She shined
a light in the dark for me that I thought I would
never see again. Because, you see, the thing you've
never been able to understand about your daughter,
Mr. Browning, is that that's what she does. She saw
Hanna's on the brink of faltering and she charged
in to save it, even when she had everything to lose.
Even when there was still a part of her that wanted
to move on and pursue her own dreams. And that
guy in Paris who conned her? I think she saw the
light in him, too. He just chose not to let her in."

Cole crossed his arms over the tabletop and
moved his shoulders over them, peering into Hudson's face. Something flickered over the man's expression. "I pity that man, Mr. Browning, because
he'll never know what I do now. That life without
that light that Briar emits is hopeless. It's empty, and
I am nothing without it."

Hudson's eyes cleared. The clarity was chased
momentarily by pain before he lowered his eyes to
the table to hide it. Cole's lips parted. "That's what
she was to you, too, isn't it? Your wife."

The flintiness was back as Hudson's gaze rose
back to pin Cole's. "Don't talk about my wife. You
didn't know her."

"Actually, I think I sort of do, sir," Cole told him.
"Briar's her mother's daughter, isn't she? Not just
in looks."

Hudson's jaw quaked as he fought against the

need to speak. He muttered an oath on an expelled breath and gave in. "The fight against Douglas Howard might've been a win, son, but it took years of her life. Five years of stress. Then she took it upon herself to fight for others. It's what killed her, you know. The stress. *He* killed her. So when Howard's daughter came knocking on my door, I knew what I had to do. You may think that I don't care about Briar. But I did what I did because I knew she couldn't win this—not without gambling something big in return. Something she couldn't afford to lose."

Cole searched the old man's face and saw the truth in the determined glint in the flinty eyes that stared back at him, challenging him to deny his best intentions. Cole didn't know which of the two of them was more surprised to hear him say, "I believe you." He cleared his throat when Hudson only blinked at him. Reaching for the thermos, he spun it around and around. "I still don't believe what you did was right. But what we do for our kids' safety or well-being *isn't* always."

"Sounds like you're speaking from experience," Hudson observed.

Cole nodded. "I did what I did for Tiffany so she'd let me see my son again."

"It's not easy," Hudson admitted, "being a father. Did you get what you wanted?"

Cole thought of the papers Tiffany had delivered to his motel room days before. "Yes, but I'd love to give him what Briar showed me I could have again—a family. Home."

Hudson reached for the thermos and took it from Cole's hand. He lifted it in acknowledgment. "Then it seems, Mr. Savitt, that, against all odds, we understand one another." The bracket between his eyes appeared once more. "And it seems, where my daughter is concerned, there's quite a bit of making up for lost time to be done by both of us."

CHAPTER TWENTY

OLIVIA FROWNED AFTER her uncle closed the door behind him, leaving her apartment over the tavern. After a moment, she turned to Cole, who leaned against the granite countertop of her kitchen, and shook her head. "Unbelievable. Do you know how many times I've tried to knock some sense into my uncle's head? You show up here with coffee and, in ten minutes' time, you two are all but chanting 'Kumbaya'?"

Cole slipped his hands into his pockets, a bit uneasy now that he was alone with Olivia. "I, ah… I'm sorry?"

"Well, don't be," she snapped. "If I wasn't so flipping mad at you, I'd kiss you right now."

He couldn't fight a smile. It was a small one, but he let it curve his lips. "Would you rather hit me, instead?"

She raised a brow. "You'd let me do that?"

"It's nothing I don't deserve." Letting his hands dangle at his sides, he stood up straight and took a deep breath. "Go on. Do your worst."

Her eyes narrowed as she measured the breadth of his shoulders. "I'd rather use Betty."

His mouth fumbled. "Who's Betty?"

"My rifle," she told him and grinned wickedly when his mouth fell. "I keep her behind the couch in my office downstairs. Just in case."

He pressed his lips together. "I'll wait here."

Her eyes lit with dark light as she considered. "Or maybe Glinda."

Swallowing, he asked after a moment's hesitation, "Glinda?"

"Oh, just my aluminum baseball bat from my high school days," she explained. "I keep her underneath Chuck's floorboard. And, you should know, I used to have the highest softball batting average in three counties. A couple of broken kneecaps ought to make me feel *loads* better."

"If you're trying to intimidate me, it's working," he told her. "Then again, you don't need Betty or Glinda for that."

Her lips quirked and the dark light in her eyes vanished, replaced by true mirth. Face softening, she relaxed. "Damn it, I still like you." Moving past him into the kitchen, she went to the refrigerator and pulled out a carton of orange juice. Grabbing a glass from one of the cabinets above the clean countertop, she asked, "Why did you come back?"

"To talk to you," he said truthfully.

"You assumed I would let you." Turning, with the glass full of orange juice in her hand, she leaned against the counter and sipped. "Brave man. Question: Is the ex-wife still picking up the tab?"

He scowled. "As far as I know, she's gone. I'm done with her in any case."

"Must've been a job well done if she's left you alone."

Sighing, he hid his hands in the pockets of his jeans again. "Ever since the break-in, I've done my best to rid myself of her, to give Briar what she deserves."

"And what's that?"

"Honesty," he said instantly. "Something real and solid. Someone she can always count on being there for her. I thought about taking out a loan to pay off the inn's debts—"

Olivia pursed her lips. "Oh, I wouldn't worry about that." At Cole's bemused look, she continued. "A couple of last-minute investors paid off Briar's tab before the worst happened. Their help is well on its way to taking care of all the bills still owed for my aunt's medical care."

"And Tiffany?" Cole added. "She just…moved on?"

Olivia snorted. "It *did* help that Adrian and I figured out for ourselves that she was behind the break-in. Since our sit-down with her to discuss our terms, she backed off real cooperative-like and we haven't seen or heard from her since. I don't think she'll be returning."

"So the inn's safe." His heart pounded hopefully. "Briar's in the clear."

"Yes," she replied and watched relief spill across his face.

He blew out a breath. "I'm glad Briar got everything she wanted. I never wanted anything else."

"Not everything," Olivia said. Setting the glass down with a clack on the counter, she boosted herself up to sit on the edge. "Do you know she cried for days over your betrayal? Don't think for a second hearing her grieve like that didn't make me want to peel the skin from your bones one inch at a time. She may have the inn back, she may have restored Hanna's legacy, but she didn't get everything she wanted—you left a hole."

"I want to fix it," he told her. "I want to be the man she saw in me. I love her, Olivia. Tell me, please, if there's any chance of making things right?"

She studied him scrupulously from head to toe, weighing him. "Nobody knows the power of forgiveness more than Briar." Hopping off the counter, she crossed the room to him. "You want to be that man she believed in, prove it now."

"Just point me in the right direction," Cole said.

Smiling up at him, she tilted her head. "How did it feel, finding out you had something in common with Uncle Hud?"

"Scared the hell out of me," he replied. Seeing himself in the broken shell of a man across the table from him had made his need for redemption even more drastic.

She nodded. "Good. That means you're desperate—you're going to need that."

CONTINUITY. IT WAS enough, Briar told herself as she gazed at the inn. She'd been working in her garden when the sun's gleam against the windowpane above her head caught her eye. Unable to help herself, she'd taken a seat on the garden bench to simply look at what she had saved.

She'd saved it. Somehow she had saved it all from disappearing. *Thank God,* she thought, closing her eyes and breathing in the smell of jasmine blooms and gardenia. She would stay with Hanna's, and Hanna's would stay with her.

She sat still, listening to the waves lap gently to shore and the birds cry from overhead. She heard the whisper of the trees and the early chirp of cricket song. A dull pulse rent the air, Olivia's tavern music just barely audible on the soft breeze.

Peace. It had been a while since she'd encountered it. Despite her surroundings, and her future and Hanna's finally solidified, peace had eluded her still.

She knew what was missing yet she refused to dwell on it. She wouldn't dwell on misplaced dreams or the man she'd built them around. She was done wishing for what could have been.

She would never love another, not enough to let him all the way in. The inn would be filled with voices for a long time to come, as she'd wished...

even if a family of her own didn't come with the happy partnership she'd envisioned. She had Olivia, Adrian and Roxie. One day, they would all bring their families into the fold. They would grow and flourish, just like the new vegetable buds she'd replanted that were already ripening on their stalks and vines.

She could be content with that.

She *would* be content with that. Just as she would try and forget what she had wanted to build with the man she had loved. And in quiet moments like these, she would meditate, and remember the ones that really mattered.

Fairies. Fairies dancing.

Briar opened her eyes and looked out toward the bay. The sun had lowered to just the right angle... and fairies danced over its restless blue crests.

Sighing, she braced her hands on either side of her. Trying not to ache for the past, she stood and bent to pick up the bucket of gardening tools she'd abandoned next to the vegetable patch.

"Hey, cuz," Olivia said, emerging from the back of the tavern. She was dressed for a long night of bartending in a black halter dress, tights and black boots. "Wow," she said, looking out toward the sunset, shading her eyes from the glare of the sun by visoring one hand over her brows. "Hell of a night for daydreaming."

Briar tucked her bucket against her hip and crossed

the lawn. "It's almost too late for dinner now. I've wasted so much time staring at it."

Olivia slung an arm around her shoulders as they walked back to the screen door of the inn kitchen together. "Sounds like time well wasted to me."

"It's a Friday night," Briar observed. "How are you not swamped behind a bar right now?"

Waving a dismissive hand, Olivia opened the screen door with a creak and let Briar pass through first. "It's nothing Monica can't handle long enough for me to check in on you."

Briar sighed and bent to place the bucket back under the sink where it belonged. "How many times do I have to tell you I'm fine?"

Olivia picked a green apple from the basket at the center of the nook table. Taking a hearty bite, she made herself at home in one of the chairs. "What happened last night didn't settle well with me. He's my uncle, your father, and you were on the receiving end. Stop trying to convince me it didn't affect you."

Giving in to the impulse, Briar seated herself at the table across from her cousin. "I actually ran into him."

Olivia paused in the midst of raising the apple to her mouth. "When?"

"Around lunchtime," Briar explained, thinking back to the strange interlude. "At Flora."

"Oh, yeah?" Olivia took another bite and talked around the mouthful. "What did he have to say for himself?"

"He was…actually kind of pleasant for a change," Briar remembered. She tried not to dwell on the hope that had been born out of the chance meeting with her father. Hope that things could change—that he could change. Lifting a shoulder in dismissal, she added, "He apologized profusely for last night. And for scheming with Tiffany Howard."

"Did you forgive him?"

"I'm not sure I'm ready to," Briar contemplated. "So, no, not there on the spot. But I agreed to dinner one night this week. He said he wants to talk things over, on my terms."

"Hmm," Olivia hummed. She motioned toward Briar with the apple. "You believe him?"

"I kind of do," Briar admitted. At Olivia's raised brow, she shook her head. "I know. Apparently, I'm subscribing to Roxie's line of thinking and becoming a hopeless optimist. But, Liv, I caught him buying flowers for me."

"No way."

"Yeah," she said, nodding. "Crazy, right? When I asked who they were for, he got this sheepish look on his face, got all red and stammery and said they were for me. Though he couldn't be sure what my favorite flower was. He looked so ashamed. He said, 'I guess that makes me a horrible father.'"

"Huh," Olivia said, slack-jawed. Recovering herself, she studied the half of the apple that she hadn't devoured. "Ol' Uncle Hud's becoming a kindly gentleman. What is this world coming to?"

The sound of knocking echoed from the entryway. Before Briar could shift to rise, Olivia was up and moving. "Sit," she commanded, pointing to keep Briar in place. "I've got it."

Briar blinked as Olivia quickly disappeared down the hall. "Okay," she said belatedly.

"Special delivery," Olivia announced, walking briskly back into the kitchen moments later, her arms laden with a large crystal-cut vase full of sunflowers in full bloom and vibrant color.

"What—" Briar's voice faltered when Adrian entered behind her, carrying more sunflowers in crystal. "Oh, my—" Again, she lost her voice as another vase full of flowers rounded the jamb, Roxie beneath it. "Um...that's a lot of sunflowers."

"Apparently, you have an admirer," Olivia pointed out helpfully.

"To say the least," Adrian said, shifting underneath her vase. "Who's got the card?"

"Me," Roxie said, turning as Briar finally found her feet.

The little greeting card was buried in the sunflower stalks on Roxie's far side. Briar pulled it off its plastic stand and frowned at the blank envelope with Flora's insignia stamped in the top left corner. "They're from Daddy." She knew already. "I just... didn't expect so many."

"Read the card, cuz," Olivia said with a smirk.

Briar eyed her curiously. She looked a smidge

impish. Turning to Adrian, she asked, "They are from Daddy. Right?"

Her eyes, a tad overbright, widened in forged innocence. "Ah...sure."

Out of the corner of her eye, Briar saw someone else round the corner into the kitchen. Someone tall, dark and broad. Her heart threw itself against her ribs, and that ache she'd been trying so hard to ignore over the past few weeks swelled to life in her breast.

She sucked in a breath, preparing for the onslaught. Reluctantly, she lifted her gaze from his trim jean-clad legs over a charcoal-hued T-shirt with three buttons at the neck and up over the devastating face of the man she'd loved. Between his hands was a single yellow dark-eyed bloom.

He looked wonderful, she noted...and probably smelled nice, too. Quickly, she expelled the wayward thoughts. She'd tried not to get near enough to smell him or look at him too closely last night. She'd tried not to think about him during the whole long, sleepless night that had followed.

Why was he here? Clearing her throat, Briar addressed the others who still stood with their large bright offerings, observing and motionless. "There better be a good explanation for all this."

"Don't be angry at them," Cole said. "This was my idea."

"And what exactly is *this*?" she asked, gesturing

to the bevy of flora crowding her kitchen. "Your plea for forgiveness?"

"Partly." He nodded, dark eyes combing her face. "I *did* have my thoughts together. I thought I could prepare myself, but…you're so beautiful, Briar. Now I can't string two words together looking at you."

She sucked in another sharp breath, this time involuntarily. Her heart thudded like a wild thing in her ears. Her head felt disturbingly light, and she couldn't draw a deep enough breath to clear it. "Explain yourself quickly, Cole," she said with a shrug. "But I warn you, there's not much you can say at this point to change things."

"Briar," Olivia interjected.

"You're defending him?" Briar asked, incredulous, as she whirled on her cousin.

Sighing, Olivia lifted the bottom-heavy vase onto the counter behind her. Then she planted her hands on her hips. "Hear me out first. Last night I didn't think there was much he could say for himself, either. But when I went up to check on Uncle Hud, he was still there. He stayed until morning. He shoved him under a cold shower so I wouldn't have to. Then he left and came back with coffee for the both of them. And then they sat down and talked."

Olivia nodded when Briar's lips parted in question. "You were wondering what happened to kick some sense into your dad. It was Cole. It was all Cole." Her gaze shifted over Briar's shoulder to

Cole, warming in appreciation. "I've never seen anything like it."

Briar looked to Cole, too. "Is this true?"

Cole stood for a moment, flexing his hands, as if debating something inside himself. He gave up, crossing from the door to her. "I spoke to your father," he acknowledged. "The way of it isn't important, as long as it has changed things, if he's back in your life in a good way. If he's willing to support you, like he should've from the beginning."

"You did all that?" Briar asked, unable to take it in.

"The flowers are from me," Cole admitted. "But they come with your father's blessing." Glancing sideways at Adrian, he added, "Or so I'm told."

"He's telling the truth." Adrian nodded.

Briar blinked several times, surprised at the sting of tears. She couldn't fight the fact that she was touched. Three vases full of her favorite flowers didn't come as near to breaking through the ice encased around her heart as what he'd done for her and her father. "But I thought you two hated each other. I don't know how he listened to you, much less how you got through to him."

"I guess I appealed to him, as a father who would do anything for his child. Even when that method isn't right."

Briar shook her head. The ache inside her split open and spread, constricting her chest until she didn't think she'd ever breathe right again. She gulped, gathering her strength as best she could. It was impossible with his eyes drinking her in like that—as if they'd been starved for a glimpse of her. "Cole, you left," she reminded him. "I asked you to leave and you left." Still, to this day, she couldn't say whether it was her reasons for asking him to go or the fact that he actually *had* that haunted her.

"I missed you," he replied. "I missed you more than I can say."

Adrian cleared her throat, setting the flowers she carried next to Olivia's on the counter. "We should probably go." She tugged on Roxie's arm when she didn't move. "That means you."

"Aw," Roxie said, though her smile didn't melt in the least as she set down her vase and followed Adrian out through the screen door. She touched a hand to Briar's shoulder. "Hear him out, hon. You were right about him from the get-go." Sighing, she looked back at Cole in a dreamy sort of way. "He's a keeper."

Olivia moved to follow them. Briar looked at her, distressed. "You, too?"

"You don't need me," Olivia assured her. "I'll see you later. Both of you."

With Olivia gone, Briar knew she didn't stand much of a chance. Turning reluctantly back to Cole, she could feel her willpower sliding away as she met his dark, wrenching stare. Steadying herself, she lifted her hands. "You left. You left me here alone. Just like everyone else."

He grimaced. "I thought…it was what you wanted."

She gulped at the ensuing tears. Her voice broke and she cursed. "I thought so, too."

"Briar, listen to me."

He was closer now. "Please. Don't touch me," she begged. "Don't." When he hesitated, she let out a ragged breath. She wouldn't be able to stand up against him or the apology she saw in his eyes if he touched her.

After a moment's tension, the muscles working against the frame of his jaw, he shook his head. "I can't. I can't stand here watching you hurt and not hold you."

He touched her, lifting his hand to her hair, letting his fingers curl into it as he cupped the nape of her neck. He closed in, crossing the marked space between them, bowing her restraint like an ill-laid buttress. "I'm sorry, so sorry. I shouldn't have walked away, no matter what was said. I shouldn't have left until you understood exactly what it is I feel for you."

"Don't do this," she whispered. "Please, don't, Cole."

He lifted his head, his dark eyes awash with regret…and love. "I would have given anything to stay with you."

"Everyone leaves," she repeated. "You would have left eventually."

His gaze heated at the words. She hadn't thought there was space left to close between them, but his arm wound around her waist and he pulled her into him, against him. "How could you say that? I love you. It feels like I've loved you forever—I can't remember who I was before you."

His arms tightened around her as he turned his face into her throat. "I realized I loved you the first time I kissed you. Here at the inn, with the bay around us. I kissed you and felt things inside me I didn't think I'd ever feel again. It was in that moment that I realized I'd somehow found home again."

A sob shook Briar. She couldn't hold them back anymore. With everything in her, she wanted to reach out to him, return his embrace. Enfold, accept him. "I can't...."

"Believe me," he murmured. "I do love you, Briar, and if I could do it all over again, I'd never hurt you. I wouldn't lie and I wouldn't walk away. Not for a single moment."

Her lips trembled. "When Tiffany told me what you'd done for her, I felt so alone. I've never felt so alone in my life as when I found out you'd betrayed me."

Brushing the hair back from her face, he skimmed his thumb over her cheek, smearing tears. "I never want you to feel that way again. I'll do whatever it takes to make sure you don't. I want to make you feel loved every moment for the rest of your life. I want to make this a home again—a real home. I want there to be a family here."

She gasped at the word. *Family.* Even when she'd

been alone, it had remained the single most precious dream. More than keeping the inn alive or going back to school. Even when she'd told herself it would never happen, it had lived on inside her.

He cupped her face in his hands until her eyes lifted to his. And there she saw it—that dream she'd desperately wanted again.

He must have seen the softening in her eyes because he smiled, touched his lips tenderly to hers, so softly the sweetness of it stole her breath. "Wait here?" he pleaded.

She swallowed, nodded, unable to speak.

His lips warmed into a smile, hands squeezing hers briefly before he walked around her to the door. She moved only to reach over and wrap a bracing hand around the back of the closest chair. The orange-red, neon-tinted light of the horizon spilled through the windows and shined through the sunflowers' petals, giving the scene a dreamlike quality. She felt something building inside her. At its crest, forgiveness rode in all its shocking, gilded glory. And behind it…all the love she'd thought had been lost with Cole's betrayal.

"Briar…I'd like you to meet someone."

Turning, she took one look at the man and boy standing in the doorway and clasped a hand over her heart. The man stood behind the boy, hands gripping his shoulders in a supportive stance. As she looked from one face to the other, what little of herself she'd been holding back instantly melted.

Cole's eyes were soft, his voice gentle and low. "This is my son, Gavin."

Briar pressed her lips inward to control the emotions building in the back of her throat. When she was sure she could speak, she took a step forward. "Gavin. It's lovely to meet you."

Cole's hands squeezed Gavin's shoulders as he lowered his head toward the boy's head and murmured, his tender eyes never straying from hers, "And, Gavin…this is the lady I was telling you about. Briar."

Gavin stepped forward and extended a hand in greeting.

Briar couldn't help the smile that broke across her face as she lifted her hand to grasp his. She simply held it, lowering to her knees so they could be eye to eye with each other.

Gavin scanned her face. His expression was curious, if a bit hesitant. He licked his lips then finally said, "Dad says your cinnamon rolls are awesome. Will you make some for me?"

"Gav," Cole said on a laugh.

"It's all right," she assured Cole. Lifting her other hand, she held Gavin's in both of her own and said, "Of course. I'd be happy to."

He grinned back at her, revealing several missing teeth. After a moment, Cole cleared his throat quietly and Gavin's shoulders straightened. "Oh, yeah," the boy said. Reaching into his pocket with his free hand, he pulled out a small box. "For you."

She touched a hand to her lips. The box was blue velvet and ring-sized. It fit in Gavin's palm, but just barely. "Oh…" Air escaped her in one long, staggering rush. "Oh, my…"

Cole put his hands on Gavin's shoulders again. "Thanks, chief. I'll take it from here."

Gavin turned, placing the box in Cole's hand. He tugged on the fingers clasped around the velvet box until Cole followed his urging and lowered his head to his level. Briar heard him whisper over the pounding of her heart in her ears, "I like her already."

Cole chuckled quietly and touched his lips to Gavin's brow. "That's my boy."

Gavin rushed from the room. After a moment, she heard the drone of the television from the next room. Then Cole shrank to one knee and his eyes found hers and the rest of the world disappeared completely.

He opened the box and lifted it so the single diamond on the band within caught the flaming light, reflected pinpricks shining on the walls around them. "I bought it after that afternoon we spent together in the rain."

Her mouth fell open as her gaze sought his, unbelieving. "No. No, you didn't."

His mouth split into a wide grin. "I did. I knew then what I say to you now. Whatever happens from this day forward, I'll love you. I'll take care of you. And I won't let *anything* hurt you, Briar. I swear it."

It was a promise he had made before. But this

time he would make it last forever. She knew it in her heart.

"Do you believe me?" he asked.

She scanned his face with eyes that brimmed with tears. A sob shook her again, but a smile bloomed on her lips. "Yes," she breathed. "Yes, I believe you."

Releasing the ragged breath he'd been holding, he placed the ring on her finger. Then he pulled her against him, into him, as the day faded and all the things she hadn't dared hope for and more sprang to life for them both. Turning her lips against his ear, she held him close and whispered, "Come home. Stay with me forever."

He pulled back, raising her hand to kiss it. "Forever," he agreed, lifting his loving gaze to hers and holding it. "And then some."

* * * * *

LARGER-PRINT BOOKS!
GET 2 FREE LARGER-PRINT NOVELS PLUS
2 FREE GIFTS!

◆ HARLEQUIN

super romance

More Story...More Romance

LARGER-PRINT BOOKS!

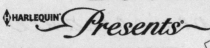

HARLEQUIN *Presents*

PASSION GUARANTEED SEDUCTION

GET 2 FREE LARGER-PRINT NOVELS PLUS 2 FREE GIFTS!

YES! Please send me 2 FREE LARGER-PRINT Harlequin Presents® novels and my 2 FREE gifts (gifts are worth about $10). After receiving them, if I don't wish to receive any more books, I can return the shipping statement marked "cancel." If I don't cancel, I will receive 6 brand-new novels every month and be billed just $5.05 per book in the U.S. or $5.49 per book in Canada. That's a saving of at least 16% off the cover price! It's quite a bargain! Shipping and handling is just 50¢ per book in the U.S. and 75¢ per book in Canada.* I understand that accepting the 2 free books and gifts places me under no obligation to buy anything. I can always return a shipment and cancel at any time. Even if I never buy another book, the two free books and gifts are mine to keep forever.

176/376 HDN F43N

Name	(PLEASE PRINT)	
Address		Apt. #
City	State/Prov.	Zip/Postal Code

Signature (if under 18, a parent or guardian must sign)

Mail to the Harlequin® Reader Service:
IN U.S.A.: P.O. Box 1867, Buffalo, NY 14240-1867
IN CANADA: P.O. Box 609, Fort Erie, Ontario L2A 5X3

Are you a subscriber to Harlequin Presents books and want to receive the larger-print edition?
Call 1-800-873-8635 today or visit us at www.ReaderService.com.

* Terms and prices subject to change without notice. Prices do not include applicable taxes. Sales tax applicable in N.Y. Canadian residents will be charged applicable taxes. Offer not valid in Quebec. This offer is limited to one order per household. Not valid for current subscribers to Harlequin Presents Larger-Print books. All orders subject to credit approval. Credit or debit balances in a customer's account(s) may be offset by any other outstanding balance owed by or to the customer. Please allow 4 to 6 weeks for delivery. Offer available while quantities last.

Your Privacy—The Harlequin® Reader Service is committed to protecting your privacy. Our Privacy Policy is available online at www.ReaderService.com or upon request from the Harlequin Reader Service.

We make a portion of our mailing list available to reputable third parties that offer products we believe may interest you. If you prefer that we not exchange your name with third parties, or if you wish to clarify or modify your communication preferences, please visit us at www.ReaderService.com/consumerschoice or write to us at Harlequin Reader Service Preference Service, P.O. Box 9062, Buffalo, NY 14269. Include your complete name and address.

HPLP13R